# THE VISCOUNT AND THE THIEF

EMMA ORCHARD

Boldwood

First published in Great Britain in 2024 by Boldwood Books Ltd.

Cover Design by Rachel Lawston

Cover Images: Rachel Lawston

A CIP catalogue record for this book is available from the British Library.

Paperback ISBN 978-1-83561-074-9

Large Print ISBN 978-1-83561-073-2

Hardback ISBN 978-1-83561-072-5

Ebook ISBN 978-1-83561-075-6

Kindle ISBN 978-1-83561-076-3

Audio CD ISBN 978-1-83561-067-1

MP3 CD ISBN 978-1-83561-068-8

Digital audio download ISBN 978-1-83561-069-5

This book is printed on certified sustainable paper. Boldwood Books is dedicated to putting sustainability at the heart of our business. For more information please visit https://www.boldwoodbooks.com/about-us/sustainability/

Boldwood Books Ltd, 23 Bowerdean Street, London, SW6 3TN

www.boldwoodbooks.com

*I've always been inspired by Georgette Heyer's formidable ladies of a certain age, in particular the magnificent Lady Aurelia in The Unknown Ajax. This book is for the real-life versions: for my Heyer friends, dowagers every one, and in loving memory of my husband's late aunts, Zia Luisa and Zia Rosa, who were best of all.*

# PROLOGUE

## THE LONDON SEASON, JUNE 1803

It was a glittering, glamorous scene from a generation ago, before the Terror, before the King and Queen and so many others lost their heads to Madame Guillotine. The theme of the costume ball in the grand mansion in Mayfair was Old Versailles. The ballroom was white and gold, lined with tall mirrors, before which sat great pyramids of highly scented flowers in the same colours – a perfect setting for the small orchestra and the whirling dancers.

The height of fashion now demanded austere modern simplicity: straight white Grecian muslin gowns for the debutantes, set off by a backdrop of plain dark evening coats in the masculine style made so popular by Mr Brummell. But the young ladies and gentlemen present seemed to be enjoying the rare opportunity this evening gave them to parade in all the splendour of bright silk, lace, velvet and embroidery, as their parents and grandparents had not so long ago. They flirted behind fans, and bowed and curtseyed to each other with exaggerated politeness, laughing as they did so, as though they were children playing at dressing up as princes and princesses.

Many ladies, and some of the more daring gentlemen, had

painted their faces in the old style and placed velvet patches here and there to enhance their beauty. Few people had gone so far as to set ridiculous tall wigs upon their heads, but some of them had chosen to powder their own hair silver, and most of the ladies sported elaborate old-fashioned coiffures adorned with ribbons and feathers. It was a colourful scene, and cheerful, unless any of the participants chose to reflect that it was all an illusion, and a recreation of a way of life, now gone forever, that had ended in disaster.

It wasn't a masquerade ball. Nobody was disguised, apart from the unfamiliarity granted them by the costumes and the unusual ways they'd dressed their hair. Rafe, self-conscious in pale blue velvet embroidered with silver, shaking his hands free from trailing lace shirt cuffs, reflected that for him the shelter of a mask would have been most welcome. He was aware, as he always must be when mixing in society, of the sidelong glances and muttering that followed him about, and of that whispered word that he had come to hate, and yet could never avoid, because it was his own name, and his father's: Wyverne.

He knew exactly what people were saying, even if he couldn't overhear the actual words, since such poisonous gossip had been the constant backdrop to his life for years now, though he was barely three and twenty. He didn't need to hear the scandalised enjoyment in their voices to know it was there. 'That's Wyverne's boy, Lord Drake. Yes, the tall, young fellow in blue with the dark eyes. The Viscount. Eligible? Well, I dare say he is, if all you care for is the great fortune and the title. I suppose it is no great surprise he was invited, and since he is here, he clearly has no shame. But would you want to ally yourself with *that* family? Would you really care to be on visiting terms with them? The father is quite bad enough, as all the world knows, but let us not forget the stepmother, if you can call her that. A common hussy from the stage – and that's the more respectable portion of her career! My dear, you *must* have heard the latest shocking rumours...'

It was no wonder Rafe generally avoided such gatherings, and lived his life in the country or in Oxford, as far away from London as he could. As a student and a green boy, he'd sometimes tried to argue with people who looked at him askance, to confront their prejudices head-on, but he was wiser now; he'd realised through painful experience that you might as well try to reason with the weather, or command an avalanche to stop tumbling down a mountain. He hated with a passion being the subject of scandal, but it was a fact of his life. He'd have said that nobody could enjoy such notoriety, except that it was perfectly clear that his father did enjoy it – revelled in it, took pleasure in provoking such shocked reactions, and in proving to the world that he wasn't as bad as he was rumoured to be – he was much worse. The Marquess of Wyverne, he knew, was in London too this June, staying in his town house, for purposes Rafe didn't want to consider, but his son and heir was not sleeping under his roof or calling on him there. He never did. He had as little to do with his father as was possible. At least the Marquess was most unlikely to be here tonight; this was hardly his sort of party.

But Lord Drake's close friend and neighbour Simon Venables, who had been his youthful tutor at Oxford, was to be married in a few days, and Rafe had found himself included in the cheerful wedding party. It really would have been excessively ungrateful and churlish to refuse to participate in such a joyous series of celebrations. God forbid he should cast even the smallest of clouds over Simon and Elizabeth's innocent pleasure, especially since he was best man. So he was staying in Simon's family home in Half-Moon Street, and had agreed to come to this ball, and other, similar events. It would do the Viscount a great deal of good, Simon had said, to mix with people. To mix with young ladies, in particular, as any man of three and twenty should.

Simon was the best of friends, but he was also a minister in holy orders, and he believed – despite strong evidence to the contrary provided by Rafe's father's disastrous marital career, or even his grandfather's – that the wedded state was the source of all human bliss. Rafe was perhaps a little young to settle down, even in the Reverend Mr Venables's estimation – but he was showing worrying signs of becoming a recluse, and therefore this was an excellent opportunity for him to spend time in refined feminine society for a change. To show his willingness to be sociable, Rafe had already danced with Elizabeth, the bride-to-be, and with her sisters, and with Simon's sister Mary. He was not well acquainted with any of these ladies, but they were all perfectly pleasant and friendly. No doubt they had been reassured in advance by Simon and his mother that, despite his family's atrocious reputation, Rafe himself would not offer them any insult, nor whisper words in their ears that would bring a blush to their innocent cheeks. He was, whatever the world might think of him, not his father.

And here was Lady Venables again, wider than she was tall in a flowered gown with huge panniers, like a sort of mobile sofa, bustling him away. She was obviously bent on continuing her son's campaign to raise Rafe's spirits, this time by presenting him to a young lady who was not a member of their own party, which made him suddenly nervous of the girl's reaction, in case she should recoil from him in horror, to the embarrassment of all three of them. But Simon's mama was inexorable. 'Mademoiselle de Montfaucon,' she said firmly, refusing to meet Rafe's gaze, 'may I present Lord Drake to you as a partner for the next set?'

He bowed correctly, inwardly wincing, uttering a polite greeting. It was clearly far too late to withdraw without insulting the debutante who stood before him, which he had not the least desire to do. Perhaps, he thought desperately, since her name suggested that she was a French émigrée, she might not be aware of the Wyverne reputation, or the horrible rumours that swirled about his own name in particular. She was smiling at him shyly, and murmuring acceptance, so that appeared to be so, thank goodness.

She was a beauty. Rafe had no interest in young ladies making their come-out, and no intention of involving one of these innocents, ever, in the slowly unfolding disaster that was his family. But he was a healthy twenty-three-year-old, and could not help but notice the young lady's sweet, expressive face, her lively brown eyes and spectacular red-blonde curls, piled up on her head in a style that became her greatly. The heavy coiffure emphasised the graceful curve of her neck, and her queenly bearing. Presumably she was indeed an aristocrat whose family had fled the Revolution; she'd have been a small child in 1793. Too young to remember anything of that dreadful time? He had quite a lot of experience of children, through his younger half-siblings, and he thought not. But whatever her private feelings might be on this occasion – he wouldn't be at all surprised if she considered it more than a touch tasteless – she was composed and exquisite in pale green silk embroidered with pink, and perfectly in tune with the theme of the ball, as if she'd stepped straight from a painting by Boucher or Fragonard.

Mademoiselle de Montfaucon put her hand in his, and he bowed over it, and led her to the dance floor, saying, 'It would be my pleasure, mademoiselle.' He realised with some surprise that it would, in fact, be a pleasure. His partner had not yet cultivated the boredom that debutantes soon understood was required of them; she did not sigh, look about her wearily and say languidly, 'It is a sad crush tonight, is it not, sir?' As the dance began, her dark eyes were sparkling with infectious enjoyment; brighter, he thought, and far more naturally appealing, than the enormous and impressive pink jewel she wore about her neck, striking fire in the candlelight as they twirled about.

Any observer, standing aside and watching them, must surely have thought that they made a pretty pair in their silk and velvet finery, both so young and handsome, the lady fair and vivacious, the dark gentleman perhaps more serious in nature, but still looking down at her now, plainly charmed by her delight, an attractive smile transforming his previously rather stern, forbidding young features. Perhaps five years separated them in age, and it would require a heart of stone, surely, not to be touched by the picture they presented in their fairy tale costumes, if one could ignore the rumours for a moment or two. They could easily have been Cinderella and her prince.

But Rafe would not have been so carefree if he had seen who was tracking their movements from the shadows at the edge of the room, eyes hot and avid, gaze unwavering, pale face set in harsh, cynical lines. The watcher – who appeared to be perfectly capable of resisting the innocent charm of the scene that was playing out before his eyes – was a man in his sixties, dressed even more opulently than the rest of the throng, bearing several elaborate jewelled decorations upon his black velvet coat and diamond rings upon his thin fingers. He seemed quite at his ease, even though nobody spoke to him and there was a little space around him in the crowded room that suggested an odd reluctance of fellow guests to stray too close, as if they feared some physical or moral infection. Again the scandalised whispers raced around the room at lightning speed; again those ladies and gentlemen whose self-control was less than perfect craned their necks quite blatantly to see. Even those who professed complete fashionable indifference shot a sly glance or two the old man's way, since one surely could not be blamed for wishing to set eyes upon the notoriously wicked Marquess in the flesh.

It was Lord Wyverne, and he watched his son and the lovely young girl as they danced not with fatherly pride, or even aristocratic indifference, but with the dark, intense, pitiless focus of a hunter with his prey.

# 1

## SPRING, 1811 – EIGHT YEARS LATER

Sophie, which was not her name, stood with self-possession in front of the Marchioness, while that lady surveyed her keenly from head to foot. The older woman – she was perhaps forty, lushly beautiful, voluptuous, skilfully painted even in her own boudoir – saw, she knew, a perfect lady's companion in every tiny detail of Sophie's appearance. She was immaculately presented, in a demure, high-necked gown of sober grey hue, which the Marchioness might assume had been given to her by a previous employer (it hadn't). She was of medium height, and medium build, and her locks, which were an unmemorable shade of dark brown (they were dyed), were drawn back sleekly into a bun at the back of her head. Her hair was dead straight, and did not draw attention to itself in any way, as was entirely proper. She wore no rouge or perfume; her prospective employer was wearing enough for both of them. Sophie's eyes were large and dark, quick with intelligence, and she could hardly have appeared any more French if she had been singing the Marseillaise and waving a tricolour flag, instead of standing sedately, hands folded, in a lady's sitting room in Brook Street. Her insistent Frenchness might have been a drawback in other circumstances, in these desperate times of war, but no; for this situation, a Frenchwoman was specifically required. She had counted on that.

She'd told the Marchioness that she'd been brought to London as a tiny infant, Monsieur and Madame Delavallois, her parents, having fled the Terror like so many others, losing everything – their modest fortune, their small estate in Picardy – except their lives. The Delavallois family had really existed, though they were conveniently dead now – all this could be checked, if anyone cared to do so, and the affecting tale, if she were in fact their daughter, would make her twenty-one. She was in reality fully five years older, but Lady Wyverne, if she noticed, didn't appear to care. Perhaps she thought, with some justice, that such a life as Sophie's aged a girl before her time. The lady would know more than a lady should about such matters, since it was common gossip that she'd been born in poverty and made a living as an actress of sorts before her extraordinary, scandalous marriage to a marquess.

Faux Sophie had good references, which would stand a great deal of scrutiny, though they were all of them purest fiction. The first lady she had supposedly served, when she'd been a mere girl of sixteen, had gone to India to join her parents, leaving a very affecting and entirely uncheckable testimonial behind for her young companion. (It should be affecting; Sophie had written it herself.)

Mlle Delavallois had next, so she claimed, been the chief support of the wife of a dashing young cavalry officer, left alone while her husband served overseas for prolonged periods. This lady, who did actually exist, was of high birth but recklessly impecunious. Lady Wyverne was not to know that the pressing nature of the woman's debts put her entirely in the power of others, most unscrupulous others, and anxious to retain their favour. She had been more than happy to put her name to a reference for an employee she'd never met.

Sophie had then apparently bettered her situation by entering the household of a widow, relic of the younger son of an earl. This lady had no debts to speak of, a matter for congratulation, but she did have secrets, and a spurious letter of recommendation was a small price to pay to see that they were kept. Sophie had, she said, attended her noble employer on visits to several notable country houses, and could reassure her prospective mistress that she knew exactly how to go on there. Rosanna Wyverne had unwittingly this much in common with her supposed predecessor – she too had secrets aplenty. But Sophie knew them all already.

The Marchioness asked why Mlle Delavallois had left her most recent employment. 'You were not dismissed, I hope?'

'Mais non, milady.' Sophie was very French just now. 'Her ladyship remarried, to a country gentleman, and so was no longer in need of a companion. In any case, they intend to live a very quiet life, residing entirely on his small estate in the county of Cumberland.' Cumberland, pronounced by Sophie, had a great many syllables, which somehow conveyed a strong impression of uncouth remoteness. 'It was a great romance.' Sophie produced the words 'small estate' as another might say 'dung-heap', and 'country gentleman' as another might say 'ratcatcher'.

The Marchioness smiled, showing teeth. She was amused, and her silken gown – it was red, and very elaborate – rustled. 'You do not care for small estates in the remote country, Mademoiselle Delavallois?'

'Non, madame. Pas le moindre.' She shuddered; it might have been considered excessively theatrical, perhaps, but she knew what was expected of her.

'Nor do I,' said Lady Wyverne. 'So excessively tedious, I am sure. Setting aside my poor mother-in-law and her odd requirements, which I am sure you will fulfil admirably, I think we shall deal excellently together. Or we shall as long as you always remember your place.' Her voice was suddenly sharp, as were her eyes, and her voice grew markedly less genteel and languid as she said, 'You are young, but I do not think you are foolish. Do what you are employed to do, and no more. I don't give a fig if you engage in squalid intrigues in the servants' hall. You may take a tumble with half the footmen and all the grooms for all I care. That's your affair entirely. But if I catch you flirting with members of the family or any of my guests, you will find yourself cast out without wages or references so fast your feet won't touch the ground. Do you understand me, missy?'

Sophie reassured the Marchioness that she did, and she was perfectly sincere in her assurances. She wasn't there to flirt, and had no interest in romance or any kind of intrigue. The footmen and grooms would be perfectly safe, as would the men of the Wyverne family, who were truly the last people on earth she wanted any involvement with. The woman was unnecessarily warning her newest employee off her husband, which might be considered natural enough, especially given the Marquess's atrocious reputation, but also her stepson, Lord Drake. As all the world so shockingly knew, Lady Wyverne's interest in *him* could hardly be described as motherly.

But all this scandal in high life was no concern of Sophie's, unless it could somehow work to her advantage, which seemed unlikely. She would be a very good companion, discreet and industrious, so that the Marchioness would be entirely satisfied with her work, and very happy with her own wise choice. Until suddenly she wouldn't be.

Everything was arranged to both women's satisfaction, and afterwards Sophie left the tall house and disappeared into the dusk. Ladies could not walk unaccompanied about the streets of

London, but Sophie was not precisely a lady, or at least not one of the least consequence. She was, or appeared to be, an unremarkable female in a modest bonnet and a simple grey cloak, and nobody paid her the least attention. She walked, and enjoyed the freedom.

The partial freedom. She was always alert, naturally. If men looked at her, she cast down her eyes meekly – not too meekly, just the correct amount of humility – and maintained her pace. She was brisk, purposeful; above all, she was not prey. Meeting anyone's glance could be dangerous. Being a woman abroad alone could be dangerous. It was a little early for a gentleman to be drunk – no, that was ridiculous, a gentleman could be drunk at any hour. She could not afford to be careless, and was not.

Her route was somewhat circuitous, and if anyone had been following her through the darkening streets – but why should they? – they would soon have found it impossible to keep their eyes upon one nondescript little figure among all the evening bustle of the great, dirty city.

She left the fashionable part of town soon enough, and London changed as she walked eastwards. Oddly for such a respectable-seeming woman, the confidence of her posture seemed to grow when it should have declined. She was in Seven Dials now, the Rookery, a place where the constables would hesitate to go, and certainly would not go alone. But she stepped around piles of noisome refuse and groups of disreputable-looking loiterers as though she had not a worry in the world. People watched her, but did not attempt to accost her. When a drunken costermonger lurched accidentally into her path, the sharp look she sent him made him shrink away, babbling apologies.

At last she reached a low tavern, a boozing ken, the unlikeliest of destinations for an honest woman, and made her way confidently inside. The ancient, panelled room was not well lit, and very crowded, but she passed surely through the haze of pipe-smoke and tallow fumes, and when the patrons saw her they drew apart as best they could to make a path. It was odd that they should show such deference to one so unremarkable and unintimidating in appearance, for some of them, men and women both, had the aspect of creatures out of nightmare. Their persons, their faces, and above all their watchful, glittering eyes, told a disturbing story. Any objective observer with a modest degree of imagination would surely have said that the room looked to be full of robbers, whores and murderers, which indeed it was. But the young woman seemed entirely unconcerned. She slipped behind the bar, saying, 'Hello, Fred, all well?'

The tapster – a tall, imposing man with the battered features of a former prize-fighter – nodded and let her pass into the inner room, saying, 'He's waiting for you,' as he closed the scarred wooden door behind her.

She threw off her drab cloak and untied her bonnet, setting them down upon a chest beside the fire. There was a man there, seated behind a desk, looking through some papers, and he did not speak, but raised an enquiring eyebrow.

'Yes,' she said in response to some unspoken query. 'She gave me the position.'

'As we knew she would.'

'Indeed. One of the other candidates, a young woman with excellent references who was expected an hour before me, did not appear, and sent no word to explain why. Lady Wyverne was highly vexed.'

'Most unaccountable,' he said calmly.

'She wasn't harmed?' Hard to say if this was truly a question.

Again the mobile eyebrow shot up. 'Of course not. She is a little better off than she was yesterday, and the next plum situation that arises will be hers. I have said so.' This rather odd statement was uttered with supreme confidence. 'She was... persuaded that to work at Brook Street and, most of all, at Wyverne Hall would not have suited her constitution, and given the nature of the place, this may even be true.'

'It may not suit mine.'

'I dare say it won't. But you can look after yourself.'

'As you taught me.'

He inclined his head. He was a man past his middle years, and his neutral speech – he used no low cant, just now, nor did he swear – made it difficult to place him, for anyone who didn't know exactly who and what he was. He didn't look or sound as though he belonged in this place, which could have been described with perfect accuracy as a notorious den of thieves. Yet this was plainly his private room, and he seemed entirely at home here. He was short, spare of frame, nondescript (this had been useful in the past). His eyes and hair were of no particular colour, and his clothes were as unremarkable as they could be. In a society where status and position were everything, he gave little away. He could have been a tradesman in a small but prosperous way, a middling clerk in some government office, a solicitor in a backwater town. A confidential servant, perhaps, to a gentleman of rank. Yes, that. He projected an air of quiet confidence, and competence. One would instinctively trust such a man.

One would be seriously mistaken.

## 2

His name was Nate Smith – that was what he said, and nobody was inclined to argue – and he was a thief. A prince of thieves. If you stole something, especially something valuable, in London and didn't give him his share, you'd be looking over your shoulder, and while you were looking over your shoulder you might trip and break your neck. It had happened. And why would you be so foolish? Nate Smith could make things disappear. Things, and people. But if you helped him, he'd help you. He could be very helpful, and fair, by his lights.

He'd helped the girl who was now Sophie Delavallois. It could be said that he'd created her. Unlike everyone else, he knew where she came from, what she'd been before, and he hadn't told a soul. This seemed almost incredible in such a dog-eat-dog world, but it was true.

A lesser man might have seen a short-term, obvious profit in a penniless, friendless and very pretty girl who could claim descent from various kings of France, and who had the manners to match. An auction could have been arranged. Several auctions, human ingenuity being what it was. Maidenhead was a valuable asset, and only a fool would imagine that it could be sold only once.

This sort of thing went on all the time, and Nate Smith had no bone to pick with anyone who chose to make their living in that particular way. He wasn't sentimental. Flesh was a commodity like any other. But it had seemed to him to be a waste of potential, in this instance. He'd seen something in the girl when he'd met her. She'd been destitute, alone, bereaved and dazed with grief, but she hadn't given in to despair, and he'd been aware of a spark of something in her that gave him pause. If he'd made the obvious arrangement eight years ago, as he easily might have done, if he'd sold her on to some madam or other, the girl wouldn't be convincing anyone she was of royal blood by now, he thought as he looked at her. He'd always enjoyed looking at her. She still held on to her youth, and he was glad to see it. Of course, she might have made a go of whoring – some rare women did – and spent her days riding in a fine carriage down Bond Street and her nights as some great lord's particular favourite, but more likely she'd be walking the streets of Covent Garden and painting her face an inch thick to hide the pox sores. Or dead in a gutter: wasteful.

He could, he supposed, have found other women who could pass as upper servants (though not a fraction as well as she did) and find their way into the most exclusive houses in the country. He'd done similar things before, when the stakes were lower, when it was just a matter of a doxy taking a few shillings to leave a door or a window open and looking the other way. This was different. The thing about thieves and criminals and their strumpets – and he was aware of the irony of this – was that you couldn't trust the bastards. His reputation, won in blood, though not his blood, ought to ensure he'd never be double-crossed again. Normally this would be the case. But when it came to very valuable things, to extreme temptation, people were so stupid. They could lose their heads. And Lord Wyverne had an awful lot of valuable things – a fortune, a king's ransom. Nate Smith wanted all of it. Sophie – best to think of her as Sophie now – just wanted one particularly precious trinket. Her fair share.

It wasn't as though he'd trained her just for this particular caper. She'd earned her keep a thousand times over. She could empty a pocket like nobody he'd ever seen, though she'd started at it late. She could pick a lock as easy as winking. She could pass as a lady, or as a tavern wench, since she'd been both. She could read and write, in several languages. She could draw you up a letter that looked as though the old Queen had had the scriving of it, or any lord or banker you could name, which was surprisingly useful.

She could stab a man who attempted to lay rough hands on her, if it came to that, and be a hundred yards away before anybody noticed, including the victim; she didn't care for that side of the business, but she'd done it. Who'd suspect her, with her pale, little face and big, dark eyes? She could go anywhere, and do anything, from Carlton House to a Charley's shelter. She could be anybody, from a duchess to a foul-mouthed doxy, a Frenchwoman, an Italian. She was fearless, quick, bold and clever. A woman after his own heart, if he'd had such a thing. And he was supposed to have sold such an exceptional woman into the life of a lightskirt – an expensive baggage and then, almost inevitably as time wore her down, a cheap one? Madness. He'd made her, and she was his creature. And together they would pull off the greatest, most audacious theft of the new century. It wouldn't be long now, if she could hold her nerve. He trusted her – as far as he trusted anybody, which was to say, not completely. Never that.

## 3

Sophie took up her new situation the next morning, and carried her modest possessions to Brook Street in a hackney. The previous companion had already left, it seemed, and her services were required immediately. And a day after that, Sophie travelled to Buckinghamshire with Lady Wyverne's upper servants, who were civil enough to her throughout the tedious journey but engaged her in little conversation and asked her no personal questions, which suited her perfectly. They didn't seem a particularly cheerful group of people, nor did they appear eager to reach their destination – but that was no concern of hers.

As the only newcomer, she found it hard to restrain herself from leaning forward and staring as the heavy coach passed through tall gateposts topped with dragons – wyverns, she supposed – and made its way down a long, long carriage drive and across an ornamental bridge. It rumbled slowly up a rise and then the house – the palace, it was nothing less – came into view. She could not repress a gasp at the sheer size of it, the height of the soaring stone columns and the length of the curving frontage

– and some of her companions chuckled a little at her reaction. 'You'll get used to it, miss,' one of them said drily.

'She will if she's here long enough,' another muttered. And then it was time to descend, and if she'd been inclined to ask what was meant by that, there was no time. It was late, dusk was falling, and after a snatched meal in the housekeeper's cosy room she was conducted up to her mean little attic chamber and left alone to unpack. The next day, she knew, she'd be settling into her new situation, meeting the woman with whom she'd spend most of her waking hours, the Dowager Marchioness of Wyverne.

In other circumstances, in her other, lost life, Sophie would have been fascinated to make her acquaintance. The old lady was a survivor, a French aristocrat of the real Ancien régime, close on a hundred years old now, and had been in her youth, it was whispered, the mistress of King Louis XV. It must be said that this was a distinction she had shared with very many women, of high birth and low, including Sophie's own great-grandmother. They were practically related; they probably were related, somewhere back in their tangled aristocratic family trees. Sophie, without a close relative left alive in the world, no longer had access to that sort of information. Who could she ask, if she'd genuinely wanted to know? And there was no point to it. All that was far behind her now.

The Dowager Marchioness, her daughter-in-law had explained during that first interview, was more or less confined to her rooms, saw few people, and had forgotten, or did not care to remember, most of the English she had ever known. This must make communication between mother-in-law and daughter-in-law almost impossible, but perhaps they had little to say to each other; perhaps it was in fact a fortunate circumstance. The old lady's chief recreation was to converse in French and to be read to – novels, naturally also in her native language. She had exacting requirements as to the voice and accent of the reader. And yet the material she desired to be read... it was a little awkward. Previous companions had either not met her standards, and been summarily dismissed, or objected strongly to the nature of the material and left of their own volition in a cloud of moral indignation. Lady Wyverne was not without a certain pungently amusing turn of phrase, and as she listened to her description of the problem Sophie was obliged to bite the inside of her cheek in order to keep from laughing. She had murmured placidly that she would endeavour to give satisfaction; when she'd told Nate later exactly what she'd been employed to do, he'd let out a sudden crack of laughter. He rarely laughed, and though she was aware that it was weak of her, she'd felt a glow of pleasure when she'd heard it. 'Dirty books – they're employing you to read dirty books...'

'*French* books, remember,' she'd said, eyes sparkling, a wicked smile tugging at the corners of her mouth.

'Dirty books, in French, to a hundred-year-old woman!'

'Apparently.'

'And paying you forty pounds a year for it, board wages. Not bad!'

It wasn't bad; high pay, for a woman who could claim no particular formal education or skills. It wasn't, she imagined, quite as much as Lord Wyverne's valet was making, but it was almost certainly more than his wife's abigail received, women's work being generally cheap.

Even setting aside the peculiar circumstances of what Sophie would be called on to do, it was well known in London that the Marchioness had a certain amount of difficulty retaining servants, and had to pay somewhat over the odds for decent ones. Rosanna Wyverne had a very bad reputation, and while many noble ladies were just as notorious, *they* were of high lineage, and she'd been on the stage, and exhibited her manifold charms in other, even less respectable places, before Lord Wyverne had taken up the crazy notion of making her his third wife. It wasn't the immorality that society objected to so much – it was the low birth. Respectable servants were obliged to take such matters into consideration, too, and if Sophie had really been what she appeared to be, she'd have been unwise to enter Lady Wyverne's service, despite the healthy salary being offered her. How long could the Dowager be expected to live, a year or two at the most, surely, and what would happen to Sophie afterwards? She couldn't expect any proper lady to employ her next, if she spent at all long in the Marchioness's household. A couple of months might be excused – after all, a girl had a living to make. To take up such a position and then leave it quickly, that was one thing. One could imagine a lady saying to an intimate friend, 'An excellent young woman, my dear, I assure you. She was employed by that dreadful Wyverne creature, to be companion to the poor Dowager, naturally, but only very briefly. I did not ask for details, of course, and she is too discreet to say, but her face told the whole story. Of course she could not stay there, for she is a decent little thing. She was employed only in Brook Street, and when the move to Wyverne Hall was proposed, she took fright at the thought, and no wonder. My dear, have you heard the perfectly scandalous stories of what goes on there?'

It was fortunate, then, that Sophie had not the least intention of seeking other employment after she left the Marchioness. Apart from anything else, even disregarding the lady's terrible reputation, it was highly unlikely that she would be writing her any sort of recommendation. On the contrary. Once the truth came out, Lady Wyverne would be frantic, setting the Bow Street Runners on her trail, but they wouldn't find anything, because Sophie Delavallois would have disappeared without a trace.

But in the meantime, she had her duties. Lady Wyverne didn't conduct her to the Dowager's chambers – this was a pity, because Sophie had a wicked desire to hear her speaking French – entrusting that duty instead to the Dowager's maid, Marchand, a Frenchwoman who was herself not young, and who regarded Sophie with a level, weary gaze that seemed to say, *Enfin*, another one! Let's see how long this one lasts.

She followed Marchand's straight-backed, prim figure into the spacious room, and curtsied as she was introduced, trying to keep her gaze low and not to look about her in too obvious a fashion as she did so. Under her demurely lowered lashes she saw a beautiful silk-hung chamber full of lovely, fragile pieces of French furniture, and she was obliged to stifle a gasp as the memories it evoked threatened to overset her. It was similar, so very similar, to her grandmother's room in Paris; even the light, elusive scent of the place seemed almost the same, and she was pulled back into her childhood, she was six or seven years old again, not long before her family's world fell apart for the first time but not the last... She blinked, and pushed away the unwelcome memories.

She knew that only French would be spoken here, the aristocratic language of her childhood, and she must bear it, however difficult it turned out to be. A low, musical voice – and she would not dwell on how much that too reminded her of her grandmother, dead at the hands of Robespierre and his ruffians these many years – said, 'Come closer, child, sit by me, and let me look at you. My eyes are not what they were.'

Sophie, still shaken, obeyed. She moved closer to the sofa where her mistress lay, and sank into a chair at her side, and they regarded each other with varying degrees of composure but equal amounts of interest.

Delphine Wyverne was tiny, and looked every one of her hundred years. It seemed she disdained the face-paint and wigs of her youth, but showed herself bravely as the ancient creature she was. There was little colour in her face, and none in her hair. Her thin hands on the richly embroidered shawl that covered her were almost transparent. But her eyes were full of life and intelligence, and Sophie found them uncomfortably sharp. 'Delavallois: a name from Brittany, of course, and Lorraine,' she said now.

'My parents had a small estate in Picardy, madame la marquise,' Sophie responded with tolerable poise.

'I did not know the family. But of course, I have lived in England for so long now, and it is many years since I was in France. It could scarcely be otherwise.'

'Yes, madame.'

The old lady shifted a little, as if she were in pain and sought some momentary relief from a change of position. 'You fled the Terror, of course.'

'My parents did. I was a tiny child, an infant at the time.'

Perhaps Sophie imagined the spark of disbelief in Lady Wyverne's eyes, but in any case if she had doubts of her true age she did not voice them. 'Your parents still live?'

'No, madame. Things were... difficult after they came to England; they were able to bring little with them, they fell ill... they are both gone now.' Unlike anything else she'd said so far, this was true, at least in part. It had been difficult – so much more difficult because of the actions of this woman's son – and now her parents were indeed dead. Again she pushed away the unwelcome memories, the sight of the disorder, the blood, her mother's frantic screams.

The quiet voice was gentle, and Sophie blinked away tears. 'You have experienced much suffering, I perceive. But you are strong. You have survived it.'

She took a breath. 'Yes, madame.' She had. She would do more; she would triumph.

'I think perhaps now is not the time for you to commence reading to me. Later today, or tomorrow perhaps, you shall read. Silly novels, but they amuse me, and I understand you do not object to the nature of what you shall read. It has been explained to you? I am fatigued almost to the point of extinction by the thought of all your predecessors, to whom it was not adequately explained, evidently, or who did not listen to the explanation, or who, it transpired, could not read in a pleasing manner.'

She could not keep saying, Yes, madame. She said, 'I do not object, madame. I hope you will find that I am able to read to your satisfaction. It is a little while since I have had the opportunity of speaking French each day, but I am sure it will swiftly come back to me.'

'I am sure it will,' said the old lady. 'It was evident that you were a little overset at first, and understandably so, but one's mother tongue, one does not forget. Is that not correct, Rafael?'

A deep voice, from a winged armchair over by the fireplace, also speaking French. 'Of course, Grand-mère. I am sure that Mademoiselle Delavallois will... perform admirably. I look forward with great eagerness to hearing her myself, I must confess.'

# 4

Sophie had not known that anyone else was in the room, and she suppressed a start when the Dowager Lady Wyverne addressed another person, and that deep, lazy voice responded. The maid Marchand had curtsied and left after presenting her, and she had been deeply absorbed in the old lady's words, her sheer presence, and in the unwelcome recollections all of it had called up. She had in recent years prided herself on her excellent reflexes and her constant vigilance, but they had betrayed her here. She flushed with mortification, and was aware she did so. She must be more careful.

Lady Wyverne's frail voice was amused. 'Ah – this is my grandson, Lord Drake, Miss Delavallois. It is apparent that the young lady is not greatly enamoured of the idea of reading to you, Rafael. And why should she be? It is most improper. If you wish to be read to – and I would be the last person to judge you for it – you must find another woman who is prepared to do so along with her other... duties. One imagines such creatures must exist.'

'Improper, Grand-mère? Really?' There was clearly an excellent understanding between the pair; he too was amused, and his tone was warm, fond and intimate. It was a seductive voice, there was no denying that, but Sophie was not in danger of being seduced by anyone in this house.

Delphine laughed, and then winced with pain, and let out some most unladylike words that made Sophie blink in surprise. 'I see I have shocked you, child,' she said. 'I dare say you will become accustomed to it, however. I assure you, old age is the very devil.'

'It is better than the alternative, *ma mie*,' her grandson said.

'I suppose so. But it is no small thing, to outlive all one's friends, one's lovers, and most of one's family. It can be so melancholy... But there is no point repining. I will sleep now, I think. Leave me, both of you, and send my woman to me, Rafael.'

Sophie rose, and stepped away, curtsying, as Lord Drake approached his grandmother's side and leant down to kiss her wrinkled cheek.

'I will see you later,' he said, 'if you find yourself a little better. I suppose I would be wasting my time to suggest that you might be more comfortable and rest more easily in your bed?'

'I am not an invalid, my dear, only devilish old,' the Dowager said. 'Now go!'

He held the door so that Sophie could precede him through it. After he had closed it behind him, she presumed herself to be dismissed and turned to leave.

His voice arrested her. 'Mademoiselle!'

She could not pretend she had not heard him, though she wished to, and looked back at him, keeping her face impassive with a studied effort. What could a man of his standing possibly have to say to her, a mere servant, his grandmother's paid companion?

He did not recognise her, of course. There was no reason why he should. The girl she used to be, the one he'd met so many years ago, had been a debutante, descendant of a noble French house, and of royalty. There had not been much money after her parents' flight from France, but still she'd been delicately nurtured, loved, and sheltered as far as possible from the harsh realities of life. At eighteen, though, when she'd danced with him just once, she was not destined to be sheltered for much longer. A matter of days only, to remain pathetically naïve and happy.

Sophie looked back on her younger self with a sort of fond exasperation – if she met that innocent girl now, she'd want to shake her out of her complacency, to shout at her and tell her to be careful. But what difference would it have made, after all? Disaster had been coming for her, and she couldn't have stopped it, no matter what she'd done. She'd had no weapons, no armour. Now she had both.

His unwelcome voice broke into her reverie. 'I am curious to know a little more about you, since you will be spending so much time with my grandmother and she is important to me. Would you care to walk a little in the grounds? It is a fine day, and not cold.'

She hesitated. It would be absurd to fear recognition, but his scrutiny must be most unwelcome. And so she had absolutely no desire to share her confected story with him, or to spend another moment in his company, but she could see that she had little choice. She felt her effort at resistance to be feeble even as she murmured, 'It is not appropriate, for you to spend time with me, my lord. You must surely see that this is so. I have been especially warned in no uncertain terms against fraternising with the family.'

He laughed. 'You echo my grandmother, with her talk of impropriety. I assure you, far more inappropriate things occur in this house every day. And night, of course.' I'll wager they do, she thought, and you an enthusiastic participant in them. 'If you are

concerned about your reputation, I assure you that you have
nothing to fear from me. We will stroll a little, where anybody
might see us.'

'That's what concerns me,' she said drily.

His dark eyes sparked with some emotion she could not hope
to interpret. 'You would prefer to be alone with me where no one
can see, in one of the secluded temples or grottoes, perhaps? No!'
He held up his hand to forestall her rushing into speech. 'I am
teasing you, and I should not. I know a woman in your situation
must be cautious, though one might point out that a truly
cautious lady would never have come to Wyverne Hall in the first
place. Walk with me for half an hour by the lake. If anyone asks
me, or even if they do not, I shall say that I was quizzing you as to
your suitability to be my grandmother's companion.'

'You have made a habit of this, perhaps?' she said with great
cordiality, distrusting him with every fibre of her being. What had
happened to her family hadn't been his fault, but he wasn't an
innocent either, and she was not likely to forget it.

'I have not, so far,' he admitted. 'Your predecessors – your
many predecessors – were all of them older.' She said nothing,
merely looked at him, and he went on, an edge of what she
thought was frustration entering his deep voice, roughening it.
'I'm not helping my case, am I, Mademoiselle Delavallois? I
assure you once again that, despite my maladroitness, I have no
other intentions than to walk with you and converse with you a
little. It was very evident how those other poor creatures came to
be here, how little choice they had in the matter; with you, it is
not so, or does not appear so to me.'

This hardly improved matters; the last thing Sophie needed
was any member of this household taking it into their head the
idea that she was somehow different, or interesting. She was
supposed to be a person of no consequence whatsoever. She

wasn't meant to be having conversations outside the course of her work, least of all with him, the Marquess's eldest son and heir to Wyverne and all its ill-gotten treasures. If his intent regard, the sheer relentless focus that he brought to bear on her, sparked an unexpected and treacherous little flame of interest and excitement deep within her, she knew she must ignore it. She would not be distracted from her purpose by any man, least of all this one. If he was attractive, and he was, she had no business admitting it even to herself. No Wyverne man could possibly be trusted. But she had little choice in the face of his insistence, and so she said, 'Very well, my lord, I will walk with you, if you insist. I must get my bonnet and my shawl.'

He bowed. 'Thank you. I will wait for you outside the main entrance to the Marble Saloon in ten minutes.' He saw her uneasy reaction to his words and interpreted it correctly, saying firmly, 'Yes, there. There is nothing clandestine about our meeting. That really would be dangerous – you must know that I am right. We are perfectly at liberty to take a short stroll together.'

She climbed the many stairs to her attic room and picked up her things, running lightly down to meet him at the top of the grand steps that led down to the lawn and the lake – one of the lakes. A marquess couldn't be expected to make do with just one lake, after all. One of the expressionless liveried footmen – James, she thought – held open the great door for her and she walked through it, assuming an air of calm composure that she did not feel. The servants would know she had met with Rafael – with Lord Drake – and by arrangement; they'd been wary enough of her before, and this would only make things worse. She was in an anomalous position, neither one thing nor the other, and she didn't want or need their friendship, but she hoped to avoid their overt hostility.

He did not seem to hear her coming, lost in a brown study,

and she examined him while he was unaware of her presence. Obviously he hadn't changed as much as she had in eight years, living in ease while she had not, but he'd been little more than a boy then, and he was a man now. He was perhaps five years or so older than she was, she thought, in his early thirties. She knew he wasn't married. He was highly eligible, apart of course from the scandalous entanglement with his stepmother that all London whispered avidly about. Presumably that reduced his marital prospects somewhat, even in the moral swamp that was the haut ton. Unless you were truly desperate for a title and a fortune, you'd not want to be brought here as a bride, or sit down to dinner with your husband's mistress, the notorious former actress, and be obliged to call her Mama. That was without even considering the atrocious reputation of your bridegroom's dear papa, many of whose exploits were too shocking even to be alluded to. Rumour had him capable of anything, and Sophie was in a position to know that in this instance rumour did not lie. Lord Wyverne, this man's father, was, if anything, even more wicked than he was painted.

So perhaps the harpies and the matchmaking mothers of the London Season were wary of Lord Drake, despite all his many natural advantages, which went far beyond those of fortune and noble birth. For it would be idle to deny that he was very, very handsome. Sophie's head still barely topped his shoulder – his broad shoulder. He was quite plainly an athlete, one of the Corinthian set rather than a tulip of the ton, and his muscular form seemed to owe nothing to padding or to clever tailoring, his buckskin breeches and coat fitting him to perfection and admitting no concealment. His hair was dark and shining, arranged with studied carelessness, and his strong features were finely sculpted, and supremely masculine. But with all these attractions he could not be described as approachable; his habitual expression – except when he had been with his grandmother, Sophie had observed – appeared to be withdrawn, aloof, closed off and somewhat cynical. His eyes were dark and enigmatic, somewhere between stormy grey and indigo blue, and as he turned now and saw her watching him Sophie flushed with mortification that he'd caught her out. That was all it was; she was no green girl, blushing because a gentleman laid his eyes on her. She moved closer – not too close – and said, 'Let us go, my lord. I fear the weather is changing.'

# 5

Rafe hated being here. He had few unshadowed happy memories of this house, the house his mother had lived miserably and died cruelly young in, tearing his world apart and banishing any real sense of security forever. From his earliest years, he'd been aware of her deep unhappiness and shared it, knowing without ever voicing the knowledge that it was caused by Lord Wyverne. His father had been a cold, critical, sarcastic presence and a constant source of unease and confusion, if not outright fear, that affected everyone around him, including the servants and the estate children who'd been young Rafe's only playmates. After his mother's death, his first stepmother had soon taken her place, and she had been kind to him, though of course she could never replace his mama, but she too had lived unhappily and died early.

Wyverne Hall remained his father's chief residence, show-place for his treasures, thoroughly imbued with his sinister personality, and had been – still was – the scene of his most notorious debauches. Now, of course, his father's third wife presided over it. Rosanna.

Rafe wasn't obliged to actually live here. That was something.

He had a small estate of his own a few miles away, inherited from
his uncle, his mother's brother, so he need never sleep under this
roof again, not while his father was alive. If it was too late or too
dark to ride all the way home, he stayed with his friend Simon at
the rectory in the village.

He wouldn't be here at all, he wouldn't so much as set foot in
the place, if his grandmother weren't here. It wasn't really clear to
him why his father insisted on her living here, and certainly she'd
have been more than welcome in his own home. If Lord Wyverne
ever went to see her in her suite of rooms, he must do it at odd
times of the day or night, because Rafe never encountered him
there. It would be ridiculous to assume that there was any great
affection between them. She never spoke of him unless she had to
(and God knows he, Rafe, never raised the topic with her). If the
mother and child bond – mother and firstborn son – was prover-
bially the strongest in nature, something had gone seriously
wrong here, and many years since.

It had sometimes occurred to Rafe that Lord Wyverne kept his
elderly, fragile mother in his principal seat chiefly so that he
could enjoy the sight of her being obliged to acknowledge and be
civil to the woman he had taken as his third wife. It was, perhaps,
a twisted form of punishment, though Rafe was unsure what
crime his father believed the Dowager had committed to merit
such treatment. She'd not been faithful to her husband, true, but
he'd been a legendary womaniser long before he'd met her and
throughout their marriage, so to judge her harshly hardly seemed
fair. But when had the Marquess ever been fair to anyone?

It might even be the case that Wyverne had married Rosanna,
with all her shocking past, not in spite of the fearful scandal it
had caused, but precisely because of it. Certainly he took a
perverse pleasure in flaunting her in the face of the world, and
especially in the faces of his own family – his mother, his heir. But

if it hurt Delphine to accept Rosanna as her successor as marchioness and mistress of the house and the estate, she never showed the least sign of it. Not in public; not, as far as Rafe knew, in private either. Whether this lack of obvious reaction was a disappointment to his father or not, he could not venture to say. It would be an enormous understatement to say that they were not close.

Rafe stood on the steps and looked out over the artificially natural landscape that would one day be his. Wyverne was damnably beautiful, there was no denying that. It was spring, and a light breeze ruffled the surface of the nearest lake. Clouds scudded fast across the eggshell-blue sky, daffodils nodded bravely under specimen trees, and leaves were just unfurling in freshest green. Each eminence was crowned by a temple or a folly, each ride ended in an obelisk or a statue, placed with supreme taste and confidence in exactly the right place. The scene was heartbreakingly lovely, implausibly idyllic, but there was no place for him here now, and if he could not be with his grandmother he should be at home, where he was needed.

He felt eyes upon him, and turned to see that the Frenchwoman was standing waiting. Watching him with those big dark eyes. A slight flush had crept up into her pale cheeks once more – he presumed she was irked that he had caught her observing him – and she spoke some inconsequential words to gloss over the awkward moment. He offered his arm, she took it with poorly concealed reluctance, and they descended the broad steps together.

It was perfectly true, as she had most impudently implied a few moments ago, that he had taken very little interest in his grandmother's previous companions. He wanted Grand-mère to be happy, and therefore he wanted her companion to suit her, but he was beginning to think that the woman who'd do that – who'd read those ridiculous novels to her satisfaction, and converse to her amusement, and not bore her to death in a week – did not exist. Or if she existed somewhere, she was living a life of her own, not looking for employment as a paid companion. There had been so many of those, and none of them had lasted long. There was no reason this girl should be any different.

And yet... she was different. It wasn't just that she was somewhat younger than all the rest. That was of no consequence; the world was full of young women. It wasn't that she was attractive, though she was that too. The world was full enough of attractive young women, for that matter. Women whose charms were all too obvious, displayed to tempt the casual observer. There was nothing obvious about *her*, and she wasn't laying out any wiles to catch his attention. If he'd been forced to describe her in words, nothing he'd be able to say would have conveyed any special sort of allure. She was inconspicuous, or should be: not tall, not short, not thin nor plump, not especially graceful in her movements though not clumsy either, her hair a sober brown, her eyes dark brown too. Her skin was good, it was true, her hair lustrous, her features regular, and she appeared to be in excellent health and have her own teeth. But one might say as much and more about a horse. A spaniel bitch. There was nothing in any of this to hold the gaze. To hold *his* gaze, in particular. But... earlier in his grandmother's room and now, he couldn't look away. Something about her sheer presence, her enormous self-possession, and the depth of feeling that he was positive lay beneath it, though she almost never let it show, drew him. Held him.

And the devil of it was, he was certain he'd met her before. He knew in his bones he had. And not a fleeting, casual contact; she hadn't passed him by common chance in the London street or anything of that nature. They'd met, been introduced, conversed.

Which was surely impossible.

## 6

The uneasy pair made their way across the velvety lawn and by tacit agreement headed for the edge of the closest lake. Neither of them spoke. In the momentary silence, Sophie thought that she might as well enjoy this unexpected opportunity to breathe fresh air and feel the spring sun on her face, unobscured by the smoke and stench of London. It had been years since her life had been such that she had walked on fresh grass and seen trees and flowers. There were parks in town, where the wealthy and sometimes even the poor took their ease, but her path hadn't lain in that direction. She'd missed all this; she'd grown up running free and innocent in the countryside, in France… But she couldn't afford to lose herself in memories again. She needed all her wits about her with this man.

This damnably observant man. He said, 'You appear more easy, mademoiselle, now that we are outside. You enjoy the country air, I see, and the prospects that Wyverne offers.'

She had no time to consider if he meant anything more than the obvious and platitudinous by his comment about Wyverne's prospects. She said sedately, 'It is lovely; one must admire it. You are very fortunate, sir, to live here.'

'I suppose it might appear so. But you are incorrect, in point of fact, mademoiselle. I do not reside here now, but on my own small estate, a few miles away. I spend time here only to visit my grandmother.'

And your mistress, she thought but did not say. You come to meet clandestinely with your mistress, who is also your step-mother, here, in your father's house. To make love to her. But his comment offered much safer ground for discussion, and she seized on it. 'She is a remarkable lady, the Dowager.'

'That she is. And I care greatly for her. Which is why I should prefer to get to know you a little better, since you will be spending so much time with her.'

It was plain he didn't trust her, though she had no idea why. Of course he was quite right not to, but how could he know it? Another woman in her situation might have chosen to ignore the disturbing implication behind his words. Sophie, though, as was her nature, went on the attack. 'You are concerned for her. For some reason I cannot fathom – is that the correct word? – you distrust me, and do not think I am fit to be in her company.'

He did not answer her for a moment. She was sure she had surprised him, but with an effort she suppressed the impulse to look up, to see the effect her reply had had on him. He said slowly, 'I don't know if I distrust you. I don't know you. But I'm not a trusting sort of a man as a general rule, that's perfectly true.' Half to himself, quietly, he said, 'Perhaps it is only that.'

'Your concern for your grandmother is quite natural. She has reached a great age, and is not in perfect health. And you ask yourself, why am I here?' This was reckless folly, but she pushed on. 'Well, I am here *tout simplement* to make a living, my lord. I am obliged to do so by the circumstances of my life now. And I am being well paid, to read a few novels and converse in my native language. I count myself lucky, I assure you; it is no hardship. Not compared with several other positions I have taken up in recent years.'

Sophie had observed previously that wealthy people greatly disliked being confronted with the bare fact of others' poverty; they considered it bad taste, that such a thing should be mentioned, and it made them feel uncomfortable, even possibly slightly guilty. Guilty was good, guilty was right. Let him be thrown off balance.

Annoyingly, he didn't seem to be discomposed in the slightest. He said, and his voice just now was very deep, 'You are young, and yet it seems to me that your manner, your self-possession, are those of a woman of infinite worldly experience. And so I am intrigued. Tell me about these other... positions.' He had stopped, and so Sophie stopped too, and now she did look at him. Could he possibly be attempting to flirt with her? He must be – what other construction could she place on his words? Clearly his bad reputation was deserved, and he was shameless. He was like his father, a libertine, and one woman could never be enough for him. She should rebuff him, she should escape his company as quickly as possible and avoid him in future. In her perilous situation, she could not afford to attract his attention like this. If only she were free to simply walk away from him.

But then their dark eyes locked, and the moment stretched between them. The air seemed to crackle with electricity, and the soft natural sounds that surrounded them – water lapping, birds calling, dry reeds rustling at the edge of the lake – faded and vanished. Though there must be dozens of people in the mansion at their backs, within call, they were entirely alone in the world in that moment.

Sophie recovered first, or spoke first, at least. She would

always fight back. She laughed lightly and said in an amused tone, 'My lord! Are we to have a conversation such as those in your grandmother's novels, where we speak of one thing and mean quite another? I warn you, if we are, French is much better for the purpose of double entendre. Do not try to tell me that you are not proficient.'

He let out a sudden, startling crack of laughter. 'I suppose I deserved that. Shocking, to try to draw a young lady into such an improper discussion, and you are quite right, that is what I was doing. A moment of... distraction, I can scarcely say what I was thinking. I beg you to accept my apologies, mademoiselle.'

She had beaten him, almost she had shamed him, if such a thing were possible; no doubt that was why her heart was racing. But nothing of it showed on her face, she was almost sure, or in her voice. 'I must accept them, sir. And if you do truly wish to learn where I was employed before this, and in what circumstances, I am quite happy to tell you. I have no secrets.' This was a truly monstrous lie; she was proud of her ability to utter it so calmly.

'Do you not? It is a rare person who can say as much. But no. No doubt... Lady Wyverne took up your references. It is her proper sphere, not mine. Oblige me by forgetting that I mentioned it.'

Sophie could not fail to notice the tiny pause, the merest hitch in the smooth flow of his speech, before he uttered his stepmother's title. 'I believe your mother did pursue my recommendations, yes,' she said with sweet serenity.

His tone was suddenly arctic. 'Lady Wyverne is not my mother.'

'I beg your pardon, my lord; of course she is not. My English sometimes fails me. Your... belle-mère, of course. Your stepmother. She is not old enough to be your mother, so I do not know how I could be so foolish.'

'No, No, she is not. And now you must excuse me, mademoiselle. It is past time I took my leave.' He turned, began to stride away, but then he swivelled back to face her and said abruptly, 'Whatever else you truly are, Mademoiselle Delavallois, and I confess I do not have the least idea – yet – though I promise you faithfully that I will make it my business to find out, I would be most surprised if anyone had ever called you foolish. Good day!'

She stood and watched him go, and only her enormous and habitual self-control prevented her from stamping her foot in anger and frustration, or otherwise making an exhibition of herself for anybody who might be watching. She had come out much the better from this encounter; she had bested her opponent, and greatly shaken his composure, even though he'd had the last word. But at what cost to herself? She must consider it a Pyrrhic victory, in a battle she should never have been drawn into at all. Oh, he was dangerous, this Lord Drake. Despite all her efforts to appear entirely harmless and ordinary, a woman in sadly reduced circumstances working for her living and nothing more, she had clearly failed somehow, because this man distrusted her by instinct, he had been flirting with her simply in an effort to learn more of her past, to trap her, and his promise to discover more about her was a serious threat to all her plans. His interest in her could be fatal. Literally so. She would have to be very, very careful.

But then, she'd known that already.

## 7

Sophie took up her duties properly the next day. The Dowager Lady Wyverne would not permit her grandson to be present when Sophie read to her, and for this she could only be grateful. She did not know if hearing her read such matter aloud would affect Lord Drake in any way, but she feared that it might seriously disturb her. That moment, when their eyes had met...

She might as well admit privately that she was powerfully attracted to him, despite the many excellent reasons why she should not be. It was almost laughable. He was the son of the man she hated most in the world, the man she was determined to destroy. If she succeeded, his family would suffer – him included, not just the rest of them. Should he discover what she was about before she did it, he'd have her thrown out of the house, if not locked in jail or beaten. If he found out afterwards, her situation would be even more desperate – he'd see her hanged, and no doubt think it exactly what she deserved. And quite apart from any of that, she could set herself up as no moral arbiter – she was a thief, after all – but the man was rutting with his father's wife and all the world knew it. If she was a sinner, surely he was much worse. And he was suspicious of her already, after just one meeting. It seemed it didn't matter. She felt a strong pull towards him, but she need not give in to it. After all, she wouldn't be here long. He could be nothing to her.

Sophie was, as he'd said, a woman of a certain amount of experience – though she wasn't sure that he'd meant it as any kind of compliment. She'd had a lover, a man she'd chosen when she saw the desire in his eyes and felt the response in her own body. They'd pleased each other for a good while, until the trajectories of their lives had pulled them apart. She knew, then, the power of animal physical attraction, not to mention the even more insidious appeal of making a connection, however fleeting it might prove to be, with another person. But she also knew, as anyone with eyes to see must, the trouble all this uncontrolled desire could cause in anyone's life, let alone hers, here and now, with a man she should run a mile from because of who he was, who his father was, and who she was. This was no time for self-indulgence.

She could only be wary at all times, and on her guard in particular when Lord Drake was near.

Perhaps fortunately, she saw little of the Viscount over the next few days, and less luckily she made no progress with her obsession – her reason, her only reason, for being at Wyverne Hall. The matter of the jewels.

Well, that was not entirely true, for in her free time, in the afternoons when the Dowager was sleeping, she explored the enormous building. It was necessary that she know her way about the place; not only must she locate what she had come to take, but she might need to flee as quickly as possible once she had taken it, or even, if things really went awry, to hide herself for a time if she was being pursued.

It was a labyrinth. The palace, for that in sober truth was what it was, had replaced an earlier and much more modest building, she knew from her research and Nate's, some hundred and fifty years ago, and from the outside it presented an appearance of classical regularity, with its two great pillared façades, like vast Grecian temples. One side, the side that faced the largest in a series of lakes, was more or less flat in aspect, though the central part was higher than the wings; the other frontage, no less grand, curved forward symmetrically at each side in a huge colonnade and sheltered a carriage entrance below ground level. But inside... Perhaps some traces of the older house remained within the newer one, and besides it must have been added to more than once over the centuries, modified according to the changing whims of its aristocratic owners. To attempt to count the hundreds of rooms would have been a Herculean task. It was difficult enough even to begin to get it all straight in her head.

The main public spaces were impressive, even awe-inspiring, arranged in long interconnecting series that ran out on either side from the vast domed marble atrium: ballroom, formal salons, a library, dining rooms of varying sizes. But she wasted little time on them. She was interested in the family's private rooms, and even more in the back stairs, the little closets, the forgotten corridors, the unused, dusty chambers where it seemed no one ever went.

She imagined trying to search this great beast of a house in any methodical way. You couldn't; it would be quite impossible. And if you'd been robbed, if there was a window open or a door apparently forced, you'd assume the thieves had fled, and taken their booty with them. Wouldn't you? A thief would be very stupid, or very cool and daring, to commit such a crime and then stay here, along with what he'd stolen. What she'd stolen.

It was going to be somewhat bulky, her loot. A fair weight to it – all those jewels, all that gold – but manageable. If the Wyverne woman could wear it, Sophie could carry it. It would be enough to fill a small portmanteau, perhaps, or a cloak bag. And she was looking for somewhere safe and clever to hide it. Because she wasn't going to take it and run; she was going to stay and enjoy the chaos she had created, enjoy the dawning panic on their faces when they realised what they'd lost. That was the whole point. She'd had such an experience herself, had known such a devastating loss and all that had led from it – she was never likely to forget that terrible night – and now they would endure it too. Lord Wyverne, chiefly, but all of them. They'd suffer what she'd suffered. And how she'd love it.

There was an area of the house that she found particularly promising. She discovered a servants' staircase in a small vestibule behind the state dining room. Perhaps it had once gone all the way down to the kitchens in the semi-basement, perhaps it had once bustled with activity, but the kitchens had been moved, she thought, and its descent ended in a blank wall now. It led up still, though, and on the first floor emerged behind a panel at the end of a corridor that led to guest bedrooms. They weren't currently in use, and there were grander ones in another wing – Sophie believed these ones would only be opened up if the house hosted a full-scale ball with dozens of noble visitors staying overnight. Since the current Lady Wyverne was not received into polite society, and probably never would be, she thought that was most unlikely to happen.

There was nothing particularly secret about these neglected rooms. But the staircase climbed higher still, up towards the attics. These were not the attic chambers the maids and menservants inhabited – those were far away on the other side of the house. There was a maze of unused rooms up here, and it was hard to see what their purpose had ever been; now, some of them were empty, hung with cobwebs, and some full of lumber and sad, discarded furniture. They'd been fine once, and several of them were large and hung with beautiful, costly old wallpaper. The paper concealed secret doors, which led to short corridors and yet more chambers. A virtual maze. In one, though, there was nothing but a single piece of furniture: a huge, decaying four-poster bed; old, probably valuable once, and far too big to move unless it were disassembled, presumably with enormous trouble that no one had ever been inclined to take. Some impulse propelled Sophie to look under the frame of it, and there she saw the outline of something, a change in the floorboards – a trap-door, almost obscured by the dust of decades. She wriggled under the high bed-frame, glad she'd thought to change into her oldest gown.

A while later, she emerged, breathless and triumphant. She'd found it: exactly what she needed. Between the floor of this room and the ceiling of the next was a windowless space, forgotten somehow and left behind in the deranged way this house had been changed and changed again. It was tall enough to stand in, a sturdy ladder led down into it, and it was full of rubbish and nameless broken things.

She would bring up a broom and sweep away all evidence of her footsteps in the dust. She could cease looking now; she was one step closer to being ready. She made her way back through the maze, and into the largest room, the one with the lovely, faded old wallpaper in soft blues, greens and yellows. This chamber had a tall sash window that looked out sideways across the roof, towards the central section of the great house. She must be near the back of the mansion, away from the carriage entrance; this part of the building was higher that the section it adjoined, and so she could, if she wished, dare to open the window and climb without any difficulty down onto the roof. She did wish – she'd be up above everybody for once, exulting in her secrets and their ignorance.

The window's sash mechanism was stiff with disuse, and for a while she thought it would not budge, but at last it gave to her insistent pressure, and she was able to push it up. It creaked on its ropes but moved, creating an opening that was easily big enough to allow her to duck agilely under and climb out onto the leads.

There was a decorative stone parapet, more than waist-high, and she stood with her hands upon it, taking in great lungfuls of air and looking out and down. It was another beautiful day of fast-moving cloud, and the intense new green and fertile brown of rural England in spring spread out below her – the shining string of lakes, the park with its tall specimen trees and stone follies, and then a patchwork of fields, trackways, hedges and small stands of timber rising to more heavily wooded heights in the distance. From here it seemed unreal, a toy landscape scattered with tiny toy buildings and tinier toy people, and this was correct in a fashion, because all of it belonged to Lord Wyverne, to handle as he wished, as if he were some overgrown, irresponsible toddler. He had been given so much from his earliest years, she thought, an idyllic little kingdom to possess, and still he could not be content with all he had, but must steal from others who owned almost nothing. She knew that her own family had also – through no merit of their own, but just because their ancestors were strong, ruthless brutes with swords, horses and knights – become inheritors of a great deal, and no doubt had taken it for granted and thought it their just deserts while others struggled to live, to feed their children. In the last eight years she'd been hungry and frightened, had seen starving children and other terrible sights that had shaken all she'd once believed without question. She could not deny the painful truth of what she now knew: her happy childhood had always been built on the most unstable of foundations and on the sweated labour of others. But those days of ignorance were gone, and her family had paid the highest price for their transgressions and those of their forebears. They'd been left in the end with very little, and what little they'd had Wyverne had taken from them. They had all suffered cruelly and were now dead – her mother, her father and her sweet little brother Louis – and Wyverne still lived in luxury. He hadn't killed them, not directly, but he might as well have done. He was a wicked, wicked man, that she knew for certain; nothing she had ever done came close to his enormous crimes. Well, she was just one woman and she couldn't take all he had away from him – but she could take a great deal.

'Mademoiselle Delavallois!'

Once again Wyverne's heir had surprised her. And of course it had to be him – who else? She looked along the parapet – it ran for thirty feet or so and led, she now saw, to another window mirroring the one she'd climbed out of. It was open, and standing by it, in the right-angle between the building and the edging wall, was Lord Drake, leaning at his ease against the golden stone. He was in shadow – she told herself that that was why she hadn't seen him immediately – but as she looked at him he stepped out of the shade and crossed the leads to her side. Too perilously near for her peace of mind.

'I must confess,' he said, 'I am surprised to find you here – to find anyone here. I generally have the place to myself.' He had taken off his coat and his highly polished riding boots, standing in shirtsleeves, waistcoat, buckskin breeches and stockinged feet, and the breeze had disordered his dark hair. Somehow all of this combined to make him appear younger, and less formidable, more like the boy she'd danced with in another life, though no less powerfully attractive. She fancied she could see his warm skin, the dark hair on his muscled arms, through the fine fabric of his shirt. Sheer folly.

She shivered, though the day was not cold, and then, conscious that she still had not answered him, she said, 'I am sorry, my lord. You are quite right, I have no business being here, and I will go immediately. Will you excuse me?'

Why must he stand so close? She could even smell him, she noticed for the first time, or the first time with conscious awareness. He smelled of fresh linen and spices, leather, and clean man. He said, 'No. No, I won't excuse you, in fact. My room is just there.' He nodded in the direction from which he had come. 'But your room is over that way, quite on the other side of the house, up in the attics, and gives no access to the roof. I think it not unreasonable of me to ask what precisely you are doing here.'

This was very dangerous. She must not panic, though, and so as was her habit she went on the attack. 'I confess I was curious, my lord, and looked to find a way of coming out onto the roof. I like high places, the open views they give. The solitude. You cannot say that I am neglecting your grandmother, if that is what you were thinking – she is asleep this afternoon and set me at liberty. But I will go now, so that I do not trouble you any more. I did not realise that this was a place servants were not permitted to be.'

'But you do.' She looked up at him questioningly. 'You do trouble me. When you are present, and when you are not.' She thought his cheeks had flushed slightly when she'd reminded him of her lowly status but he showed no other signs of being abashed that she could see. It was frustrating, but there was an odd exhilaration, too, in sparring with him. He was a worthy opponent.

'Still you distrust me,' she said steadily.

'No – well, yes, perhaps. As I think I said before, my trust is not easily given. But that's not why the thought of you preys upon my mind. I must admit, after our last meeting I find myself thinking about you a great deal.' His voice was so deep, so seductive, with an undeniable strength underlying it, like the softest velvet and silk sliding over hard muscle and hot skin.

Sophie was very aware suddenly of how alone they were up here, and it did not help, to know that the attraction, the compulsion that she felt, however she chose to name it, was a mutual thing. She had thought it must be. A woman knew what the light in a man's eyes meant, the spark of interest, when they lingered on her, and she was no longer a naïve girl.

She was about to make some light answer, to turn his words aside if she could, when his hand came out to brush her cheek, a soft touch that lasted only a fraction of a second, and yet still seemed to linger and to burn. 'You had a cobweb there,' he explained. 'Another, in your hair. You really have been exploring, have you not? Let me...' His gentle fingers caressed the side of her head, above her ear, for a moment, and then with a sort of inevitability his head lowered and his lips found hers. Claimed them. It was not an urgent kiss, or deep, it was not passionate or demanding, but Sophie found that she closed her eyes against the sheer sweet rightness of it. She sighed against his mouth and felt herself sway towards the warmth of his big body, so tantalisingly close and so very tempting. To hold, to touch, to be held and touched; no longer to be alone for a precious little while... But as she leaned towards him, his lips found her ear and he whispered very low, his breath tickling her sensitive flesh and making her shiver, 'I know I've met you before. I am positive of it. And one day soon, mademoiselle, I will remember, and then – why, then I will know exactly who you are, and what you are doing here. For you are not who you claim to be, or what you claim to be. And you are quite right – of course I do not trust you!'

Her eyes sprang open in shock, but before she could patch together any sort of answer he was gone, moving fast and sure as a great cat across the walkway and stepping quickly through the window into the shadowed room behind.

Sophie turned and walked slowly away in the opposite direction, prey to a multitude of roiling emotions in which anxiety, anger – at herself as well as him – and thwarted desire warred for prominence. Eight years ago, she'd have been shaking if anything remotely similar had happened to her: the kiss, with all its false, seductive sweetness, and then the challenge. But not now. She'd faced down worse men than Drake in the intervening years, and been in greater danger, and escaped. Or survived, anyway. Prospered, in a fashion; grown hard and made a plan.

It was easy to tell herself all this, and another thing to believe it entirely. She could not be certain if he were watching her or not as she left him, not really, but she thought he must be; she felt his stormy dark eyes boring through the fabric of her gown and all the layers of garments beneath it, right through to her bare skin and her naked self.

# 8

Sophie had so far not met Lord Wyverne, her host, the man above all others in the world whom she hated the most. She'd had him pointed out to her when riding in Hyde Park, centuries ago in her previous life, and her father had known him socially, of course, to her whole family's ruin, but he hadn't been in Brook Street when his wife had interviewed her, and he'd been absent from Wyverne Hall since her arrival. But now he was back, with a few guests, and holding a dinner party. The household had been in turmoil for days before his arrival, the servants frantically cleaning and polishing rooms that had already appeared immaculate to Sophie, dusting the statues and the pictures with anxious care; clearly, the Marquess was an exacting master.

The Dowager, summoning her to her side one afternoon, was perturbed; Sophie knew her well enough by now to be aware of this. Her distress, if that was not too strong a word, showed not in her voice, her face or her words, but in a certain restless motion of her frail hands, twisting involuntarily on the bright shawl that covered her lap, playing with the fringe of it, plaiting and unplaiting. She said, 'My dear child, I have something unpleasant to tell you. This morning I received a note from my son, demanding my attendance at dinner this evening. He does this to me occasionally. I could plead illness, of course, but... in my experience that would be unwise.'

Sophie had not realised that they were estranged, though living in the same house. It struck her now that Lady Wyverne had never mentioned her son in her hearing before, and now that she did, the emotion that coloured her voice seemed to be nothing less than fear. 'I am sorry for it, if you should dislike it, madame,' she said. She was indeed sorry, but to show her sympathy too plainly could hardly be pleasant for the old lady, proud as she was.

'I do dislike it, to speak frankly. Setting aside Wyverne's company and whether it pleases me or not, the nature of the people with whom he surrounds himself cannot be... that is why he insists upon my presence, of course: because he knows how much I hate being obliged to meet them, and how much more I loathe to see them with free run of this house. Prostitutes, scoundrels, degenerates, men and women of the worst possible character!' Her voice was fierce with anger and for a moment she sounded much younger, stronger, and then the brief moment of passion faded and she added almost in a whisper, sounding frail again, 'But that's not why I speak of it. On these occasions he also insists that my companion accompanies me, to help me, so he says.'

Sophie made some involuntary noise or movement, she knew not what, and the Dowager said, 'I am sorry, my dear. I believe in the past he has gained amusement from the great discomfort some of my previous companions have felt in the company of his... friends. The ladies were not harmed – I may be a weak, useless old woman, but I would not stand for that – but there was mockery. It was most displeasant, and drove one or two of them away, which I expect amused him. I am not sure, in point of fact, if his wife has spoken of you to him, and told him that you are young and attractive. From what I know of her, I would imagine that she has not done so; she is a viciously jealous woman, and I am positive she would not have hired you if there had been any alternative. No doubt they have not discussed you, and he may not even know I have a new companion, because in general he takes little interest in me. But in any case, I must beg that you attend. I am afraid we have no choice in the matter. It is quite possible that he will pay scant attention to you, but if you were to refuse to come... that would be the surest way to attract his notice. And you do not want that. Believe me, child, you do not.'

Sophie could easily accept the truth of this statement. She'd prefer Lord Wyverne never set eyes on her, at any rate not until her mission was accomplished and the jewels safely hidden away. The last thing she wanted was to spend several hours in dangerous proximity to him now, even if it was indeed true that he would likely barely speak to her. The only thing that could make the prospect of such a nightmare evening worse was...

'There is just one consolation,' the Dowager said, in what seemed to Sophie to be a conscious effort to raise both their spirits. 'When he heard of the plan, and realised that Wyverne demanded my attendance and yours, Drake reassured me that he would come also. This is most unusual, I assure you, since in general he takes great care to avoid his father's company, and he is even less enamoured of his so-called friends than I am. But there has been no open breach between them, or at least not recently, just an enormous coldness, so if he wishes to attend, he is able to do so. Again, to see Rafe's disgust at the nature of the other guests – my son enjoys that. He knows Drake must be thinking, My God, if I were master here, such creatures would not so much as enter the gates, let alone sit at table. But he is not master yet, and

Wyverne merely raises his glass and smiles, that smile of his that chills the blood.'

Her companion could not control a slightly fevered snort of laughter. 'It sounds as though it will not be a dull evening, at least!' she said.

'Oh, yes, but it will,' the old lady sighed. 'Perhaps you have not had the occasion to observe, but people who are highly conscious of how terribly wicked they are, what notable sinners, are the dullest people who ever walked the earth. It is because they have no characters to speak of, outside their bad behaviour. Ask any one of them if she or he has ever read a book and see how they answer.'

Sophie laughed again, this time with genuine amusement. 'I'm sure you're right, madame. Most of all, I suppose, if there are persons present who are *not* so famously bad, and therefore they, the wicked ones, must exert themselves to be especially shocking.'

'Indeed,' the Dowager sighed. 'So very tedious. It will be you who must be shocked – not me, perhaps, for they might be aware that I have a past, but then I am impossibly old, so they may have forgotten it. They will not want to imagine me young, for that must mean that they too will grow old, if they live so long, which probably they shall not. No, I promise you, you will be stifling yawns. And it is not as though you or I shall have Drake sitting beside us to entertain us, for Wyverne will not wish me to have his support, and madame la marquise will want him near her, you can be sure of it, and very far from you. Oh, how vulgar one becomes when one is forced into contact with vulgar persons! It is contagious. Let us speak of something else, dear child, or we shall soon be as bad as they are.'

'Willingly,' said Sophie, happy to cease discussing who was wicked and who was innocent. 'But madame, I do not know what

I am to wear at such an event. I have an evening gown of sorts, but I scarcely think... I suppose I am there simply to be mocked, though, so my shabbiness does not signify.'

'Nonsense!' said the Dowager with some robustness. 'Of course I had thought of that. There is no time to obtain anything new, but I sent Marchand to see if she could find my daughter-in-law's gowns that were put away in lavender when she died – the previous Lady Wyverne, you understand, my son's second wife, poor sad creature that she was. I think you are of much the same height and build, and though they will be sadly outmoded they will at least not be shabby or tawdry. We shall see, in any event. If any rapid alteration is needed, Marchand will do it, for she is very skilled.'

Sophie could only murmur her thanks. 'As for me,' the old lady went on, 'I shall be *en grande tenue*, as if the foolish Austrian queen were not in her grave these many years. And though his guests may find me ridiculous, my son at least might feel some slight pang of shame, if he has indeed any speck of it left, that he obliges me, whose father was a friend and companion of the Sun King himself, to consort with this *batterie de canaille* under his own roof.'

There didn't seem to be anything that Sophie could usefully add to such a bravely sweeping statement, and so she did not make any attempt to reply, but turned the subject and awaited Marchand's appearance with the gowns. She had no illusions that she would be choosing one herself: Delphine would pick, and she did not grudge her this small illusion of control, when in reality she was so very helpless at this final stage of her life, except for her indomitable spirit.

She had little time to untangle the roiling mix of emotions that assailed her, and perhaps that was fortunate, for it was a great deal to cope with. There was dread at confronting Lord

Wyverne at last; concern that she would not keep her wits about her when finally she saw him; worry that she did not attract too much attention from him or anyone else, including his wife; and underlying everything else a strange, uneasy mixture of apprehension and hectic anticipation which she traced to its source in the prospect of spending time, even among others, with Lord Drake. She knew it was foolish, and probably dangerous, to entertain the idea, but she could not help herself. A dinner party; it was eight years since she had attended anything resembling a dinner party.

She wasted no time worrying about the dubious company which she had been warned against. That, at least, she was used to. They might mock her, in their ignorance, but they could not hurt her. Let them try, and they would see who came off worst.

Many of the old gowns were found to be quite unsuitable, but a few of them held some promise. The second Lady Wyverne had favoured the Grecian style, it seemed, which in its austere simplicity had the advantage of not dating too terribly, and at length Delphine decided upon a gown made up in that fashion. It consisted of draping layers of fine black muslin, a mourning dress, and its shape was undeniably not quite in the latest mode, but it had a pleasing line to it, with loose sleeves that covered the shoulders and the upper arms, and a hem and neck – low, but not excessively so – beautifully embroidered in silver in the Greek key pattern. Marchand found long black gloves to match it, and Sophie had slippers of her own that would do well enough.

The gown was found to fit her tolerably well, needing no alteration, and as the dinner hour drew near Marchand, expressionless as ever, came up to the stuffy little attic chamber and helped Sophie into it, dressing her hair for her also. Her impassive façade cracked a fraction as, wielding a hairbrush, she said abruptly, 'You will help madame la marquise, I trust, mademoiselle, as far as you are able? Protect her, even, if it should be necessary? You have not been in this house long, I know, but it must be evident to you – I perceive that your eyes are of sufficient sharpness – how much she dreads this evening, and the toll such disgraceful events take on her?'

Sophie, seated on her one chair as the older woman moved around her, said with all the reassurance she could manage, 'I will, of course, if she should need me. I will not let my vigilance lapse. And Lord Drake will be there too, don't forget.'

'That's true,' the abigail said, though Sophie could not tell if the thought gave her any comfort. 'I am done. Let us go down, mademoiselle, for it is almost time and madame will be anxious.'

Sophie was as ready as she would ever be, and thanked Marchand for her help with some warmth, though the woman had retreated behind her barriers again and showed little reaction. In silence they hurried down the stairs to the Dowager's chamber, and as Marchand stood by watchfully she helped the old lady to her feet, highly conscious of her birdlike frailty, and complimented her sincerely on the court gown of silver brocade and costly lace and on the elaborate powdered wig she wore. Now the Dowager was painted in the fashion of her youth; all of it was armour, Sophie realised, and despite it the old lady's slight frame was shaking with tension. She had not imagined, before she came here, that she had it in her heart to feel the least sliver of sympathy for any member of this family, but she now knew that she had been wrong. It had not taken Marchand's words to set all her senses on high alert for what might occur tonight.

A tall, expressionless liveried footman had been waiting, and now picked the Dowager up and carried her gently and carefully, as if she weighed nothing, which was no doubt almost true, along the corridor and down the grand staircase towards one of the larger dining rooms, Sophie following in his wake. A low chuckle floated back to her over his broad shoulder, and after it a whispered comment that made her smile: 'Seventy years ago, my handsome young man, this little excursion might have ended very differently, I assure you!' The footman, William, was wise enough to make no answer, but Sophie thought she heard him stifle an appreciative snort of laughter as the back of his neck grew red. The woman was incorrigible.

They were the last to arrive, and a dozen expectant faces, most of them unknown to her, turned to watch them as they entered. Sophie did not return their stares, concentrating on helping the Dowager to her chair. It was not until she was seated by her side that she had the chance to look about her.

Her eyes refused to be drawn to Lord Drake, darkly handsome in his evening black, sitting on the other side of the long table, not directly opposite her but at the right hand of his stepmother. His mistress. She could never afford to forget that, nor to be drawn into wondering if his father knew the scandalous fact. Surely he must, since all of the rest of the world certainly did. And could his grandmother really be ignorant of the gossip? Surely she must know and disapprove greatly, despite her obvious love for him. But none of this was Sophie's concern. She had other matters to worry about. She must push his seductive kiss from her mind, and remember instead the blatant threat that had coloured his words to her: he sensed somehow that she was not who she pretended to be, and that distrust, even if it never grew into knowledge, must always be a grave peril to her.

She dragged her eyes away from him – it was all the harder because she was aware that he was looking intently at her, a little frown between his strong dark brows – and focused her gaze first on his father, some distance away at the head of the table. The Dowager Marchioness should by all rules of precedence and simple courtesy be in some place of honour, probably at her son's right hand, but she was not; she was halfway down the table, with Sophie at one side to help her, and on her other side a man of raddled and disreputable appearance who presumably had been selected, if Delphine was correct in her assessment of her son's motives, for his outstandingly disagreeable qualities as a dinner companion. But he was currently fully absorbed in flirting outrageously with the woman on his right – he had just taken snuff from her bare wrist – so the Dowager seemed safe for now.

It was odd, Sophie thought, how insignificant-seeming the Marquess was. She'd known it already, but she hadn't seen him for eight long years, and perhaps inevitably she'd built him up into a nightmare monster that loomed large in her imagination. He must be seventy or so now, and he *was* a monster, but an observer could see little of it in his countenance or his manner at table. He was a man of medium height and spare build – his son was much taller and broader – and though his face should by rights be lined with deep grooves of dissipation, it rather disappointingly wasn't. His eyes were blue-grey, like Lord Drake's, their only point of similarity, and the rest of his features were entirely unmemorable. He could easily pass unnoticed in a crowd, and the person of Sophie's acquaintance whom he most resembled was, with a biting irony she was well able to appreciate, Nate Smith, that equally unremarkable-looking master of thieves and of the London underworld. In the highly unlikely event that they ever encountered each other, they'd be obliged, if they were honest, to remark upon the undeniable likeness. And Nate, like this man, was far more formidable and dangerous than he appeared. Monsters, she thought, should advertise their qualities upon their faces for all to see, not masquerade, as this one did, as normal men.

And then he smiled at her, obviously conscious of her regard, and she revised all her earlier facile opinions. It was, as his own mother had said, a smile that chilled the blood. His dark eyes, so like his son's in other respects, were dead and cold and merciless. She struggled to repress a shudder, and looked hastily away.

A simple white soup was served first, which she and the Dowager ate in silence, but once it was removed a huge variety of different dishes were laid out by the footmen in the old-fashioned style, à la française. The table was soon covered with platter after platter of different types of meat, fish and vegetables in enormous profusion, many of the dishes smothered in rich and elaborate sauces. It was a deliberate display of wealth and abundance, of excess, and in her present mood Sophie found it sickening.

Her uneasiness was not lessened when she realised that other eyes were upon her. She didn't seem to be attracting any attention from the other diners, who were helping themselves from the plates close by to them with great enthusiasm, but Lady Wyverne, in her place at the opposite end of the table from her husband, was watching her. Sophie smiled, and bowed her head politely – she had seen almost nothing of the woman since her arrival at Wyverne Hall – and Rosanna shot her a glance that said very plainly, I have my eyes on you. She was magnificent in gold lace; her gown was cut very low across the chest, and her splendid bosom was on full display. Many of her female guests were similarly attired, but only she was wearing one of the world's largest diamonds nestled between her breasts, striking pale fire with every small movement she made, every exhalation and drawing in of breath.

Like all notable jewels, it had a name: because it was pink and had originally been crafted in Italy, it was called the Stella Rosa, and it belonged to Sophie.

**9**

Sophie hadn't set eyes on the diamond for eight years. She'd never seen anyone but herself actually wearing it before, for that matter, or if she had, she'd been too small to remember it afterwards. It was the great treasure of her family, brought to France, so it was said, by Marie de' Medici when she married King Henri, and passed down by some irresponsible or love-struck descendant of hers – if Sophie had ever known which, she had forgotten it – to the noble lady who was his mistress and Sophie's ancestor. It had been a possession of her house for more than a hundred years, and it was supposed to be cursed.

It was certainly true that it had not brought her parents any luck. It had been smuggled out of France during their desperate flight in 1792, sewn into her mother's clothing, and when they had at last acknowledged that they were down to their last few coins, with Sophie's come-out to pay for, her father had taken the decision, which she knew had been a very difficult one for him, to sell it. There was no point trying to pawn it – they'd never be able to afford to get it back, her mother had argued persuasively. They should let it go – sell it and make a fresh start. Sell it to Lord Wyverne, who made no secret of the fact that he had always coveted it, for a fair price. An enormous price, one which would have kept her whole family in modest comfort for many, many years. But it had not been sold – it had been stolen. And because of that theft, because of the terrible circumstances that had surrounded it, everyone Sophie had ever loved was dead, and she was here. To take it back.

She had been mechanically helping the Dowager to a few morsels from some of the less rich dishes set in front of her, though even they would surely be indigestible for one who was almost an invalid, all the while feeling dazzled and overset by the sight of the Stella Rosa, when a voice too close to her ear drew her attention from her dark thoughts.

Her dinner companion on her other side was claiming her attention now, having presumably assuaged the worst of his hunger, as the stains on his clothing attested. She smiled at him politely, without warmth, as she turned to face him. He wasn't any more prepossessing than the Dowager's neighbour further down the table: perhaps fifty, and wearing fully as much rouge and powder as any of the scantily dressed women who surrounded him. The points of his shirt were so high as to make it a labour for him to turn his head, his cravat resembled nothing so much as an enormous bandage, and his padded purple coat was very tight on his corseted frame. Sophie knew he was corseted because he creaked as he moved, edging towards her in a confidential fashion. She discarded her cursory smile, and looked at him stonily. If he intended gallantry – and he had that look in his bloodshot eyes – he had picked the wrong woman, and this of all nights was the wrong night.

He said, 'We haven't been introduced.' He wasn't looking at

Sophie's face as he said it. This seemed perverse, for Sophie and the Dowager were the only women at the table who hadn't chosen to display almost all of their embonpoints. There was plenty of ripe flesh on display elsewhere, if your taste lay in that direction.

'No,' said Sophie. 'We haven't. But my breasts don't have names. I'm up here.' It was liberating to realise that she felt no need to be civil to this creature, nor to observe the social conventions.

He laughed loudly. He was, Sophie realised, quite inebriated already. '"Don't have names!" Dashed witty!' he said, his slack mouth leering wetly. 'So you are, and very nice too. You're the old girl's companion, I hear.'

There was no point giving him a lesson in courtesy; it was clearly far too late for that. 'I am companion to the Dowager Marchioness,' she said between gritted teeth.

'Must be devilish dull, for a young thing like you, cooped up with the old crone for hours on end. I hear you read to her; you could read to me.' He waggled one painted eyebrow suggestively as he said this.

'In French?'

'Oh, yes!' he smirked. 'Not that I'd understand every word, can't claim to be a clever sort of a fellow, but I dare say I'd get the gist, if you know what I mean. And if I didn't...' He paused for emphasis, and Sophie had a sense that she knew precisely what he was going to say next. 'If I didn't, I dare say you could always show me.'

Sophie felt suddenly very tired, and couldn't summon the energy for a response.

'I said,' he persisted, 'you could always show me. I'd like that. And I could make it worth your while, you know.'

'I seriously doubt it.'

It took a little while for the implications of that to sink in, and when they did, as Sophie had expected, his face took on a purple hue, not unlike that of his coat, and lust was joined, as it so often was in her experience, by a simmering anger, and the lurking threat of violence. He reached out across the little space that separated them and put a damp, heavy hand tight about her wrist, hard enough to bruise. 'Look here, you impudent little hussy, I'll teach you—'

She said, 'If you don't take your hand off me right now, I'll take this fork I'm holding and stab you in the leg with it. Hard.'

'You wouldn't dare.' His hand still held her, but his grip had loosened.

'Yes, I would. And you know what these people sitting around this table would do, when you screamed and swore? They'd laugh. And so would I.'

There was something in her voice or her manner, it seemed, that convinced him she was entirely serious. 'You fucking insolent little—'

'I might just do it anyway,' she said. 'For the pure fun of it. And I will, if you don't let me go this instant.'

He swore again, but released her, almost pushing her away in his eagerness to be free of her, and ostentatiously turned his back on her in a display of such utter petulance that she could not help but laugh. She sat back smiling derisively as the broken meats and the dirty plates were removed and an equal profusion of desserts was placed before them. Would this meal never end?

The Dowager said, startling her, 'I almost wish you had done it, my dear. It seems that I was wrong when I told you that this dinner would be utterly tedious.'

'I had not known you were watching, madame,' she replied, her mirth fading.

'Of course I was. And so was my grandson. He was about to

leap to your defence, possibly by going across the table at that revolting creature and taking him by the throat, but it proved unnecessary. I suppose it is just as well, as enjoyable as it would have been to see.'

Sophie's eyes leapt up, and she saw that the old lady was right. Lord Drake was looking steadily at her, his face closed and enigmatic, and when she met his gaze he raised his glass, toasting her, and made an ironic little bow in her direction. His stepmother, beside him, tugged impatiently at his sleeve, but he ignored her. The great pink diamond flashed its fire as her bosom rose and fell, and once again she darted a poisonous glance at Sophie.

The two women sat for a little while in silence, ignored once more by their table companions, some of whom were feeding each other with spoons and licking them suggestively. The Dowager seemed to have lost what small appetite she'd had, and did no more than toy absently with a syllabub for several minutes before saying drily, in an obvious effort to distract herself and Sophie from their surroundings, 'I suppose the annals of legend and history must contain examples of worse social occasions, where the guests hated each other more and behaved even worse, though I confess I cannot call one to mind just at the moment.'

'Dinner with Diane de Poitiers and Catherine de' Medici,' suggested Sophie promptly, in the same spirit, just stopping herself from adding, My illustrious relative. Hastily she went on, 'A banquet in the House of Atreus. Taking tea with the Empress Livia, or her great-grandson Caligula. Or almost any member of their family, for that matter.'

For some reason her response caused a sudden expression of trepidation to creep across Delphine's painted countenance. 'About that...' she started to say, but at that moment her daughter-in-law stood, indicating that the ladies should leave the gentlemen to their port, even though it was plain that not everyone had had their fill of pudding, and the moment was lost. 'We will speak of it tomorrow,' the Dowager said. 'When we are alone. I must warn you of the danger you face.'

# 10

Rafe had not sat down to break bread with his father for a long time. Generally he left Wyverne Hall before the dinner hour, though sometimes he dined early and alone with his grandmother in her rooms. She ate little these days, but she liked to see him make a good dinner, as if he were a pale, grief-stricken child again, in need of any comfort she could give him, even the most basic one of a meal. She was, in every way that mattered, his mother – his own had died when he was small, and he struggled to remember much about her, beyond the tears she'd tried to conceal from him and her pervasive unhappiness. He thought he recalled a gentle voice, a soft, warm embrace, a feeling of safety when he'd been in her company – but he might be deluding himself. There had been his first stepmother, who had done her timid best in the short time she'd had, but there had always been Delphine, who he could not doubt loved him fiercely in her own fashion.

After his mother's death in childbirth, his father had troubled little about him and rarely seen him unless to dress him down severely for some small error. It had hurt him when he'd been a lonely boy desperate for his approval and love, before he'd known what the man was and realised he could never get either of those things, but now he must think it a blessing. His influence could only have been malign. Wyverne had no interest in children, no scrap of parental feeling, and now his oldest son was glad of it. This lack of normal human emotion had meant that after his stepmother had also died, the Marquess had raised no objections when her uncle and aunt had descended and swept her two young children, Rafe's half-brother and -sister Charles and Amelia, up into their care. They'd never lived with their father again, and Drake meant to ensure that they never did. They were *his* charges now, in daily reality though not in legal fact, and he made sure that they were kept as far from their indifferent parent as could possibly be contrived. The Marquess could at any moment choose, as was his right, to take them away, to uproot their lives on the lightest whim, and Drake would have little chance of stopping him. His only weapon, if he chose to go that far, was the fact that he didn't imagine any court in the land would consider Rosanna fit to have charge of an innocent girl of seventeen, or – he shuddered at the thought – a boy, another stepson. He'd been such a boy once – who could know better than he how unsuitable she was as any sort of maternal influence?

As ever, his father's thought processes remained a mystery to him, but perhaps even Wyverne, who appeared to be so utterly indifferent to the good opinion of others, might just hesitate to do anything that would provoke his heir to stand up in open court or any other public place and say in plain words and from his own experience precisely why Lord and Lady Wyverne should never be allowed to have Charles and Amelia living under their roof. He'd do it, if he must, and he thought his father knew that, even though the family had seen more than enough notoriety already, and Rafe hoped it would never come to that.

They circled each other warily, the two of them, in a sort of armed standoff, neither of them ever letting down his guard for an instant. They were icily civil – or to be accurate he was; his father usually seemed to be lazily amused – on the rare occasions that they encountered each other, as tonight, and it was many years since there had been open, blazing hostility between them.

Rafe, then, didn't usually attend these dinners, when his grandmother was sometimes, not often, forced to come down and join a most disreputable party for his father's cruel amusement. He wanted to protect her, conscious of her frailty, but she'd told him a thousand times that she could take care of herself, and that his hovering over her couldn't help and might only make things worse. It wasn't as if he feared that anyone would do her violence, and he didn't claim fully to understand the nature of her damaged relationship with her son; his thoughts about it were little more than guesses. But she'd raised no objections to his staying tonight.

He knew why he was here, and he must assume that his clever grandmother knew too, though she had so far said nothing, for which he was grateful. It was Sophie.

He still didn't know who she was, though she wasn't Sophie Delavallois, he was sure of that. He no longer had the least suspicion that she had any intention of harming the Dowager – he'd observed that affection was growing daily between them and he could see their bond as he sat here now across the table – but still she had some ulterior motive for being at Wyverne, he was certain. He could tell himself that that was why he was present now, to learn more of what she was about, but it wouldn't be true. He just couldn't keep away, that was the bare fact of it.

This overheated room was full of women who'd undoubtedly be delighted to take him to their beds. Some of them were prostitutes and some of them weren't, but without vanity he knew it made little difference. He really wasn't flattering himself; it was nothing to do with him, Rafe, the person. There was no need to entertain such a ridiculous notion. After all, he was a viscount already. He was rich enough in his own right, and he was Wyverne's heir besides, due to inherit all this magnificence and the more exalted title of Marquess one day. Wyverne was nigh on seventy and lived a highly irregular life, so that day surely couldn't be terribly far distant. Some of them would want him, Drake, for the money and status they thought they might get from him, some for the novelty, some didn't really need a reason, and Rosanna – well, she had her own twisted motives. But he didn't desire any of them. He'd realised that, despite himself, despite his mistrust of her, he wanted Sophie.

He'd been watching her across the room as the raddled popinjay beside her made his advances to her. The fellow hadn't even tried to court her before he propositioned her, hadn't taken five minutes to try to charm her, and Drake had known the moment he'd crossed the line of decency by the way her mouth twisted in a sort of weary disgust and her eyes flashed in anger. And then he put his filthy hand on her. His grandmother saw too, and only her brisk head-shake and emphatic gesture of denial had prevented him from thrusting back his chair and seizing the revolting creature by the throat as he so richly deserved. But he saw the cur's face redden, then grow pale, as Sophie uttered some low, emphatic words. And he released her, turned away from her with unmistakeable emphasis. She had defended herself with ease – she didn't need him to save her.

He saw conflicting emotions chasing each other across her face, the remains of disgust warring with triumph and even amusement, and their eyes met. Scarcely knowing what he was doing, he raised his glass to her. She was so fierce, so brave, no matter what else she might be that he didn't know yet. Rosanna, entirely disregarded at his side, put her hand on his arm when she saw, and the gesture was so utterly unwelcome that he barely managed to restrain himself from shaking it off. That would be unwise.

Sophie turned to speak to his grandmother. A short while later they were laughing together. She couldn't be too deeply affected by what had just occurred, and he studied the pure line of her throat with a kind of hungry urgency, hoping this didn't make him as bad as the creature she'd just repulsed. Distrust fought desire and made him a stranger to himself. The impulse that had driven him to seek out her company the very first time he'd encountered her had not left him, had only grown stronger as he'd seen more of her, as he'd given in to overmastering impulse and kissed her. It was madness, and yet he wanted more of it.

The other women here had managed the seemingly difficult trick of being simultaneously underdressed and overdressed, but she was cool in simple black muslin with a touch of silver, her shoulders covered and her neck unadorned. Her dark hair was piled up on her head, with a few ringlets falling in seeming casualness about her ears. Her lips – he'd tasted them, too briefly – were full and sensual, rose-pink, and he wanted to feast on them again, properly this time. He wanted to kiss his way down her throat and along the neckline of her gown, where the slightest tantalising glimpse of the swell of her upper breasts appeared. He'd barely touched her, just that swiftest of kisses and a moment's caress of her hair, her cheek. He desperately wanted to. It was a powerful, irresistible compulsion rising up in him, despite himself, despite his wariness of her. He had no time for such distractions, but God, he'd never felt such need, such burning passion in every inch of him. Was this what his father had felt? Was this what had impelled Lord Wyverne to possess

Rosanna despite all the many excellent arguments against it? He didn't want to think so. The last thing he wanted was to be anything like him. He refused to be.

Rosanna stood abruptly then, in defiance of all proper etiquette, and led the women from the room; his grandmother and Sophie would have more to endure at her hands, though he knew it wouldn't be long before his father would signal that his male guests should follow them. There would be gaming tables set up; Wyverne wouldn't want to miss that. And then, Drake hoped, his father's attention would turn to gambling and the other dubious delights his party offered him, and he'd let the two women, the outsiders, leave.

So it proved. It was scarcely fifteen minutes later that Rafe was able to escort them away – he could hardly flatter himself that he had rescued them. He'd done nothing; he had so little power here while his father lived. But he dismissed the footman and carried his tiny grandmother upstairs himself, smiling wryly as she reproved him, as he'd known she would, for denying her the plea-sure of another few moments in William's strong arms. She was like a chicken, or a very fluffy cat – she appeared substantial in her finery, but weighed almost nothing. Less, he thought, than she had when last he'd done her this service. His heart clenched at the thought that it surely could not be long now before he lost her forever.

Sophie opened the door for him, and they gave the Dowager over to Marchand's tender care, and were shooed firmly away a moment later, left standing together once more outside the closed door of her chamber, Sophie holding a bedroom candlestick in one hand.

'Your first evening of pleasure at Wyverne House, mademoi-selle,' he said drily. 'I shall not ask you if you enjoyed it. Was the time you spent with the, er, ladies of the party very bad?'

'Well,' she said judiciously, 'for the most part they ignored us. They did not speak to us, at any rate, though they made great play of staring and giggling behind their hands. But your grandmother kept me entertained with a very frank assessment of their dress and deportment, and their charms in general. I learned several new French words, which are bound to come in useful one day.'

He laughed. 'I hate to think what they might be.' And then he said abruptly, 'How do you generally spend your evenings?'

'I eat early with your grandmother in her room,' she replied tranquilly, 'and then sometimes we play cards, for vast imaginary sums in the old French money. I owe her a king's ransom – I suspect she cheats! And then I go to bed. She does not sleep well, as I am sure you know, and often wakes early and calls for me.'

'It's not much of a life for you. You must be lonely.'

She shrugged. 'It is no hardship. I am fond of her.'

'I can see that.' And then he said, 'I doubt she will rise early tomorrow – tonight will have tired her, and Marchand will insist she stays in bed and rests. Come up on the roof with me. It's a moonlit night, so it will be beautiful up there, and the air is fresh and clean, as it was not downstairs.'

'That's true,' she said. 'So much perfume, so much... flesh.' She seemed to hesitate, he thought she was about to refuse him, then she said suddenly, as if surrendering to an impulse that she might easily have chosen to resist, 'Very well. I will come.'

'In that case...' Scarcely knowing what he was doing, refusing to consider where all this might lead, he put out his hand, and she took it, following him along the corridor and up the nearest stair, her candle casting flickering shadows as they headed up into the darkness.

## 11

Sophie stood on the roof and took a deep breath. Drake was right; it was beautiful. The sky was clear apart from a few ragged clouds which did not obscure the moon. It was almost full, and laid a path of sparkling silver down across the largest lake. There was a light breeze up here, and the air was indeed very fresh, not cold, but full of the green scents of spring. There was not a light to be seen anywhere, and it was very quiet – if the party so far below was growing noisy by now, which seemed likely, no hint of it drifted up here to disturb the tranquillity of the scene.

Once again they were entirely alone, in a way one never was in London. She was reluctant to break the silence, which might seem magical if she were a more fanciful woman, but she had no appetite for a moment of seductive closeness followed by a reproach, for the bitterness that so often lurked beneath the sweet honey. If that was why he had brought her here, to interrogate her again, to try to trap her, she'd sooner know it now. So she said, 'Last time we spoke, you made what sounded like a threat – you were determined to dig out my so-called secrets. Is that why we're here, in truth? Because if it is, I'm tired...'

'No,' he said. 'No. Enough of that. I too am tired. Tired, apart from anything else, of always being sensible and safe. Of making calculations, of having nothing at all in my life for myself. That probably sounds foolish, ridiculous even, and I have no idea why I'm sharing this with you, of all people. I know that I am very fortunate in so many ways, and yet...'

There was little of safety in Sophie's life now, there had not been for years, and nobody could call her fortunate apart from in not being dead in a gutter, but his words must still strike home with her. She realised with a pang of unexamined feeling that really he was telling her that he was lonely. And so was she. He knew it – he had said as much.

He hesitated for a moment and then said, with the air of a gambler making a desperate throw, 'What I'd really like more than anything in the world is to kiss you. I spoiled it last time with my crass stupidity, and every time I recall how you closed your eyes and sighed so very softly, I have been regretting it. I wonder, have you?'

'I'm making no admissions.' Up here, alone with him, a recklessness seemed to possess her. She was all too aware she shouldn't have come here, and that she ought to run from him, and however much she wanted to kiss him she knew too that she shouldn't. It was nothing less than madness. And yet... 'Stop talking, will you, and kiss me before I come to my senses?' she said.

He laughed, and drew her close, whispering, 'Madam, I am at your service.' When his lips found hers, it was less tentative this time, since they'd both admitted what they wanted, which was this. He still wasn't rough or demanding, his mouth was soft and warm, but as she opened to him he deepened the kiss, and she met him eagerly, her tongue darting out and tracing the sensitive flesh inside his full lower lip. He groaned, and she nipped at him with her teeth, which caused him to suck on her lip, gently and then harder. His strong hands were holding her tight about her ribcage, just below her breast, and she slipped her arms about his neck to pull him closer.

He trailed hot kisses across her cheek, and when he came to her ear he whispered into it, 'I do have one thing more to say.'

She swore fluently in French, using his grandmother's words, and twined her fingers in his glossy hair, tugging at it ungently, pulling his mouth back to hers. Now that they'd started this, she had no wish to stop, or hear anything unwelcome.

'Just a few words,' he breathed raggedly against her, 'but important ones. Rosanna isn't my mistress. I can't possibly explain now, it's a horrible story from long ago that I'd rather put from my mind, but she isn't and she never has been. I swear it on Grand-mère's life.'

'Good!' she said, and claimed him once more. Later she reflected that it was odd that she should not think to disbelieve him, but now was not the time for thought.

Time passed, though they were unaware of how much or how little, absorbed in exploring each other with growing urgency. Her impatient hands had tugged his shirt from his black satin breeches and slid under it, exploring the hot skin and the corded muscles of his chest and back. He'd run both his hands down her gown until he found her buttocks, and bunched up the thin layers of muslin to grip her tight and pull her against him. He was kissing her neck and shoulders, his clever mouth evoking delicious sensations everywhere it touched her, murmuring endearments between kisses, and she could feel his hardness pressing into her belly. Once again there was a perfect rightness and inevitability to all this, which was strange, because it was all so very wrong, given who he was, given who she was, given what she was here to do. She wasn't here for *this*.

'Sophie!' he gasped against her mouth, his hands still tight about her, one having crept up to her breast, his thumb just brushing one erect nipple through the thin layers that covered it, tantalising her. She moaned softly, eager for a more complete contact, but he did not oblige her. 'I'm sorry always to be talking, and God knows I don't want to, but I have to ask you... what's that pressing into my leg? It feels like...'

'It's a knife,' she said.

**12**

---

'A knife...' he repeated, seeming a little dazed.

'A very sharp knife, in a sheath, in my garter,' she explained reasonably.

He hadn't pulled away, she had to give him that, and his voice was tolerably steady. 'And do you intend to use it on me?' he asked with a fair assumption of simple curiosity.

'I might, if you don't stop talking. No, of course I don't. I thought I might require it tonight, for protection – not from you. But I only had to threaten that horrible man in the purple coat that I'd stab him in the leg with a fork. I didn't need the knife at all.'

'A fork. You would have done so.' It wasn't a question.

'*You* looked as though you wanted to knock him down. Would you have done so?'

They were still embracing tightly, and one strong, warm hand was still on her breast, the other on her bottom. She still caressed his muscled back. Their faces were very close, and they were both breathing hard. She wanted his hands, his mouth, to continue their exploration, and she wanted to touch him as well, to kiss and taste him, without the barrier of their clothes. But there was something undeniably erotic, too, about this pause, about the intimacy of their low voices, their stilled hands, their racing hearts – she had a dangerous sense that anything might happen, and it was heady, exciting. Perhaps it wasn't touching each other like this that was most perilous – perhaps the real danger came from talking, from the illusion of sharing an intimate moment across the gulf that separated them. If you didn't speak, you couldn't lie. Or be lied to...

He said, the whisper of his breath caressing her and threatening to drive all rational thought from her mind, 'I was filled with rage towards him when I saw him manhandling you, and shame that such a thing should happen in my father's house, so, yes, I think I would. And,' he said very low, 'what's more, I would probably have enjoyed it.'

'So would I,' she said. 'It seems we are the same.' He was still hard against her belly, and she pressed against him, her desire equal to his, the last vestiges of caution slipping away from her. What was she doing?

'Perhaps we are. Sophie...'

'Mmm?'

'Will you show me the knife? I don't mean just take it out of its sheath... I mean show me, now.' And as he spoke, he sank to his knees in front of her, and looked up, expectant, in the moonlight in a way that utterly disarmed her.

She did not hesitate. She bent and took up the hem of her gown, making sure she gathered up all the draped layers and petticoats too. Slowly, she edged them up, over her ankles, calves and knees, until her pale thighs were exposed. Her stockings were black, and so were her garters, and so too was the wickedly narrow leather sheath that sat in one of them. 'Ah,' he sighed. There was a lot of feeling in the single exhalation of breath. And then, 'You've shown me this much, and I am honoured. Will you show me more?'

Deep inside her Sophie had known, in truth had hoped, that he would say that. She was still holding the edge of her gown, and pulled it higher, uncovering herself fearlessly to him until the fabric sat around her waist, and she was naked below it save for her stockings.

'You could take your very sharp knife,' he said, and now his voice was unsteady where it had not been before, 'and cut me off a curl that I could treasure. And I would treasure it, I promise, Sophie.'

'I could,' she said, 'or I could let you do it.' She was on fire now, with no intention of turning back, intensely aroused by the sight of him at her feet in what felt like worship, and his hot gaze on her, and the anticipation of his touch. Some part of her still knew that he was a Wyverne and an enemy, but the faint little voice that called out a warning had no power over her just now.

'You trust me with your blade?'

'I do. Take it.'

He was still kneeling. His left hand held her thigh steady while his right pulled out the stiletto, bright and deadly in the moonlight. She was leaning back against the roof, which rose at an angle behind her, and she spread her thighs a little, settling herself more comfortably, offering herself to him. With his left hand he reached out and chose a curl, twirling it around his fingers, brushing her skin with his fingertips as he did so. A tiny moan escaped her. Then he took the blade and with infinite care sliced off the lock, and tucked it securely away in his pocket. 'Thank you,' he said. 'You did not lie when you said it was sharp. I could shave you with it, I should think.'

'I'm not entirely opposed to the idea,' she whispered. 'But I think I might prefer you to do it when the light was a little better.'

'You doubt my steadiness of hand?' As he spoke, he sheathed the blade again, holding her once more for safety as he did so, lest the wickedly sharp thing should slip and wound her. But he did not remove his hand when he had done. It lay on her thigh, warm against her bare skin, just above the leather and the lace.

'Anyone's hand may tremble,' she said. 'I myself... might move.' She could hardly prevent herself from squirming as she spoke. He would claim her soon, and she was more than ready.

'It's true, you easily might,' he agreed, and he leant forward a little, and pressed an intense kiss on the place from which he had taken the curl. His lips were warm against her, and he was so tantalisingly close to where she needed him to be, his breath feathering across her sensitive skin, making her shiver with anticipation. Her nipples were hard pebbles, aching with desire, and she was wet for him. She could call a halt, even now, but God, she didn't want to. Then he groaned and buried his face in her, edging forward on his knees and pressing the length of his chest against her legs.

'Oh, yes,' she gasped in welcome. 'Yes.' With hands that shook, she bunched up the fabric of her gown and petticoats, pulling it up further and pushing it behind her body where her weight would hold it, freeing herself so that she could touch him too, her fingers tight on his head, in his dark locks.

He had a big hand on each thigh now, caressing her tender flesh with his thumbs, spreading her more, and she moaned deep in her throat and moved, so that he could reach her better. He pulled his head back and teased her with his tongue, the very tip of it upon her pearl of Venus. 'God, so good,' he moaned, and then, before she had to urge him, he fell to devouring her in earnest, kissing each of her lower lips as he had kissed her mouth, nibbling on them, drawing them in, sucking on her, tonguing up and down between her engorged nub and her entrance. His hands still gripped her thighs but had slid out and round to hold her more tightly, and the sheath of her knife must be pressing into him again, but if he noticed it he didn't seem to mind.

She'd thrown back her head and neck, and could feel the lead of the roof cool beneath her. She felt fierce and primitive and glorious. 'I could pull out my knife...' she gasped, very close to losing control, her fingers still tangled in his hair.

His tongue slipped from her, to be replaced by his finger, by two fingers. She arched her back and her legs almost buckled at the strength of the sensations he was evoking in her. 'Do it,' he whispered against her core, and then he drew her nub into his mouth and sucked on her hard. 'Do it!' he repeated close against her, his clever fingers still working her ruin. 'In this moment I can't think of a better way to die.'

She cried out as she came, and he held her and tongued her, prolonging the waves of ecstasy and then burying his face in her once more until the last tiny little spasm had faded. She still cradled his head between her thighs, and after a while she said, 'If you let go of me, or if I let go of you, I will slide to the floor, and possibly off the roof. You have killed me.'

She could feel him smiling against her skin. 'Despite your threats, though, I am still very much alive. I'm not the man I was – I may never be – but I live.'

'Can you stand up?'

'I doubt it. I should think I'm frozen in this position forever. It has its advantages, there's no denying it.' His wicked tongue crept out and licked her long and slow where her thigh met her body, and he whispered, 'Who needs to stand up and walk about, after all? These things are overrated. I could...'

Sophie tugged sharply on his hair. 'I'm not asking you to walk about. I had another form of exercise in mind. Just lean against the parapet.'

It was astonishing, how quickly he scrambled to his feet, holding her about the waist so that she did not fall when he released her thighs. She subsided to her knees, still a little dizzy, probably not very graceful but he didn't seem to care, and sat back and looked up at him. He was enormously dishevelled and grinning down at her, his hair in wild disorder, his cravat a wreck, his shirt hanging loose and his knee-breeches a disgrace. Well – not entirely a disgrace. Not where it counted. 'My lord...' she said.

'You won't be needing the knife now, I hope.'

'Nor the fork,' she murmured wickedly, reaching up and working intently at the buttons that closed his breeches fall. 'But it's true, I am still hungry.'

'In that case, how can I deny you?' he said shakily, and then he said nothing more. He sprang free into her waiting hand, and she looked at him, caressed him, felt the silky skin and hard hotness of him, and liked it all, and bent her head to show him exactly how much.

It was a long while before either of them spoke again, though there were soft, urgent sounds, sighs and gasps, there on the roof, as the moon sailed across the sky and Sophie's candle, forgotten, guttered and went out.

## 13

Rafe sat at his desk, a little smile playing across his lips, though he was quite unconscious of it. He was at home – he'd ridden back through the moonlight late last night and fallen into his cool, empty bed, though he hadn't slept for a long while afterwards. He should be exhausted, but instead he was full of restless energy.

The fine weather hadn't lasted – it was raining this morning, and the wind was gusting, throwing sudden fierce showers against his library window every now and then. But it was warm here, a small fire crackling in the grate, and blessedly quiet. He was alone except for the servants, about their business elsewhere in the house; his brother Charlie was in Oxford, nearing the end of his first year there, and his sister Amelia had gone on an extended visit to her cousins on her mother's side. His guardianship was a relatively new thing; they'd only been with him permanently for a couple of years, since their aunt had died, but he was very fond of them both and missed them when they were absent as now. They brought life to the place, and laughter, and all the things his own childhood had to a large extent lacked. They were astonishingly happy and carefree, despite the sad losses they had sustained, and perhaps this was because they were so far lucky: unlike him, they knew their father not at all. He intended to make sure matters stayed that way, and a great deal of his time and energy was devoted to their care. Today, though, he welcomed the solitude.

It was good to be away from Wyverne Hall for a time, to gain a little much-needed perspective. He couldn't tell if the powerful emotions and sensations that had overwhelmed him over the last few days were genuine, or some sort of reaction to the torrid atmosphere the place always generated when his father and Rosanna were in residence. He wasn't someone who normally gave in to his impulses – he'd seen all too clearly where that led – but he'd done so last night, and though he could not regret it in the least he did wonder why. Why this woman in particular affected him so deeply, when he had guarded his emotions and his desires so carefully for so long.

He reached into his pocket and pulled out the curl he'd cut from Sophie last night. At the thought of it, let alone the sight, he was instantly hard again, could almost feel the wonder of her mouth on him once more, and his mouth on her delicious wetness. He pushed away the unwelcome thought of how unlike him it was to do such things, to take such a shockingly intimate token, and how like his father. He refused to accept that. He was no libertine. It wasn't a trophy, proof of conquest, and he certainly wouldn't be showing it to anyone or boasting of it, as his father undoubtedly would in his place. It was deeply private, he was a deeply private person, quite apart from the fact that his best friend, his only friend, really, was a minister of the Church of England. The thought of sharing such a secret with Simon, or anyone, made him let out a little snort of wry laughter.

But if it wasn't a trophy, what was it? He looked at the bright curl as he held it, frowning, fighting his insistent arousal, trying to think. It wasn't as if he needed a souvenir to remember last night by; while he lived, he thought he'd never forget it. It was... he wanted to say that it was a pledge. A recognition. She had said, at some point in that incredible evening, that she and he were the same. She'd been talking about an impulse to violence, a desire and a willingness to protect oneself and others in the most primitive of ways, but he realised now that she was right in more ways than that. There had been no missed step in their time together on the roof, no momentary awkwardness. He'd never thought of himself as reckless, he'd had every reason not to be, but he'd been reckless last night, and so had she. They'd been in harmony, wanting the same things, claiming each other, barely needing to put any of it into words. In that magical moment out of time and away from all the world he'd been the man who'd ask for such a token, and she'd been the woman who would give it freely, and – above all – trust him to take it. She had not hesitated or been surprised. She had not laughed or mocked him. It ought to be vulgar – anyone who heard of such a thing would surely think that it was – but in his mind it was very far from that. It had all been so right and so perfect, despite the fact that he barely knew her. And he wanted so much more.

Of course, it could not lead anywhere. It could be nothing more than a brief interlude that he might one day look back on with fondness and no little astonishment that he had ever been so daring. But he could see even now how precious the memory might become.

He looked down at what he was holding. Something about it nagged at him... Good God in heaven. It was the colour.

Sophie had dark hair, dark brown, almost as dark as his own. He'd never thought to question it; her eyes were dark too. But this curl wasn't dark. It was a bright red-blonde. A most distinctive colour.

Dark brown eyes, bright locks... How many women in England, how many Frenchwomen in particular, could there be with that particular combination? He couldn't recall if he had ever seen...

And all at once he knew exactly who she was.

## 14

He'd danced with her. Christ, but he had. Just once. Rafe remembered it clearly now. He spent so little time in London, so little time in society – being whispered about and stared at had always been a torment for him – but his friend Simon Venables, before he'd given up on him in recent years and stopped trying, had occasionally endeavoured to persuade him that it wasn't healthy for a young man to shut himself away from all company, and particularly the company of women. Eligible women.

It must have been about the time that Simon had married – yes, eight years ago. They'd been in London for the wedding, staying with Simon's mother and his brother Philip, a light-hearted family party plus Rafe, and in the run-up to the ceremony he'd been persuaded to attend a few balls and other social events. He didn't lack for invitations, despite the unsavoury rumours that had swirled around his name even then, and had hardened into accepted fact by now. The title and the money still worked their sordid magic. And Simon was the younger brother of a baronet and related to half the noble houses of the land.

It had been, appropriately enough, a masquerade of sorts.

Simon and Elizabeth had been innocently delighted, he remembered, because the fact of their partial disguise had meant that they'd be able to dance together more often than the paltry two or three times that society normally permitted. He'd danced with Elizabeth, and with her sisters, but he'd recognised no one else, even if they must have known him for a scandalous Wyverne. He couldn't remember now who had presented him formally to the lovely young woman in flowered green silk. Someone had. Simon's mother, the Dowager Lady Venables, that inveterate matchmaker? He had no idea, and really it didn't signify in the least.

They were all of them dressed as courtiers at Versailles. He'd had his grandmother to advise him well in advance, so he could be sure his blue and silver costume was authentic. It had been amusing, he'd had to admit, to ape the more formal manners of the previous century, and he had made a particularly sweeping bow to the young lady in the pink and green gown. She'd smiled as she took his hand, not mocking him, but enjoying his enthusiasm, he'd thought. She'd been a good dancer, and he'd admired her grace. She was very young, probably in her first season – but then he'd only been twenty-three or so himself – and as they twirled and turned about the room together her fine dark eyes were sparkling with pleasure. Brighter – he might even have told her, or maybe he'd just thought it, since he was after all only twenty-three and had little experience of ladies – than the enormous, fabulous pink diamond she'd been wearing about her neck.

Good God almighty. The diamond Rosanna had been wearing last night. The de Montfaucon diamond. He thought it had another name, as these things often did, but he couldn't recall it. He remembered the jewel, though. There was no possibility of mistake.

He hadn't stopped to consider before how the treasure had come into his father's possession, and he'd never had any reason before today to link the bauble Rosanna loved to flaunt with the girl he'd danced with once and never seen or thought of again.

Mademoiselle de Montfaucon. The daughter of the Duke, one of the many noble refugees from the Terror. He struggled to recall if he'd ever heard her Christian name, if someone had addressed her by it or said it when he'd been presented to her as a suitable dancing partner. So very suitable, no wonder they'd thought of it – both of them so young, he a marquess's son, she a duke's daughter.

Yes. He did know. When the dance had ended, he'd heard someone address her: Clemence. It was Clemence. She wasn't Sophie Delavallois. He'd always known that deep down, though he'd chosen to forget it last night. He'd set his previous suspicions aside in the headiness of what had roared into life between them, and when he'd knelt at her feet in worship he hadn't cared who she was or what she was. But she was Clemence de Montfaucon. It surely couldn't be a coincidence that she was living at Wyverne Hall of all places, in his father's house, where the famous necklace that her family had saved from the chaos that had enveloped them was now kept. 'Kept', that was an innocuous little word. His father kept it, as he kept so many precious jewels that adorned Rosanna's body. Lord Wyverne liked his possessions.

He was a collector, an obsessive hoarder of the beautiful and the rare. So Rafe had always assumed that Wyverne had bought them all – the jewels, the pictures, the woman. He supposed it was entirely possible that Sophie's... that Clemence's father had been obliged to sell the precious diamond to provide for his family. The Marquess, his father, was just the man to enjoy getting something valuable cheaply because of desperation, to enjoy on top of possession the fact that the sale hurt the seller.

That would be disreputable, dishonourable, loathsome, but not...
not criminal.

He had an uneasy feeling that there were things he wasn't yet
aware of; that Sophie's reasons for having inserted herself into his
father's house would bring him most unwelcome news. But he
knew who would know more.

He must set aside for now his own feelings, the turbulent mix
of emotions that roiled within him as he struggled to absorb what
he had discovered. He wouldn't think about last night, and
whether in thinking it such a wonderful moment of escape he'd
been deluded or deceived, and what if anything he should do
about it. He needed to talk to his grandmother.

# 15

Rafe didn't want to wait, he was desperate to know the truth, but there was no point leaving now – the Dowager would still be asleep, or at least in her bed, Marchand would make sure of that, after the exertion of last night. Grandson or not, he'd get short shrift from the benevolent dragon who guarded her door if he presented himself before what she considered a respectable hour.

The hands of the clock dragged round unconscionably slowly, but at last he judged that it was time, and headed out for his stable to have his favourite bay mare, Cinnamon, saddled. John Wilson, the groom who'd known him since his youth, shot a sharp look under his heavy brows – obviously Rafe was not, to one well acquainted with him, quite his normal self today. But John said nothing, and soon Rafe was trotting and then galloping across his own land towards his father's much more extensive acres. He found pleasure, and a sort of escape from the turmoil of his thoughts, in the exhilaration of the motion.

He rode round to the stable block and left Cinnamon in the care of Tom Wilson, John's brother and Wyverne's head groom. After a few words of casual conversation, he made his way up to his grandmother's rooms. The huge house was very quiet, since no doubt gambling, excessive drinking and other diversions best left undescribed had gone on until the early hours, and the participants would still be recovering in their beds, or someone else's. He wondered if Sophie were awake, and hoped on this occasion that she was not already with his grandmother. It wasn't that he didn't want to see her – he didn't care to admit to himself how much he did – but he'd prefer to be in possession of all the facts first. He was uncomfortably aware that a careless word from him could cause enormous damage, and he wasn't even sure yet if he was going to let her know that he'd discovered her secret, and how he might approach the subject with her if he did.

His luck was in; Marchand admitted him, grumbling, to Delphine's sitting room, and then absented herself. He bent to kiss his grandmother's soft cheek, noticing with a pang how pale she was, how obviously weary. 'You could have stayed in bed today,' he chided her gently.

She shrugged. 'You know I do not sleep much, Rafael. And nor,' she said as she regarded him shrewdly, 'did you last night, I perceive. What's the matter, my dear?'

Of course she would see that he was agitated; he had never been able to conceal his feelings from her, no matter how hard he tried. 'I wanted to talk to you about Mademoiselle Delavallois.'

'Ah,' Delphine responded enigmatically.

'I realised something about her last night,' he said cautiously. He couldn't be perfectly sure how she would react to what he now knew; he didn't think she would dismiss Sophie from her service, but he supposed that rather depended on why the mysterious young woman was here in the first place. He didn't want his grandmother to be hurt, distressed, but then he did not want to cause Sophie the least harm either, and he wasn't sure now if this was even possible – it was a devil of a coil they found themselves in.

The Dowager, as was her way, cut straight through it to the heart of the matter. 'I apprehend,' she said drily, smiling a little, 'that you have at last realised who my so-called humble little companion really is. I must say, it has taken you long enough. I know you met the child at least once years ago, for I recall you told me so then.'

He was astonished. Almost one hundred years old and she could still surprise him. 'You knew?'

She scoffed. 'Of course I knew! That dyed hair and the ingenious little story of her obscure parentage did not deceive me for more than a moment or two. She bears a strong resemblance to her great-grandmother, who once upon a time was a great rival of mine. Her smile, it is just the same; the way she carries herself. I have little to do here but relive memories from long ago; I could not possibly be mistaken. And Clemence de Montfaucon vanished eight years ago, vanished so completely that none of the people I sent could ever find any trace of her, so it all fits together perfectly. God knows where she has been in the intervening time; I dread to think.'

She took his breath away. 'You were trying to trace her... Why?' And then it struck him like a dizzying blow to the stomach. 'Because of the diamond. Because Wyverne has the diamond.'

'Your wits have not entirely deserted you,' she said with a flash of her teasing spirit. 'But in truth it is no matter for humour. As soon as I saw the Stella Rosa about that creature Rosanna's neck eight years ago, and recognised it, for there cannot be another stone like it, of such size and in such a setting, I feared that Wyverne had obtained it in some dishonourable manner. I have never been able to keep track of all his terrible deeds – in reality, I didn't want to. But I was younger then, barely ninety, and I still had a little energy, and so with Marchand's help I sent Samuel Wilson to London to see what he could discover. And it was much worse than even I could have imagined.' She sighed, and her frail hands moved restlessly in her lap. 'When I confronted Wyverne with what I had discovered – I was braver then than I am now – he laughed in my face and boasted of what he had done.'

A cold dread was creeping through his body, so strong it was a physical sensation that made him shiver. 'What had he done?' he almost whispered.

'The de Montfaucons left France with very little, and when they had sold or pawned all the rest of his wife's jewels they realised, I suppose, that they must part with this last most precious thing. Wyverne wanted it and let it be known that he did – he has always had the ability to scent distress in others, where he may profit or get pleasure from it. Even as a boy he was like that. He offered to buy it – at a sufficiently low price, I am sure, but still, it would have been enough for the family to live on quietly for many years. And de Montfaucon would not want the humiliation of a public sale, to have his plight be an object of general discussion, so he was all the more vulnerable.'

'That's how I assumed Wyverne won all his treasure,' said Rafe dully. He knew there must be much worse to come. 'Pressure, taking advantage of people... I told myself that such proceedings were unpleasant, dishonourable, but not criminal. No laws were broken. Even as I said such things to myself, I despised myself for weakness.'

'He makes us all weak,' said Delphine bleakly. 'There is nothing he would not do, and this gives him great power over ordinary people, who have limits on their behaviour. In order to defeat him, one would need to be entirely without conscience, without moral scruples or human feeling. Without love. Such a person would be as bad as he, and there are few such. It is useless to reproach yourself. I, his mother, say this. I have had years to come to know just what he is capable of, and I have always tried to shelter you from the worst of it.'

'That time has long passed. Tell me, Grand-mère.'

'He met with de Montfaucon – and you must remember, Rafe, that the Duke was a broken man already, in body and in spirit, before he ever set eyes on your father. His poor mother had gone to the guillotine – he had been unable to save her – along with many of his relatives and his dearest friends. He had lost almost everything, and had been lucky to escape with his life and the lives of his wife and two children, and what jewels they hid about their persons. And then years in London, slowly selling off all they had to maintain the appearance of dignity, their lodgings growing shabbier with each move. Now his daughter was of an age to make her come-out – she was a beauty and might marry well and save them all – but they needed money to pay for this. Their credit was exhausted.

'Wyverne told me, smiling that smile of his, that he promised de Montfaucon they would meet and discuss the sale. But that was not what happened. He took the diamond from him. Took it and walked away.'

'That's not possible,' said Rafe. 'It's blatant theft. Even he would not dare to do such a thing. The damned pink diamond is well known – half of London would know it in an instant, and know who owned it. I myself saw it around Sophie's neck when I danced with her at that ball. It's a famous heirloom of her house!'

'Wyverne told de Montfaucon that he was quite at liberty to inform all the world that he had sold the jewel, and to whom. But he said – I will never forget his face as he described it to me – that if the Duke tried to go to law over the matter, to accuse Wyverne of theft, he would make sure he regretted it. Wyverne intended to spread abroad a shocking tale: that he had demanded Clemence's

maidenhead as part of the sale, and offered a higher price if that
was included.' Rafe groaned when he heard this hideous revelation, but did not think for a second to disbelieve what his grandmother was saying. 'Wyverne would say that de Montfaucon had
tried first to offer his wife up instead, such was his desperation,
but he had spurned this paltry offer, and the transaction had
occurred precisely as he wished. He was prepared to describe the
event in extreme detail – you know what he is, you cannot doubt
how much he would enjoy that. I expect he did describe how his
foul imagination pictured it, to the child's father. I expect he made
it sufficiently convincing. And he promised he would say that
afterwards, after the deed was done and the girl despoiled, in his
greed the Duke had sought more money and threatened to brand
Wyverne a thief if he refused to give it. Wyverne would tell
everyone he was simply calling his bluff, and reveal all the
distasteful details. Make sure all the world knew them. After all,
*he* has no reputation to lose – he is well known to have not the
least scruple.'

'Surely no one would believe such a farrago of nonsense. It's
nothing but a pack of diseased lies, like something from one of
your damn novels!' Rafe was almost pleading.

'I think you are wrong, my dear – I think people would believe
that Wyverne of all people could easily concoct such a Satanic
bargain.'

'But not that a father would agree to it,' he persisted. 'De
Montfaucon had a reputation as an honourable man, not some
vicious scoundrel.'

'As to that... perhaps not,' sighed Delphine. 'But you have
every reason to know the world. It scarcely matters in the end if
the tale were believed or not – the poor girl's good name would be
utterly destroyed in any case. People do not need fully to credit
rumours in order to spread them. She would be ruined, she

would be unable to marry any decent man. The whole family would be cast out from society.'

'Good God,' he said blankly. He was not attempting to argue with her now.

'Wyverne said he threw down a purse, a few miserable guineas, and took the jewel from de Montfaucon's unresisting hand – he'd brought it, unsuspecting, so they could look at it together before the sale. He said the last thing he saw, as he left the tavern room where they had met, was the Duke upon his knees upon the floor, frantically gathering up the shining coins where they had spilled in the dirt. He laughed as he told me that.' She hesitated for a moment, and then added, 'And he told me too that he'd seen you dance with Clemence while she was wearing the jewel, and thought what a pretty pair you made. So young, so innocent, he sneered. So deluded as to the real nature of the world. That gave his actions extra spice, he said.'

'Does it ever occur to you,' Rafe said in an attempt at composure that fell sadly short, 'that he is insane? Not just wicked, but actually insane?'

'Frequently,' said Lord Wyverne's mother, and her tone was infinitely weary. 'I first feared it when he was twelve years old and I found that he had tortured... But there is no point in this. It is ancient history, and I am afraid that the tale is not quite done.'

'Go on.' He'd taken her thin hand and held it some while back; he wasn't sure if he was comforting her, or she him.

'He told me, and my investigations confirmed at least the bare facts of it, that de Montfaucon went home, told his wife what had happened, and then took a pistol and put a period to his existence in front of her. I don't know if his children, Clemence and her brother Louis, who was a few years younger and never strong, saw the horrible scene or not. I can only hope not.'

Rafe had his face in his hands now. 'The mother, the brother...? They're dead now?'

'They had to leave their lodging soon after. I do not know if they asked friends for help and were refused, or if by then there was no one they could ask. Perhaps they were too proud, or too shocked. They found meaner, cheaper lodgings, to which my people were able to track them – they must have been living on the pitiful sum of money Wyverne flung down, and on the sale of their clothes and so on, whatever possessions they had left.' Delphine would not spare herself the last few agonising details. 'The Duchess, Marie-Claude was her name, I remember her when she was just a girl, and her little son, they quickly fell sick in one of the epidemics that so often ravages the slums of London. Typhus, perhaps. It scarcely matters. Wyverne killed them all, as surely as if he had shot them himself.'

'And... and Clemence?'

'She disappeared utterly. Samuel, and the people he employed – a Bow Street Runner, and others – could find no trace of her. They laid out a large sum of money, made diligent enquiries, but they could learn nothing. It was assumed that she had come to the point where all she had to sell...'

'Enough,' said Rafe very low. 'I cannot fail to understand how desperate she must have been, and how few choices she had. Enough.'

A little silence fell between them. Delphine said at last, her voice no more than a whisper, 'I would have helped them. It was only a few pitiful months too late, when I found out and searched for them. I would have helped them, Rafe. It must be my fault somehow, what he is. His father and I between us, somehow we made him what he is. I was a bad wife to a bad husband; our relationship was broken from the very beginning and it must have affected Gervais very deeply. So I am responsible for his cruelty, I have always known, and I would have done all I could to set it right...'

'I know you would. It's not your fault, though. How can it be? You had other children, and they were not like him. You are a good woman, Grand-mère.'

'I don't think I was ever that. But thank you. I have done my best by you, at least.'

He raised her paper-thin hand and kissed it, and she squeezed his fingers in response with all her feeble strength. Then with an effort he said, 'Does Sophie know that you have guessed her secret? Have you spoken of it?'

She shook her head. 'I have hesitated to say anything, for I fear to make her speak of all the hideous truth of it. She must be so angry. She must hate Wyverne more than I can easily imagine. She has every reason to do so.'

'I'm almost past the point of caring, but do you have the least idea why she is here? Do you think she has come seeking revenge?'

'And could you blame her if she has?'

# 16

Sophie awoke smiling, stretching languorously in her narrow bed, even though she knew that last night had in sober truth been a mistake that she should regret. The fact was, she didn't wish away a single second of it. Whatever she had shared so briefly with Drake wouldn't turn her from her purpose – nothing would – but it had been glorious, exhilarating and deeply satisfying, and her life held little enough pleasure, so she would not feel guilty. Guilt was a waste of time and energy.

She found that the Dowager had been up and in her sitting room for a while when she went to see how she was after the exertions of the previous evening. The old lady looked tired, and it struck Sophie that she had been crying, but she did not want to press her as to why. Lord Wyverne's mother might have many reasons for private tears, she thought.

Delphine did not acknowledge her own tears in any way, nor show any further signs of distress, saying only, 'I am glad to see you, my dear. Do not read to me, not today – I am not in the humour for it. I want to talk to you.'

A little curl of dismay rippled through Sophie's stomach. There were many topics she would rather not discuss with Delphine; the whole subject of the old woman's grandson headed the list after last night, but there was a great deal more besides. 'Yes, madame la marquise?'

'I started to speak to you last night, to warn you, but we were interrupted and I was not able to finish, but now I must. Lord Wyverne plans another gathering tonight, I am sorry to say.'

'Another dinner?' Sophie grimaced.

'Oh, no, dear child. If it were only that. It is ridiculous – at my age and with all my experience, you would not imagine that there is anything I am afraid or embarrassed to speak of, and yet I find that it is so.'

'It must be something very terrible,' said Sophie with an attempt at lightness.

'I fear it is. Did you learn Latin in your youth, my dear?'

Sophie presumed that this odd question was not the non sequitur it appeared to be, for Delphine's wits were far from wandering. 'I did, a little,' she said cautiously.

'I do not suppose that your studies included the work of Suetonius?'

'No,' she said. 'I remember I have seen his name upon a volume...' She almost said, In my grandfather's library at the Chateau de Montfaucon, but she just stopped the words in time. 'I cannot recall where. In any case, I have not read any text by a person of that name, nor heard anything that I can recall.'

'It is scarcely surprising, for his work would not have been at all suitable for a young lady. I wonder then if you have ever heard of the Empress Messalina?'

'I believe I have, though I do not know any details. Is she not proverbial for wickedness?'

'Indeed,' said the Dowager drily. 'There are many scandalous stories Suetonius tells of her, but one of them is that she once challenged Rome's most famous prostitute, Scylla, to a contest, to see which of them could... engage with the most men in succession before tiring of it. And that, I am sorry to say, is the theme of Lord Wyverne's party tonight, with Lady Wyverne, I need scarcely say, in the role of Messalina. I believe her opponent, if that is the word I seek, has been brought from London and employed at vast expense. She is quite celebrated in her own right, apparently, as such women sometimes are, and Marchand tells me that she is to receive an enormous bonus in gold if she wins. I understand that large bets are being laid on the outcome.'

'Good God,' Sophie said. And then again, 'Good God. And all this is to happen...'

'In public. In the Marble Saloon.' With a little hiccup of laughter that might easily have been a sob, Delphine said, 'It's terribly draughty in there. All that marble – so chilly. It is so typical of men – they cannot possibly have considered.'

'And everybody will be...' Sophie had thought herself beyond being astonished, but she now discovered she'd been wrong. She'd been moving in low circles, she'd thought, over the last eight years, and consorting with all manner of thieves, rogues, artists and whores. She'd seen people drunk, so often that it was no longer any sort of novelty, and in the grip of lust and murderous rage. The two things could be all but synonymous. She knew that some men, many men, harboured all sorts of dark impulses, and she knew that women could too; not by any means all the women on the streets were victims, or just victims. She'd seen women offer to sell their own children for a flagon of gin, and no way to prevent it. She wasn't an innocent; she wasn't at all easily shocked. It was possible to argue that no one would be hurt by what would happen tonight, and certainly she was no enemy of passion or of pleasure. But could this be described as passion, or even honest lust? There was something so cold-blooded about it, so deliberate. To make a contest of it…

'Everyone will be watching?' asked the Dowager wearily. 'Yes. I imagine that's the point of it. The display, the show it makes. No doubt, since she is to play the part of an empress, she will be wearing every jewel she possesses, if little else. I am sure he will insist upon that. We must not delude ourselves that this would be happening if Wyverne did not want it. I would assume that it was his idea; it certainly bears the stamp of his nature. Whether his wife is an enthusiastic participant or takes part merely in order to please him, I cannot say. I don't understand the nature of the bond between them, and I don't care to, really. She had made her bed, quite literally on this occasion. If she were ever an innocent, which I suppose even she must have been once, it was long ago. My concern is only for the servants, and for you.'

Sophie looked at her in silence; she almost feared to ask. 'There will be no maids downstairs this evening, and the stair that leads to their – to your – chambers will be guarded. They have all been warned to stay away, to make sure they are safe, and now I am warning you too. You most of all, I think, for they must imagine you entirely unprotected and friendless, and Rosanna has begun to dislike you into the bargain. I could see that well enough last night.'

'You're not just worried that I, or any of them, will see things we should not see? It's more than that. You are concerned for our physical safety too?'

'I am.' The old lady sounded very tired suddenly. 'I do what little I can. Perhaps I am over-reacting – no, I am not. I would believe anything of Wyverne's so-called friends – I cannot know what they might do, but I would not be at all surprised; recall how that creature last night tried to accost you not five minutes after you had sat down. As for Wyverne himself, I have no specific reason to think him a rapist, but I know how very wicked he is, and that he has no scrap of morality or fear of consequences to restrain him. I do know for a fact that he has blood on his hands. And I think you must know it too.' She paused and then said very deliberately, 'Your father's blood. Your family's.'

# 17

Sophie sat frozen in shock. At length she gathered together her scattered wits and said in as steady a voice as she could manage, 'How can you possibly know this?'

'My dear child,' said the Dowager with a sad little smile. 'I knew your great-grandmother Adele so very well – we were contemporaries. Rivals, for the King's affections, though it seems foolish now, when she is long dead and so is he. I remember when she married de Montfaucon, and when your grandfather was born, and your father. I knew your mother's family intimately too. She was a distant cousin of mine, in fact. I forget what happened last week, probably because very little did, but I can remember very clearly what happened eighty years ago. I can see bright pictures in my mind, as vivid as you sitting here before me. You have a great look of Adele about you; I could not possibly mistake it. Even with that ridiculous hair you have dyed to try to make yourself look ordinary. You are not ordinary in the least.'

Sophie – Clemence, as she had not been for eight years – found herself perilously close to tears. 'I did not know,' she said.

'That I resembled her so greatly, I mean. There is no one left to tell me such things. They are all dead. Every one of them.'

'I am so sorry,' Delphine said with a little difficulty. 'For everything. I did try to find you – you, and Marie-Claude, and your brother. As soon as I saw the Stella Rosa around that woman's neck, where it had no business to be, as soon as I heard what had happened to your poor father, I realised that you must be in terrible trouble. I sent people to look for you, but it was too late. They had both died, and you had disappeared. No one could find you. I did try, Clemence. Please believe me.'

She had not heard her mother's name spoken in eight years. That, and the knowledge that someone had cared enough in that desperate time to seek her family out, to try to help them, broke down the last of her defences, and she sobbed, deep racking sobs that shook her whole body, as she had not done for so many long years. She cried until she thought she had no tears left. But even as she wept, she refused to dwell on how different her life might have been, if the Dowager had come a little sooner and saved her. That would do her no good now, and she could not afford to indulge this weakness for long. The rescue that had come had been of a very different nature, and she had become the person she was now because of it. At length she took out her handkerchief and dried her tears with resolution, then said a little unsteadily, 'You do not think, now that you know all this, to ask me why I am here, and why I have deceived you?'

'You have not deceived me. Not for more than a minute or so. I was very glad to see you – nothing has made me so happy for a long, long time. I had thought you must surely be dead, and perhaps that your life had been one of such suffering that death came as a release. And as for why you are here, I think I know. There can only be one reason. Revenge. I must presume you plan to take the Stella back.'

'That and more,' Sophie said with a mirthless little laugh. 'I will take everything I can, and it still will not be enough to punish him as he deserves to be punished. But you will not give me up? Tell your son, or his wife, of what I mean to do?'

'I tell that man nothing!' Delphine said with sudden heat. 'If a pit opened up at his feet and I saw he was about to fall into it, I would not say a word. To give him power to hurt another person when he has already hurt so many is the last thing I would do while I have breath in my body. And as for her...' The Dowager made the explosive sound that is usually transcribed as, 'Bah!'

'And you do not want to ask me where I have been, how I have been living?'

'Do you wish to tell me?'

'I do not.' It was the last thing she desired.

'Then I would not dream of enquiring. However you have lived, whatever you have had to do, I do not wish to know. It is not my affair; I am merely glad that you have survived, and are here now. Understand me, child: I do not care what you intend to do for your revenge. I'd rather you didn't burn the house down with me and the servants in it, but beyond that... What can you do to Wyverne that he has not deserved of you?'

'You really mean that?'

'With all my heart. There are people I care for in this world still, my oldest grandson chief among them, but *he* is not one of them. He is a monster. And that is why,' she said, leaning forward, wincing with effort, and fixing her companion with an intense gaze, 'you must be very, very careful.'

'I am not without resources,' Sophie replied with an attempt to recover her dignity, shaken by the old lady's words but determined not to show it. She had come too far to be frightened now. She was not a helpless ingenue any longer; that girl was dead. She was not Clemence de Montfaucon – she was Sophie Delavallois.

'I hope that is true. I hope you do have resources, for you will need all of them. I hope you succeed in your aims, as long as no one innocent will be hurt by them. I would cheer you on with a clear conscience, if it were not that I am terribly afraid for you. When I tell you that that man...' Sophie noticed now that she would rarely refer to Lord Wyverne as her son; he must have a first name, which this woman and her husband had given him when he lay in his cradle, but she had never used that in Sophie's hearing either. 'When I say that he is a monster, it is no exaggeration, no figure of speech. I do not know if you are aware exactly what he did to your father – how precisely he gained possession of the Stella...'

'I do know,' she broke in. 'I overheard everything, every horrible word. What he had threatened to say about me, and about my father and my mother. All of it, and I heard Papa crying like a little child, which I had never heard before in my life, and Maman's terrified protests as she begged him no, and the shot that killed him, and her screams.' She could hear it all now, as if it had been yesterday, ringing in her ears.

'So you know then,' Delphine said heavily. 'You know exactly what he's capable of. How far he will go. I suppose it is no use begging you to think again, to walk away from this and make a new life, with my help? I would hate to lose you now I have so unexpectedly found you, but for your own sake, my dear Clemence, will you not give it up? Can you not let his fate find him, as we must hope it will, can you not let a thousand devils come and drag him down to hell where he belongs, without taking a hand in it yourself and putting yourself at risk?'

'I can't. I almost wish I could, for your sake, madame, but I simply can't. You must understand why.'

The old lady sighed. 'I do. Of course I do. Well then, I can say little more. I cannot give you my blessing – my fears for you if you take this dangerous course of action will not let me put that on my conscience along with all the other sins that lie heavy there – but I hope that you succeed in your purpose, and that your success brings you peace, and safety.'

'I don't expect peace. I'm not sure anyone or anything can give me that. But thank you.'

The Dowager shook her head. 'Don't thank me. You owe me no thanks, alas, for though I wished to help you eight years ago I did not. Be safe. That's all I ask of you. Be very careful, be safe. Survive this. Don't let him destroy you too.'

## 18

―――――

Sophie – she wouldn't think of herself as Clemence; she couldn't afford to, for she feared it might make her weak – was deeply touched by the Dowager's warning, and by the old lady's concern for her. It had been a long time since anyone had worried about her safety in a manner entirely free from selfish calculation.

Nate Smith, of course, had saved her, in a manner of speaking, when she'd been in the very depths of despair, and she must always be grateful to him, but he'd always been open with her about his reasons, in which human compassion figured hardly at all. He'd seen a spark in her when they'd first met, some spirit of defiance and resilience that had made him think that, properly trained, with her aristocratic background she might one day be very useful to him indeed. It was even possible – she knew how cool and sharp his intelligence was, with what lightning speed it functioned to calculate his own advantage – that this whole scheme had sprung fully-formed into his mind the very instant she poured out her story to him in the squalid little lodging where her mother and brother had died. Because Nate Smith, for reasons she couldn't begin to understand, was quite as determined as she was to destroy and humiliate Lord Wyverne. There must be some history between them – she had never dared to ask. Nate had always been good to her, by his lights, and she'd have been dead on some rubbish heap, or floating in the Thames, if he hadn't chosen her to be his tool, his weapon. But she was nonetheless a little frightened of him still, all the more because she knew so many of his secrets, though certainly not all.

She could not afford to fail, and the idea of walking away, as Delphine had begged her to do, was quite impossible. Even if she'd felt herself drawn to the idea, which she didn't, there was Nate to consider. He was waiting, and although he was a patient man, there were limits to his patience. People who disappointed him tended not to prosper. She had no intention of disappointing him.

So, hiding in her room tonight was simply not an option. This party – though that was hardly the correct word – might be her best opportunity, and she intended to seize it. When they had discussed the matter at great length, late at night in Nate's tavern, making their plans, he had stated what was sufficiently obvious to both of them: Lord Wyverne's huge jewel collection must ordinarily be kept safe in some strongbox or locked closet in his or his wife's private chamber. Sophie could pick a lock as well as any man, he'd made sure of that, but it was not enough. There was enormous risk in such a proceeding, and what Nate knew of the Wyvernes' habits rendered it unnecessary, or so they both hoped. It was well known that Lady Wyverne almost always wore the Stella Rosa in the evenings, and many of her other most valuable jewels besides. Sophie had seen the truth of this herself – had it only been last night? She'd scarcely spared a glance for all the Marchioness's other adornments, focused as she'd been on the precious, cursed necklace that she hadn't set eyes on for so long. But she recalled now that Rosanna had been positively dripping with other jewels, with long white diamond earrings, emerald bracelets, sapphire brooches and ruby rings, several on each finger. It had not been a tasteful display, but as an exhibition of extraordinary wealth and excess it had certainly made its point. The woman had glittered so much in the candlelight that it had almost hurt to look at her. If she wore as much tonight, as Delphine had been so sure she would, if after all her exertions she was careless in putting everything away: that would be Sophie's chance.

The problem was, how would she know when it was all over? She'd have to attend the party, that was plain. But she could not risk being seen and afterwards remembered by some curious guest or watchful servant as someone who was present and yet had no business there. That could be fatal – literally fatal, for she could easily hang for such a daring theft.

She ate a light, early meal with the Dowager that evening, and then promised her she'd go to her chamber and remain there. On some impulse she kissed the old lady's cheek when she left her, and there was a lump in her throat as she closed the door behind her. She'd been lying, of course, and she had a shrewd idea that Delphine had known as much. But she'd said nothing.

She drifted unobtrusively downstairs to the Marble Saloon, as if carelessly interested in the preparations for the party, and found the great atrium all abustle, with footmen in their shirt-sleeves moving furniture under Lord Wyverne's direction. It was vital that he of all people did not see her here, and so she shrank back into the shadows of one of the doorways and watched. Once again she was struck by how entirely unremarkable he was in appearance, like Nate, and yet how intimidating in his sheer pres-ence. His instructions were given in a low tone so that from her place of concealment she could not hear his words, he did not habitually raise his voice in blustering command nor bark orders at his servitors as so many men of his class did, but when William made some error in the placement of a thronelike chair, the few quiet words the Marquess uttered had the young man stammering apologies and looking so pale and terrified that she feared for a little while that he might actually fall down in a swoon. And William – he was the one who had carried the Dowager down to dinner so carefully last night – was a young giant of well over six feet, like all the other footmen, and could if he wished, if he dared, have picked his employer up without breaking sweat and pitched him down the flight of stone steps that led down to the lawn and gardens. It was also undeniable that a servant who looked as well in livery as he did and performed his duties so diligently and cheerfully would have little trouble finding a position in another noble house, so the hold the Marquess had over him, and most of the other servants, was even harder for an outsider like Sophie to understand.

After a little while Lord Wyverne went away – to change, she presumed – and the maids, looking frightened, clearly in a desperate rush to finish their duties and be gone, began laying out a repast upon long tables that had been set up around the walls of the great chamber. They arranged huge pyramids of fruit from the estate's forcing houses, and all manner of cold food in great profusion. They laid out costly Venetian glasses, and there was a great quantity of rich red wine, which had been decanted into jugs of silver and crystal. It was, she realised, an attempt to recreate a lavish Roman banquet.

On one table by the entrance sat a pile of what she thought looked like masks, and, once the maids had gone and she was sure she was unobserved, Sophie went over cautiously to examine them. They were made of leather, which had been moulded by some incredibly ingenious craftsman or -woman into uncannily beautiful and cunningly grotesque faces, and then stiffened and gilded so that they would hold their shape. She found what she thought must be Apollo, Venus, Bacchus, and Jove with a great curled beard, and any number of leering satyrs and coyly inter-changeable female visages which she presumed to be meant for nymphs. Each one had eyeholes, and the simpler ones left the mouth and chin uncovered. Attached to all of them were golden ribbons that could be tied about the head. This discovery was nothing short of providential for purposes of concealment, and she took the opportunity and stole one of the plainer ones, then sped off to change her gown and make the rest of her prepara-tions. It was nearly time.

Earlier she'd wondered anxiously if the guests would be in fancy dress, which would present a problem for her, but then she'd thought that if they were they'd surely have been commanded to continue the classical theme, and this she could achieve with another of the late Lady Wyverne's Grecian gowns, this time a simple draped white muslin. She put it on – stays didn't seem to be a necessity tonight – and skilfully arranged her hair in a more elaborate and fashionable style than she normally favoured, weaving a white ribbon through it and trying on her mask in the cracked and spotted little mirror that hung in one corner of her chamber. She looked at herself, and saw a blank-faced, lovely stranger, some golden figure from myth or legend. The fact that these tales often ended badly, especially for women, was something she refused to contemplate. She was ready, and made her way downstairs.

It was growing dark, and all the lamps and many-branched candelabras were lit. They illuminated an extraordinary scene, and one which she thought she would never forget. Even in daylight and empty, the large oval chamber was one of the most impressive spaces she had ever seen, and it was all the more striking now. Tall columns of purplish marble held up a frieze that ran around the room, ornamented with a continuous plaster relief of gods and goddesses and scenes from Roman life. Above it, a huge coffered dome rose to a large circular oculus that in the day admitted the sunlight, but now showed the diffuse glow of the full moon. Between the columns, niches held statues of deities or huge gilded urns, and the floor was paved in slabs of chilly white Carrara marble. It was, as the Dowager had said, a draughty space with several entrances, and the candle flames guttered wildly, casting flickering shadows across the faces and forms of the guests who laughed and talked, ate, drank and embraced. Some of them must be the people she had dined with last night, though she could not recognise them in their masks; the rest must have come specially for this event, driving here in the moonlight.

Sophie had been correct in her guess – they were for the most part garbed in Roman dress, the women in scandalously flimsy gowns of silk and muslin, many of them with breasts completely bared, and the men in robes or what looked very much like bedsheets, draped in some approximation of togas.

At one side, on the elaborate thronelike chair that William had so painstakingly positioned atop a small dais, sat a man wearing the most elaborate of the masks, the bearded one Sophie had particularly noticed earlier, and his rich crimson robe was heavily embroidered with gold. He was costumed as Jove, the master of the revels, and she could have no doubt as to his identity: Lord Wyverne. Sometimes he spoke to some guest or other who had gone over to pay him homage, but chiefly, Sophie saw, he watched.

On a low platform in the centre two mattresses had been laid side by side and piled with bright silken cushions. One bed was occupied by a naked blonde woman whom Sophie did not know – she wasn't disguised, and hadn't been one of the guests at the dinner party last night – and the other by Lady Wyverne. Rosanna was masked as Venus, but quite recognisable, and she too was naked, as far as clothing went, but she could not be described as unadorned. Her beautiful, voluptuous body was glittering with jewels that struck flame from the candles as she writhed and postured. She had bracelets of every possible colour from wrist to elbow, and others about her ankles. Her fingers were covered with rings, as many as could be worn, and chains of gold studded with gems were threaded through her hair. The Stella Rosa, Sophie was extremely relieved to see, sparkled between her breasts.

Sophie hoped she was no hypocrite. Last night she'd been given the chance of a little pleasure, a little comfort, and she'd seized it gladly. She could hardly criticise anyone else for doing the same. But to see a woman thus displayed to the gaze and the touch of others, to strangers, as though she were nothing more than one of the many precious objects Lord Wyverne possessed and gloated over... Even if Rosanna consented to it freely, it must disturb Sophie, although it undoubtedly suited her purposes.

A man was currently pawing at the jewel, and at Rosanna, as he thrust into her. The spectators, both men and women, were cheering him on from beneath their golden masks, and they were eating and drinking heavily all the while, their wet, avid mouths exposed. They clearly found the lurid scene erotic – some of the waiting men were visibly aroused and impatient to take their turn.

Sophie turned away. The scene did not entice her; on the contrary, if she spent long enough in the room, she thought, she'd be tempted to take a vow of lifelong chastity. Setting aside every other consideration, was none of them worried about the possibility – the likelihood, one might say with justice – of catching the pox? 'I wonder how they are keeping score?' she murmured to herself distractedly.

A deep voice close by her ear said, 'A reasonable question. In other circumstances, with less to distract the eye, no doubt you would have noticed the disturbingly tall and realistic representations of the male member that stand by the head of each couch. When each man has done his part, he slips a ring, provided for the purpose, over the end of it – see, one is doing so now, to great applause. They make a little ceremony of it. Lady Wyverne, I am sure you will be fascinated to know, is winning. But then the night is still young.'

Her heart was suddenly pounding harder, her blood beating in her ears. Sophie hadn't considered for a second the possibility that he of all people would be here tonight; she had assumed he'd be as far away as he could contrive, in his room upstairs, if not miles away in his own home. She didn't like to think that the man she'd shared those stolen moments with could possibly enjoy this spectacle. In her shock and disbelief she had pivoted to look at him the instant he'd begun to speak and she had recognised his voice. 'Lord Drake!'

He was not dressed according to the Roman theme, she saw, but wore his ordinary clothes, covered with a black domino. He was masked, though, and a the coldly beautiful face looked back at her impassively, hiding his expression and his thoughts most effectively.

'I had not thought to see you here,' she said. Though it was no affair of hers, since he had made no commitment, no promises of any kind to her, nor she to him, she owned herself ridiculously disappointed. She had with shocking swiftness come to believe that he was nothing like the rest of them, nothing like his wicked father, though a few short days ago, she recalled now, she'd thought that he must surely be as bad. Something had changed inside her in the meantime, and now she was dismayed to realise that she must have been cruelly wrong to begin to have a better opinion of him.

He let out a brief, unamused laugh, and drew her aside, out of the nearby door and into the corridor, where they could converse unobserved. 'Last night I told you, did I not, that Rosanna is not and never has been my mistress? Did you not believe me? If I have resisted her manifold charms for the last fifteen years or so, and I promise you that I have, despite all her best efforts to seduce me, I am hardly likely to succumb to them now, in such a public arena. If I wanted to fuck – I think we can both agree that that is the *mot juste* here rather than any of the more usual euphemisms – her, or indeed her competitor for that matter, then I would scarcely choose to do so while Lord Wyverne sits and watches. The idea fills me with horror. But actually, Sophie, I don't have the least interest in either of them. Nor, for that matter, in watching this… I don't have words for what this is. Except to say I hate it. The ostentatious public display, Lady Wyverne's involvement, the fact that those present will undoubtedly spread word of every detail of it far and wide…'

She was somehow comforted. It was reassuring to know that she had not been so mistaken in him, but still, he was here, was he not, despite all his fine words? 'So why are you not miles away, then?'

'I was looking for you – why else?' he said, his dark eyes glittering behind the mask. 'And now I have found you, have I not, Mademoiselle de Montfaucon?'

## 19

Of course. The Dowager must have told him. It was only natural, she supposed, though it was devilish awkward. 'Your grandmother...' she began to say, but he shook his head, forestalling her.

'She didn't need to tell me. I recognised you,' he said. 'I should have done so before, perhaps, but this morning I was musing over the token you so kindly granted me last night, and I came to a certain realisation.'

Sophie swore, in crude, pungent, unladylike English. How could she have been so careless? And he laughed with genuine amusement this time, it seemed to her.

'Precisely,' he said. 'One cannot think of everything, and it was dark last night, but this morning, in daylight... I have met a young lady before, I thought to myself, long ago, who had big brown eyes and hair of bright red-blonde. Who was she, and where did I meet her? And then I remembered. We danced together.'

'It wasn't me, really,' she said, almost whispering. 'It was a girl with my face, and I was acquainted with her, I admit, but she seems so distant. It was another life, certainly.'

'Before *he*...' Lord Drake nodded in the direction of the room in which his father presided. 'Before *he* ruined your life and drove your family to their deaths, and set in motion the events that brought you... wherever you are now. I do not know, though perhaps I can guess, what other pain and suffering beyond the horrors I am aware of have been your portion over the last eight years. But I do know that every part of it, every single moment of distress you have suffered, is *his* fault. I had not the least inkling of any of these terrible events before today, but I knew what he was, and have for a long time. Sophie – Clemence – I am so very, very sorry.'

She found herself quite unable to speak for a moment, and it was a while before she said, 'None of it was your fault. When I came here, I had the impression – if I thought about you at all – that you must be as bad as he. I knew, or thought I knew, that your stepmother was your mistress, so it is perhaps understandable that I believed ill of you. But I know better now. I expect,' she said with a sudden flash of insight, 'that you have been his victim too, as much as I. So you have nothing to apologise for.'

They were intensely focused on each other, very close together in the quiet hallway, and somehow the masks they both wore seemed to make it easier to speak these uncomfortable truths. 'I have been accustomed to thinking that I was his victim,' he said a little unsteadily. 'I have had my moments of self-pity, which I am ashamed of now as I stand here with you. It would be idle to deny that I have found it hard, being his son, knowing that those foul rumours were spreading about me, and that most people who heard them believed them, and there was nothing I could do to change their minds. But in reality my grandmother protected me from the worst of it, as I am trying now to protect my brother and sister. He has no interest in children, since he cares much more for things than people, and so has been an absent, indifferent parent to all three of us, and for that I must be thankful, for it might have been so much worse. And nothing that he has ever done to me approaches anywhere near what he has inflicted on you, and on your family.'

It was seductive, to be so near to him, in this little bubble isolated from the world. But she must break the spell. 'I think you must have guessed what I came here to do,' she said, hearing an undercurrent of wistfulness in her voice and hoping he could not hear it too. 'And what I need to know,' she went on more firmly, 'is whether you mean to stop me.'

'You intend to take back – I will not say steal, for it is yours by right – what was taken from you.'

'I do.' She was resolute now. 'I mean to take that, and more. As much as I can carry. It is my intention to deprive him of so many things that are precious to him.'

'And will you leave tonight, after you have done so? Shall this be our last meeting?'

'No. No, I want to see the after-effects of what I have done,' she said fiercely. 'I'll hide it all in the house, and leave traces that will make it appear that the thief has fled. And I will stay here, in his home, and watch him suffer. And I must ask you again, now you know that I shall not take only the Stella, do you mean to stop me?'

He did not hesitate for a second. 'Of course I don't.'

She was incredulous. 'Really? You will allow me to deprive your family of thousands and thousands of pounds of jewels, a fortune, and you will not raise a finger to stop me?'

'Not one finger,' he repeated. His voice was deep and cold and sure as he said, 'Apart from the fact that you are owed your revenge, apart from the fact that there may well be stories of misery like to yours behind every single bauble, can you imagine for a moment that I would wish to see my sister or a future wife of mine, supposing such a creature should ever exist, decked out in the finery that *she* now wears? In there, while one man after another makes use of her, a crowd of degenerates cheers her on and the man I must call father watches?'

'I can quite understand why you might not want that,' she said drily. It was certainly a valid point of view. But she had been desperately poor once, where he had not, and so she said practically, 'You could always sell it all. One day when he is dead.'

'I couldn't rest easy doing that. I have no idea where it all came from, so that I might give it back, and I do not know how I could set about finding out. Many of the smaller stones have been re-set and re-cut – it is one of his more innocent hobbies, to design such things to adorn his wife, and one ruby or white diamond must be much like another. Surely now I must assume that the bulk of it was acquired as he acquired the Stella Rosa from your family. Stolen, in effect. Worse than stolen – a housebreaker is benign compared to him. I want no part of it to be my inheritance. And if it hurts him to lose it, can you really think that I will be sorry?'

'So I am free to do what I must?'

'Yes. Though I hope you will be very careful.' He put his hands on her bare arms and pulled her closer, his mask almost touching hers. 'You think you know what he is, but you have never seen him thwarted. I have, and I can tell you that he will stop at nothing. I am sure he will order beatings, torture, worse, if he so much as suspects that you have taken what he believes to be his and thinks that hurting you would help him get it back. Actually, even if he didn't have such a hope, he might still hurt you for its own sake. Because he likes it.'

'I know,' she said. 'Of course I do; I can never forget what he did to my father. That's why I will contrive it so that it appears the thief has gone, has fled with the jewels. He will send men in pursuit, but of course they will find no trace, for there is nothing to find. I don't want anyone innocent – the servants above all – to be suspected and to suffer for it.'

'Then there is little more to be said. You intend to wait till they are done in there, till she has passed out – she's drinking steadily, they all are – and take it all from her body, despite the hideous risk you take by doing so?'

'Yes. That is my plan. I know it is daring, but I believe it has a good chance of success. She won't be calling her abigail to help her – the maids are all locked away and guarded tonight, on your grandmother's command.'

He said soberly, 'You may have a long wait. Would you like me to go and see...?'

She nodded, grateful that she would not be obliged to go back in there just now. He released her, leaving her alone in the shadowy passageway – she was suddenly cold in the thin muslin gown, and shivered – but in a moment he was back at her side. 'It's not over yet,' he said, 'but the crowd has thinned out considerably. Some of her earlier – I honestly can't think of an appropriate word, but some of them have already succumbed to drink, and are still present in body, but snoring and insensible. Since there are far fewer women there now, I must presume that some couples, with a delicacy you would hardly suspect them capable of, have departed, no doubt to conjoin in some privacy. It almost makes one feel affection for them in their sweet bashfulness, don't you agree? Rosanna's opponent seems to me to be flagging, and Lord Wyverne, in so far as one can judge, appears to be a little bored. It might not be much longer.' He must have seen that she was chilled, for he said in a quite different tone, 'You could come closer, and let me hold you. You have gooseflesh on your arms.'

'I do,' she said, stepping into his embrace, torn between a strong desire to be there and a certain wariness, 'but I must warn you, I am not feeling in the least amorous. I was thinking, in fact, that I might never again.'

'I am not either,' he said ruefully, slipping his arms about her and resting his masked cheek against her hair with a deep sigh. 'I have observed before that whenever I am offered the dubious privilege of an insight into the workings of Lord Wyverne's mind – and today has really been nothing but that, all day long – it drives away all lustful thoughts from me for a good long while.'

'You don't want to be anything like him,' she murmured against the dark fabric that covered his broad chest. She was warm in his arms, and felt safe, though she knew this was pure illusion. 'It's perfectly understandable. I've noticed that you rarely describe him as your father, and I do not think I have heard your grandmother refer to him as her son above once or twice.'

'Can you say that you are surprised?'

'Of course not, but I don't think you need to worry. Surely if you'd shared his... his proclivities, they'd have revealed themselves by now. The very fact that you worry you might be like him shows that you can't possibly be. You must know that. I'm sure he was a vicious child, and a vicious youth, to grow into such a man.'

'Yes, I believe he was, though the stories I have heard of his doings have come from others, from the servants mostly. It pains my grandmother to speak of such things, and she has tried to shelter me as best she could.' He fell silent, and they stood, holding each other in the near darkness, taking precious comfort each from the other.

After a little while he said, 'I know I'm not like him. My closest friend – he lives nearby, he is the rector of the local parish – tells me so, if I ever begin to doubt it. I do not share Wyverne's twisted appetites, and I have no desire to treat any woman as a possession. I've had one lover in my life, and I was faithful to her all the while we remained together, and would have remained so if she had stayed with me, though I understood why she left. Two lovers, Clemence, if I may count you. And I would like to count you.'

She was about to answer him, to reveal some of her own tightly held secrets, but a sudden noise startled them. A dishevelled man in a wine-stained bedsheet toga came lurching out of the Marble Saloon, his arm about the waist of a woman draped in exiguous white silk. They were both unmasked. 'You've missed all the fun, wench!' he confided, breathing heady fumes into Sophie's face, making her grateful once again for the protection of the mask. 'Lady W has been declared the winner. A worthy successor to Messalina. Twenty-six, to the other's twenty-four! What a woman! Makes you proud to be British, don't it? Only she's passed out now, and no wonder. The whore is mad as fire! Going off to set a few records of our own now, aren't we, my girl?' he said, squeezing his companion's bottom.

She didn't appear to be anywhere near as inebriated as he was. 'We'll see,' she said with a bold wink at Sophie. 'Stranger things have happened, I suppose. Come on – I'll have to get you upstairs first, and you might find you prefer a nice nap by the time we get there. Come along!'

They staggered away together, and Sophie pulled from Lord Drake's embrace. Whatever she had been about to say was gone forever. It was probably for the best, she thought. 'I must go and see if it's time.'

'Be careful!' he said, his voice deep and intense.

'I will. I always am.'

'You weren't last night...'

She didn't answer him. She was already gone.

## 20

When Sophie cautiously re-entered the great marble chamber, she found it almost deserted. There were indeed, as Drake had warned her, drunken men and women slumped insensible here and there – some of them had chosen to claim the vacant bed and lay there snoring in a jumble of limbs. But Lord Wyverne's throne stood empty, and his wife had been abandoned after all her exertions and lay sprawled in her tawdry finery, limbs spread across the crumpled sheets. If he had shown concern for Rosanna, even to the extent of having her carried away, it would have complicated matters; she'd have had to follow to her chamber, and would have done so despite the risk. But there was no need.

Sophie had a small bag, part of her luggage, and she'd secreted it earlier in the evening, before the party started, under one of the tables. She fetched it out now. She'd always known that this would be the hardest part – to strip the jewels from the unconscious woman's body. She was a pickpocket; she had the lightest of touches. But this was something altogether new, and undeniably distasteful as well as difficult. It would have been quite impossible, she realised now, to undertake such a daring, intimate theft if her victim had merely been asleep rather than insensible from drink and physically exhausted besides. She had been, she now admitted, insanely confident in her plan – and yet it seemed fate had played into her hands. She must not fail to take advantage of it.

She started at her ankles – that seemed easiest, and taking the Stella from about her neck, that would be most difficult. Slowly, slowly... She'd even practised for this; there was no manner of fastening that she couldn't undo, even while blindfolded. Her deft fingers found the clasp of the first diamond bracelet, and in a moment she had dropped it into her waiting bag. She breathed a little easier. She could do this.

The jewels had marked Lady Wyverne's skin in places. The candles had burned low and were guttering; some of them had gone out completely – there had been no servants here to trim or to extinguish them properly – but the full moon was high above, its powerful beams streaming down through the oculus and illuminating the extraordinary scene below. It was in truth more light than Sophie needed or wanted, and not only because of any lingering fastidiousness she might feel at being confronted with the stark reality of her task rather than being able to perform it in cloaking shadows. It was not just that; if anyone should enter the room now she would be utterly undone, exposed as guilty, but she would not let the terrible risk deter her. Not when she had come so far.

She was moving faster now, more secure in her skill and in the depth of her victim's stupor. Bauble after bauble slid easily into her bag. Both Rosanna's ankles were now bare, and she turned her attention to the woman's wrists, working swiftly. The rings, she thought, would be quite hard to remove, and she'd leave them till last. Till after the Stella.

It was time now, after so much preparation, to do what she

had really come here to do. The chain had a clasp – a curious thing, not quite like any other fastener she had come across before or since. She remembered... good God – a sudden image flashed into her mind, shocking in its clarity. It was so powerfully affecting that it made her pause for a moment to recover her composure before she dared to continue. She remembered her mother setting the jewel about her own neck, on the one occasion in her life when she had worn it, when she'd gone to the costume ball and danced with Lord Drake. Before their lives had come crashing down around their ears. She'd been so excited that evening to be trusted with the family's most precious treasure. Mama had fussed with it for what seemed like forever, careful not to disturb Clemence's piled-up hair, and then stepped back to see the effect it had made. The Duchess had smiled rather mistily and told her she was beautiful. Her father had agreed when he had seen her later... they'd both kissed her, and her brother Louis had come down in his nightgown and little cap to see her, and had teased her over how grand she looked, how unlike herself...

Enough. She took a deep breath, unfastened the clasp, and with infinite care drew the chain from about the neck of this woman who had no right to wear it. The jewel was heavy in her hand, and warm from where it had lain. She shuddered involuntarily, and slipped it into the bag with all the rest. If she could hold her nerve a little longer, she would soon be done, and then she could go, and do all the other things she needed to before this interminable evening could be over.

Lady Wyverne stirred in her sleep and made a fretful sound. Her head turned restlessly, her eyelids flickering. Clemence – Sophie – froze like a statue, wondering if there was the least chance of getting away undetected if Rosanna woke now and found herself robbed. Realistically, she knew there wasn't. She'd be seen, there'd be a scream to shatter the stillness of the night, others would wake, she'd be caught... But no. The naked woman turned her head uneasily upon the pillow again and then sighed, and slipped back into a more peaceful slumber.

Hands shaking, Sophie unwound a long diamond chain from her hair. It was agonisingly difficult, repeatedly catching and tangling, and she was pushing her luck too far now, she knew. She ought to stop. But some demon of perverse determination drove her on, and now she turned to the rings, easing one and then another very slowly from Rosanna's fingers till her hands were as bare as the rest of her body.

Done. It was done. Sophie turned to leave, had already taken a few hasty steps away, and then she pivoted, impulsively catching up a length of fabric that lay on the edge of the bed and trailed to the floor – an abandoned toga, a bedcovering or Rosanna's own gown, she did not stop to discover – and draped it carefully, delicately, over the unconscious woman. She told herself that it was only sensible – that if Lady Wyverne was not cold she'd sleep more soundly and for longer, and that the concealment the material offered was also useful, disguising the theft. But the truth was that she seemed so vulnerable lying there alone, stripped of all her jewels after an evening spent being used by a procession of men who could care nothing for her, and all this while her husband watched like the depraved monster he was. Sophie felt no remorse, she was quite sure, but she could not bear the sight of her suddenly, or the thought that the servants, men and women both, might see her thus exposed when they came in the early morning to begin tidying away the detritus of the night before.

It was time and past time that she was gone, far away from the scene of the crime. She closed up her bag and slipped out of the atrium with it, heading for the stair that led up to the place she'd chosen as the ideal temporary cache for the treasures. It was much darker here, but her night vision was good and she made her way sure-footedly upwards and through the maze of rooms to her destination: the chamber with the big, old abandoned bed frame and the secret trapdoor under it.

She had an unpleasant moment or two in the cobwebby darkness when she was trying to get down the ladder without slipping. This was the final step before she could conceal her precious burden deep among the heaps of junk that lay in the hidden storeroom. At the bottom she barked her shin painfully on some invisible sharp object, and feared for one long agonising moment that she'd destabilised the pile of rubbish and that it would come crashing down and wake half the house, or crush her with its weight so that she suffocated slowly, trapped. What a hideous way to die. But if it tottered – she could not see as she stood holding her breath – it did not fall, and she was able to do what she had come to do and close the trapdoor securely behind her. A day or two earlier she'd swept the floors quite thoroughly with a birch broom she had borrowed and later returned, so her footprints in the dust of decades would not betray her even if someone did think to search here.

She hastened downstairs again, feeling a brief sense of exhilaration at having the whole huge, silent building apparently to herself, and carried out the final part of her plan, which was to open a set of shutters and a tall sash window in one of the rooms close to the Marble Saloon. This window led rather usefully to a broad stone ledge that would offer an easy enough climb via a drainpipe down to ground level, to someone reasonably agile. This would signal that the thief, who must surely be an enterprising member of the male sex, not a mere feeble woman encumbered by skirts, had left that way, and was no longer in the house. If anyone were outside in the moonlight watching – and she could not quite exclude the possibility, knowing Nate as she did – the opening of the shutter would also signal that she had been successful in her daring escapade and the jewels were now safely in her possession.

Her final mission – and she must not grow careless now – was to regain her room, and she had feared that this might be her hardest task, since she knew that the maids' attic was supposed to be locked and guarded. It would be ironic, she thought as she climbed another steep set of stairs, now rather weary as her earlier excitement subsided, if the measures that the Dowager had taken to protect her and others were to be her downfall at last. If she couldn't regain the relative safety of her room, she'd surely be suspected, and all the rest of her meticulous precautions would have been in vain.

And the door *was* guarded. A chair had been set at the top of the staircase, in a little alcove where the steep steps met the turn of the passage, and in it sat James, another of the footmen, valiantly protecting the women of the household lest some inebriated, degenerate lord should wander up here with dark purposes in mind.

But it was very late now, the house was utterly still, and the poor boy was fast asleep. He wasn't exactly snoring, but he was breathing very heavily and regularly, and Sophie, suppressing an impulse to cross herself in thanks to a deity she didn't believe in, stepped lightly past him and approached the lock. She already knew it was a paltry sort of a thing, and with her lockpicks ready to hand – thank heaven she had not forgotten to remove them from the bag before she hid it – she made short and almost silent work of the mechanism and secured it behind her just as easily.

She'd got away with it, she realised as she reached her chamber and closed the door very softly behind her. She did not know what tomorrow might bring, but she'd pulled it off, and fashioned a fine alibi for herself into the bargain. She could not possibly have stolen the jewels, for had not she been locked away along with all the other female servants? James could vouch for the truth of that. She concealed the picks and her trusty knife under a loose floorboard, pushing them deep, deep into the cavity – she wasn't going to be tripped up by little things like that, after all she had achieved tonight – and rapidly undressed.

An hour or so later, Sophie lay in her mean little bed, too wound up to sleep. It had all gone so smoothly, she could hardly believe it. She attempted to ignore the nagging little internal voice that told her it was too good to be true. What had she wanted – failure, capture, disaster? Nonsense. She had planned and she had executed, and she'd been lucky besides. Nate had once told her that clever and careful scheming seemed to attract luck, while sloppiness drew ill fortune to it.

All that she'd wanted, all that she'd planned for so long with Nate's help, all the fierce hope and focus that had sustained her while she planned it, all her wonderful revenge – she'd done it. Every bit of it. More than she could ever have hoped for. Even if the jewels were by some mischance found – and she was reasonably confident they would not be, so clever was her hiding place – there was nothing there to link her, honest Sophie Delavallois, to them. Now all she had to do was hold her nerve for a little longer and keep her face and manner impassive while she gloried in the chaos that her actions would undoubtedly create. The hard parts were done, the easy parts lay ahead. It might not be precisely simple to smuggle the jewels out of the house – but she'd done so much already, that would be child's play.

It should be the happiest day of her life – or of her new life, in any case, the old one with its ordinary family pleasures and prospect of happiness having been left so far behind her with her old identity.

Why, then, did she feel so empty?

## 21

Rafe watched Sophie walk away from him with a disturbing mixture of emotions churning in his breast. She was so brave, he thought, so resolute. And undeniably reckless, in a manner that seemed to call up some echo of her wildness from him too. It must be her, because the rest of his life was so controlled and ordered.

She was, he supposed, a criminal in most people's eyes. A thief. Moreover, she carried a knife, and seemed confident in her ability to use it. He had not the least idea how she had survived alone for so long and found her way here at last. But he found he didn't care – no, that was wrong; he could guess at how much she must have suffered and he cared very much about that, he devoutly wished none of it had come to pass, but he didn't care about her history otherwise. He would not dream for a moment of judging her for any of it. He'd even considered offering to help her tonight, but then instantly realised that this was something she needed to do by herself. He could see that the impulse to revenge had sustained her for years and that it would be very wrong to take any part of that away from her. This was *her* moment, not his. He was desperately worried for her safety, though, and prayed that all her ingenuity and fierce determination would be a match for Wyverne's ruthlessness.

Should he spend the night here, as he never did, or ride over to the rectory as he'd originally intended? It was a dilemma – if he stayed, he'd be here in the morning when the theft was discovered, and could perhaps help Sophie if she needed him. But he had not slept here in years, and if Wyverne heard of it, as he surely would in the end, he'd think it excessively strange. Knowing the way the man's mind worked, he thought that his instant assumption would be that Drake had been bedding someone here, and that was why he had changed his fixed habits and remained. And might not his thoughts then turn to Sophie as a likely candidate, since she was the only new arrival? Could drawing attention to her thus put her in further danger?

Rafe resolved at last that it was best to go, to behave as though there was nothing unusual at all about this night as far as he was concerned. It might be useful, if matters really grew desperate in the aftermath of the theft, to sow a tiny seed of doubt in his father's mind, and divert attention away from Sophie and all the other inhabitants of the house. If the Marquess was busy wondering if his own heir had robbed him, had taken the jewels and instantly spirited them away from the estate to God knows where before their loss was even suspected, he might spend less time worrying about everyone else, including Sophie. He must know that Drake hated him, and why; the idea might give him a few extra anxious moments.

Having decided, he made his way through the dark, silent house towards the stables – he had his own keys and always locked up behind him, he wouldn't contemplate leaving a door open and risking any of the staff suffering for his neglect – and saddled his sleepy mare before trotting sedately off across the moonlit lawns and around the side of the lake. He paused for a moment when he reached the great triumphal arch at the top of the rise and, almost against his will, gazed back towards the house. There was not a light to be seen anywhere inside and nothing modern or sordid about it from this distance; it looked like some magnificent and pure temple to the ancient gods. It was so piercingly beautiful as it sat there slumbering, the tall, pillared central section with its imposing flight of steps and triangular pediment cast in sharp relief by the light of the moon, that once again his heart ached to see it. He would be ambushed every now and then like this by his love for the place, and his desire that everything could be different, so that he could look on it just once with unalloyed pleasure. But he doubted that that would ever be possible, and certainly it could not be while his father lived and while Rosanna shared the house with him.

He shook his head and rode on, through the arch and down the ride to the village. The rectory was never locked and he had a standing invitation to spend the night there; it was possible that Simon, who kept very late hours and seemed to need little sleep, would still be up reading, though he wasn't sure he wanted to face his friend just now. The Reverend Mr Venables was a curious mixture of innocence and shrewdness, and would undoubtedly be able to see at a glance that Rafe's mind was disturbed. And there was so much he couldn't tell him.

He stabled Cinnamon, the other horses whickering quietly in welcome, and made her comfortable, whispering to her soothingly as he went about his tasks, taking longer than he needed in the rather cowardly hope that Simon must surely be abed by now. But he wasn't – he could see the light under the door of the study when he had closed the front entrance carefully behind him. He sighed and went to tap softly on the panel.

Simon's cheerful face turned to him as he came in, his spectacles gleaming in the candlelight. He was perhaps ten years older than Lord Drake, his former student, a short, plump, balding little man with a sunny disposition that was written quite plainly on his face. 'You're about late, Rafe!' he said. 'I'm glad to see you. Will you take a glass of brandy with me? You look as though you could do with it.'

Rafe crossed to the desk and poured a small measure for each of them from the decanter that sat ready. 'Carousing into the small hours, I see,' he said drily, sinking into one of the comfortably shabby armchairs by the small fire and stretching out his booted legs. It had been a long day.

'Hardly,' said his friend with a smile. 'I was writing my sermon, and I rather lost track of time, hunting down an interesting reference in St Augustine... But it isn't important. You look as though you have the weight of the world on your shoulders. I hope your grandmother is not unwell?'

'She's fine,' Rafe reassured him. 'She seems most content with her new companion.' There had been no need to add that last sentence. He hadn't wanted to speak of Sophie, of Clemence, but he couldn't seem to help himself.

'Good heavens, she has another? I cannot keep track of them.'

'I thought I'd mentioned that a new companion arrived a short while ago,' Rafe said, a shade too airily.

'You hadn't, in fact.'

'Ah.'

'I apprehend that this new arrival is not a particularly elderly lady like some of her predecessors?' Simon was smiling at him as he spoke, and he felt himself colouring under the benign scrutiny.

Rafe laughed ruefully. 'It is useless to attempt to hide anything from you, is it not?'

'I didn't think you were actually trying very hard. Do you wish to speak of her?' And then Simon's cherubic face clouded over and he said, 'If she is someone you think you could be... interested in, then Wyverne Hall is surely no place for her. Lord Wyverne himself is hardly respectable – and I understand that he has guests, and can all too easily imagine what manner of persons they must be. Are you concerned for her safety – is that why you look so troubled?'

Rafe didn't answer him directly. He had no intention of telling him everything, but nor did he wish to lie. He said, 'Last night Wyverne insisted, as you know he sometimes does, that my grandmother and her companion attend a dinner party he was holding. One of his guests did not let five minutes pass before he propositioned the young lady – Mademoiselle Delavallois.'

Simon exclaimed in horror, his innocent face creased with distress. 'I am excessively sorry to hear that! Could you do anything at all to protect her?'

'I wished to, naturally, but as matters turned out I did not need to. Mademoiselle Delavallois immediately threatened to stab the creature in the leg with a fork, and he was so convinced that she was serious that he left her alone after that. Of course she was obliged to suffer the company of Lady Wyverne and her cronies for a little while longer, as was my grandmother, but at last they both escaped unscathed.'

Mr Venables could not help but smile, though his brow was still furrowed. He shot Rafe a sharp glance. 'You overheard the shocking insult that the poor young lady was forced to endure?'

'I saw it from across the dinner table, and she told me afterwards how she had defended herself.' Too late Rafe saw the neat trap that had been set for him. 'Yes, Simon, we have conversed privately – several times, in fact. Was that what you desired to know?'

It was his friend's turn to look disconcerted. 'I'm sorry. I don't mean to pry. Would it be inappropriate, or perhaps too hasty, if I said that I would be very happy if you brought this young lady here to meet Elizabeth and the children? I am sure they would be happy to know her, and it might be good for her to have friends nearby, if she should ever need them.'

Rafe gazed down into his brandy glass, swirling the golden liquid before he drank a little. 'I know you're concerned for me, and for her. But the situation is more complicated than I can possibly tell you, and – I don't believe it's a good idea. If I brought her here, everyone at Wyverne would soon know of it, and the last thing I want is to attract his attention – my father's attention – to her. At present he barely seems to have noticed her existence, and I think I would prefer to keep it that way.'

'You fear... Good heavens, Rafe, how much longer can you continue in this life? That a man should be worried that his own parent would force his attentions—'

'I know. That's not precisely my concern, though, because he does not... It is very hard to speak of such things, but if I cannot say them to you, who in the world can I tell? In plain words, then, it is my understanding from what I have heard whispered by the servants that my father does not now lay hands upon a woman – not his wife, not anyone else. What he does do...' Rafe picked up his glass again and drained it. 'What he does do is watch. He watches others while they couple, he orders that they should do so for his entertainment. And so I do not fear direct harm to Mademoiselle Delavallois from him, but that does not mean I think her safe at Wyverne by any means.'

'Good heavens! My dear fellow, what can I say? Of course, even I have heard stories...' Simon murmured unhappily.

'I dare swear they're all true. Tonight he arranged that Lady Wyverne and some notorious ladybird from London should stage a reenactment of Messalina and Scylla's famous contest, which you may recall from Suetonius. If you have not read it, my dear friend, I am sure even you must have heard of it.'

The rector gasped and grew pale. 'I must believe you if you tell me so, but I confess I can scarcely credit it. That such shocking things should happen in London I suppose I always knew, but that they should take place here in Buckinghamshire, in my own parish...'

Rafe laughed mirthlessly. 'Come, Simon! The Hellfire Club became active here long before my father was born, so there is a history of such deeds in this area, though I am not aware that he ever attended its meetings. But I'm sure he did if he was able – can you seriously doubt it?'

'West Wycombe is more than forty miles away!' Mr Venables protested naively, as if the distance served as some protection.

'Perhaps Sir Francis Dashwood's doings there merely served as inspiration, then,' Rafe said drily. 'It hardly matters, after all. I don't, in fact, have any evidence to suspect Wyverne of Satanism. The things I know he's done are quite bad enough. Tonight... I feel events are moving to a crisis, Simon. He seems to have less and less restraint, and I have a sense of impending doom. I have wondered lately if he is... unwell in a specific fashion, as the promiscuous way he has lived makes all too possible, and his mind is affected by his malady. I need not go into greater detail, I'm sure. But I don't see what in the world I can do about any of it.'

The rector was plainly deeply troubled by all he heard, and did not think to tell Rafe that his fears were foolish. 'I can see that there is sadly little that can be done. You could take the young lady away, that's one thing – bring her here, perhaps.'

'Thank you. But there is also my grandmother to consider. I cannot leave her unprotected. You must see that.'

Simon said dubiously, 'Perhaps your father would not now object...'

Rafe shook his head. 'He's told her a thousand times that he will never let her go. She believes him to be entirely serious, and she must know him best. I would have had her safe with me years ago if it were otherwise. And I might risk incurring his grave displeasure for her sake, and steal her away, if it were not for the fact that I have Charles and Amelia to think of. You know he would have the full weight of the law on his side if he ever took it into his head to take them back. I am just their half-brother. He is their father, and a man of great power. Thank heaven they are not here just now to be drawn into the crisis I sense is coming. Is it a sin, tell me, reverend sir, to wish for another person's death, and that person one's own father?'

'My conscience tells me it must be,' said his friend sadly. 'But I cannot find it in my heart to reproach you for it. I can only pray that you are wrong and that matters can reach some happy conclusion without any further pain being caused to anyone, though I confess I cannot imagine how this might come to pass.'

And you do not know all, thought Rafe grimly. You do not know the full depths of Wyverne's depravity, nor Rosanna's, and you know nothing at all of what Sophie did tonight, and the terrible danger she faces as a result. 'Nor me,' he said tersely. 'Nor anyone. Pour me some more brandy, would you?'

## 22

It was quite late the next morning when the theft was discovered. Sophie had risen at her normal hour and was with the Dowager, reading quietly – she wasn't paying a great deal of attention to what she read and she didn't think Delphine was either, but they were both by tacit agreement working hard at pretending everything was normal – when Marchand appeared with William. They both looked pale, and Marchand, normally a woman of great self-possession, appeared almost flustered. 'I have been sent to summon you, madame, mademoiselle. William is here to carry you.' She spoke in English, which in general she did not, as if to make sure she could not later be accused of sharing secrets.

'This is most unusual,' responded her employer coolly in the same language, raising an eyebrow. 'Has something occurred to upset the household?'

'I am not to say anything,' Marchand replied woodenly. 'Monsieur himself instructed me.'

'Very well,' Delphine replied. 'Come, Sophie, set down your book. The Vicomte de Valmont will have to wait for us, it seems. I ᴜᴀre say it will do him good, the scoundrel. William – I am all yours.'

He didn't raise a smile this time, and it was a solemn little procession that made its way downstairs. Sophie shot Marchand a questioning glance, but the woman merely shook her head emphatically and would not speak.

The whole household staff, as far as Sophie could tell, including people she'd never set eyes on before, was assembled in the Marble Saloon. The empty wine glasses, the spoiled food and all the rest of the debris from the party had been cleared away, but the great throne on its dais was still there, and the beds also remained, crumpled and sordid in the clear morning light that streamed in through the great oculus above. William looked about him a little wildly, but there was no other chair, so he was obliged to carry the Dowager to the throne and set her gently in it. He hurried away to join his fellow footmen where they stood, and Sophie, with Marchand, went to the old lady's side, so that she would not be entirely alone. I've caused all this, she thought. I believed I'd gone into it with my eyes open, but... what have I done? Her heart was racing.

Lord Wyverne stood to one side, and Lady Wyverne next to him. There was a space around them, as if no one dared approach, and they were not touching each other. Their guests were nowhere to be seen. Rosanna didn't look as though she'd been to her own bed – her hair was still dishevelled and she was very pale, but someone had brought her a robe, and the flimsy fabric with which Sophie had covered her lay discarded on the floor in a pool of stark red on the white marble. It looked like blood.

Apparently they were still waiting for some more of the servants to join them, and Lord Wyverne would not speak until they had. The tense silence in the chamber was disturbed after a moment or two as the stable staff and gardeners shuffled in and took their places with all the rest, then the company fell uneasily silent again.

At last Lord Wyverne said, and his tones were low, so that Sophie had to strain a little to hear him, 'I have been robbed.'

There were a few gasps, a little murmuring, but he waited till silence reigned again, and then repeated, 'I have been robbed.' He was still not speaking violently or aggressively, but his whole body vibrated with tension.

She'd seen very little of him prior to this moment, and the rest of the staff must know him much better than she did, but what shocked her, and, she thought, shocked the others, judging by their faces, was the fact that his voice wasn't steady; it shook, and his eyes were fixed and glaring. Although he wasn't shouting, or not now – perhaps he had been earlier – he had spittle around his lips, and his face was flushed and hectic. Well, she'd wanted to wound him, and there could be no question that she had done so. It ought to feel better.

Sophie's hand crept out and found the Dowager's, and Delphine did not pull away. Her hand was thin and frail, the skin soft and papery. But it was steady in Sophie's gentle grasp.

'Robbed!' her son repeated. 'And if I find that one of you here was responsible, or knows anything at all about the matter – anything! – I promise you, you will wish you had never been born. You will beg for death before I am done with you.' His dark gaze travelled slowly around the room, stopping here and there as he fixed one servant or another with a basilisk stare. They trembled and grew paler. We all look guilty, Sophie thought, or terrified, which amounts to the same thing. No one could hold his eyes for more than a moment, and although she would have liked to stare him down, she knew it would be foolish to provoke him, so when his regard fell on her, as she'd known it must because she was so new here, she let her eyelids drop after a moment, so that she would look as abashed as everyone else did, no less and no more.

'Perhaps you might tell us what exactly has occurred,' the Dowager said quietly. 'If we are being accused of something we might at least hear what it is, for at present you know we are all in complete ignorance.'

'I know no such thing,' he said shortly, his eyes bulging. 'But very well, madam. I suppose it would be ridiculous to suspect *you*, a helpless cripple. So. Lady Wyverne rather carelessly allowed herself to fall asleep here last night, on that bed, there, wearing almost every jewel that I possess, and when she woke from her slumber – which must have been extraordinarily deep, but then she had drunk a great deal, as is her wont – she found to her great consternation that all my precious things were gone, stripped from her body. It beggars belief that such a thing should have happened here, in my house, but my dear wife assures me that it is so. It was later discovered that a window was left open in the blue drawing room, so perhaps the thief left that way, or perhaps he did not and only feigned to do so, or perhaps he had an accomplice among you here. And now you know just as much as I do.' His voice was icy cold, his words clipped, and his wife flushed with mortification as he spoke and looked as if she might burst into tears. But she did not, and said not a word to defend herself.

'How shocking,' his mother replied in level tones. 'You will contact the authorities?'

Lord Wyverne's flush deepened. 'That is no affair of yours, madam,' he snapped, losing some of his coolness. I think that means no, Sophie mused, a little calmer now. Perhaps he dare not, because all the precious things that have been stolen from him had first been stolen from others. Or perhaps he doesn't want word to spread through society of how he has been humiliated, as it must if he reported the theft. And if the world should learn the manner of the crime, and exactly what had occurred here last night... Rosanna couldn't be cast out by the haut ton, because they'd always shunned her, and her husband too was no longer received or invited anywhere due to his atrocious reputation. But *this* would be a truly enormous scandal, eclipsing anything that had gone before. Could he want the whole of England to know what he had caused to be done, and the disaster that had resulted from it?

Sophie had once in Nate's tavern heard a tale of a crim con case, a scandalous divorce that had happened before she was born – of a gentleman who had encouraged men to look at his wife naked, who had perhaps watched her in congress with her lover and enjoyed doing so. She remembered the man's name, Sir Richard Worsley, for it was still repeated as a byword and a laughing-stock at every level of society, and what he had done so long ago was as nothing to Lord Wyverne's behaviour. Could he want to be known for that, for what the world would surely label perversion, and by implication impotence? Could any man?

It wasn't clear to Sophie what the Marquess had hoped to achieve by summoning all his household here – had he expected the culprit to break down and confess, intimidated so that he or she lost their wits? Or had he imagined that someone knew something to implicate another and would rush to tell it, in order to save themselves? But nobody spoke. Nobody so much as coughed. The silence stretched, and they endured it.

Lord Wyverne said at last, his voice still wavering a little, 'You have been warned. I will be watching all of you very closely. Now go about your duties. You have wasted quite enough time.' This accusation was so unjust that Sophie might have laughed, but despite their master's words it was plain that no one wanted to be the first to move; they all stood as if frozen, as still as the statues in the alcoves behind them. 'Go!' he shouted, his voice rising and cracking on the single syllable that echoed in the dome, and there was a great bustle and confusion as the room emptied out with surprising speed. William hurried over and seized the Dowager, almost running up the stairs with her in his arms, and Sophie was close behind them.

But just as she was about to reach the turn in the stair, the great main door opened with a dramatic creak. Normally two liveried footmen would be standing by it all day long to admit any visitor, but they'd fled along with everyone else, so Lord Drake thrust open the door himself and strode in, looking around him casually at the backs of the stragglers who were still queuing to escape. A little frown creased his handsome brow, as if in puzzlement at the unusual sight, and Sophie could not resist going just a little further up the stair then watching from her place of concealment. She had no clue what might be about to happen.

'You!' said his father with evident loathing. 'What are you doing here? Come to gloat, have you?'

'I have not the least idea what you mean, sir. I have come to see my grandmother, as is my daily habit.' Lord Drake's words were coolly civil, although Sophie noticed that he had not acknowledged his stepmother's presence by so much as a nod.

Wyverne's eyes narrowed in instant suspicion, and he stepped forward. 'Were you here last night, Drake?'

'I was. What of it?' The civility was fading fast.

Wyverne's face was almost as purple as the marble columns now. 'I was robbed last night, sirrah, robbed, I tell you, and I demand to know, did you have a hand in it?'

'I know we have little regard for each other, but I confess I had not expected to hear you accuse me of theft.' Lord Drake was icily controlled, in sharp contrast with his now obviously agitated parent. 'If some bauble from your collection is missing, perhaps you should interrogate your guests. Having made their acquaintance, I could well believe any one among them capable of such a crime.'

'Some bauble?' bellowed his father, enraged, spittle flying from his mouth. 'Some fucking bauble? Some treacherous bastard has taken every jewel I possessed, boy, including the Stella Rosa itself, while *she* lay sleeping here, in this room, like the stupid, lazy whore she is!'

Rosanna did not break when she heard herself so described. Her face was quite impassive, and Sophie could read nothing in it. Perhaps she was accustomed to such abuse.

'Am I to understand that some ingenious person actually took the items from Lady Wyverne's body as she slept? Such audacity,' murmured Lord Drake. He seemed to be deliberately trying to infuriate his father even further.

'Ingenious? I'll break every bone in his body when I catch him, and we'll see how audacious he is then! I'll have him whipped in the town square before he hangs! Look me in the eye and tell me it was not you!'

'It was not me.' Four chilly words.

'But you were here!' Wyverne seemed to have seized eagerly on the idea of his son's guilt, and was clearly reluctant to give it up.

'I was, but I give you my word that I did not take your jewels. I cannot prove it to you, so my word of honour will suffice – though it is ridiculous to speak to you of honour – or it will not. I cannot help what you choose to believe. I spent the night at the rectory, as I often do, and you must consider if you really think I rode there with a sack of stolen diamonds in my lap, or whether you are making a fool of yourself once more. I must congratulate you, for it seems that you have found a new way to do it, which I had not previously thought possible. Good day to you, sir.'

'You insolent cur! Do not turn your back on me! You could easily have hidden them somewhere in the park!' his father yelled after him.

But Drake was mounting the stairs, and made no answer.

## 23

Sophie considered hurrying away before Rafe should see her, but somehow could not bring herself to do so. She went a little further up the steps and halted, waiting for him to reach her. He was pale, she saw now, nowhere near as composed as he had appeared to be when confronting his father, and his mouth was set in a grim line. His expression lightened a little when he saw her, and he did not seem surprised that she should be waiting to accost him. 'We must talk,' she said in a low tone.

'Not here. Come into one of the empty bedchambers so we will not be overheard or observed. I am always glad to see you, but you take a terrible risk in addressing me where we might be watched.' He took her hand in his and led her swiftly to the top of the stairs and along the corridor, then chose a door apparently at random and drew her inside, closing it very quietly behind them and turning to look at her, still frowning slightly.

She found herself in a large chamber, the furniture shrouded in Holland covers that gave it a desolate appearance. They stood close together, well away from the tall windows, and spoke in low tones, though in truth there was little chance of an eavesdropper here.

'You were trying to enrage him on purpose,' she said. It seemed extraordinary to her. It didn't occur to her to apologise for listening – such niceties of behaviour were far behind them.

'It's easy enough for me to drive him distracted,' he answered with a shrug. 'And he me, for that matter. But on this occasion I thought it might help. My first impulse was to spend last night here, to remain close and make sure you were safe, but I then I realised that if I went away it might lead him to think that I must have taken the jewels. I could have done, after all. I imagine it would be easy enough to ascertain that I'm the only person who left the house last night. Left the estate, in fact.'

'Apart from the thief,' she said with the ghost of a smile, and she could see his response to it in his dark eyes.

'Apart from the thief, of course, through the open window.'

'I don't want you to feel you need to protect me.' Of late years, Sophie had gloried in her independence, had taken pride in the fact that she didn't need anybody. There was no reason at all why that should have changed.

'I wouldn't presume to do so. You're hardly in need of my protection. But I thought it might be useful to turn his mind away from the household.'

'He can't seriously suspect you – his own son?'

'I'm not sure he's entirely rational just now. And you must have seen that there is little filial feeling between us. But you were locked away with all the maids, were you not, when the crime was committed? So it's hard to see how you could be suspected. I congratulate you.'

'I *was* locked away,' she said serenely.

'You can pick locks?' he asked, coming closer still, the tension from the unpleasant encounter with his father visibly leaving his body, to be replaced by a different kind of tautness and focus.

'I have all sorts of uncommon skills,' she murmured. He was not the only one capable of deliberate provocation.

'I remember that.'

And then she was in his arms, unsure which of them had made the first move, but sure that it did not matter. His strong arms were about her, pulling her to him, and she ran her fingers up into his glossy dark hair and drew his head down for a kiss. 'I did not sleep for thinking of you!' he breathed against her lips, and then there was no need for talking.

There was a sort of hunger in the way that they claimed each other, but it didn't feel entirely like desire, or not at first. It felt more like deep mutual need. They'd shared a curious moment of connection the night before in the shadowed corridor, and been interrupted, and were both in a state of heightened emotion. Their kiss was deep and slow and satisfying, and for a long time it was enough. His hands were tight about her waist and hers remained buried deep in his hair; their bodies were pressed together down their whole length. It was comfort they sought as much as anything else, as it had been when they had held each other a few hours before.

But gradually and inevitably passion grew between them. Her hands slipped from his head, trailed down his broad chest and found their way under his coat; she was fumbling instinctively with the buttons of his waistcoat, pulling up his shirt, seeking his skin, and his lips had left hers and were tracing a path down her throat, where the high, modest neck of her gown frustrated his efforts to go further. He picked her up and carried her across the room to a console table that sat against one wall, and lifted her, pulling her skirts so that he could fix his hands on her bare bottom; she wrapped her legs around his waist and pressed herself eagerly against him. Her lips were at his ear; she sucked his earlobe into her hot mouth, then nipped at it and whispered, 'I thought you said that your father's activities drove all amorous thoughts entirely from your head?'

'I lied!' he groaned.

He was hard against her, his erection pressing into her belly through the fabric of her gown, and she dug her heels into his buttocks and sucked on his sensitive lobe, teasing at it with her teeth. He was kissing her face, her neck, her hair, murmuring broken endearments as though he hardly knew what he was saying. Her hands had found his skin under his shirt, and he held her, a willing captive, with his hands splayed wide and his caressing fingertips tantalisingly close – but not close enough – to the core of her.

And then he stilled. He did not release her, but he pulled back a little with one last lingering kiss. 'This is too dangerous,' he whispered against her mouth, his reluctance obvious. 'We both know it is.'

'You're right,' she said, slipping her hands slowly down his chest, then lower, where his warm skin met the buckskin of his breeches. It *was* dangerous, and just now she didn't care. But he captured her hands and brought them up to his lips, kissing them, one and then the other, and holding them to his face, cradled in his much larger ones.

He shook his head, frustration clear in every inch of him. 'I don't know how I have the strength to stop you when I want nothing more in the world than to let you continue. God knows I want your hands on me, and your lovely mouth. God knows I want to taste you again, and make you scream with pleasure, and then throw you down on that bed and take you, to plunge deep into you and lose myself. I want to see you naked, in the daylight, as I have not yet. I want to explore every inch of you, and make love to you for hours, for days, until you lose your senses, and I do too. But we can't. Not here, not now. We risk too much. You risk your life, Sophie, and you know it.'

She sighed, and caressed his face, easing herself off the table and letting her legs slide down his until her feet touched the floor once more. 'I know,' she said. 'I know you're right.' She pulled her hands from him, and he let her go, though they were still standing very close. She rested her head on his chest, just for a moment, and he raised one hand and cupped it. 'It feels so safe, when you hold me like this. As though nothing and no one could touch us. But it's an illusion, isn't it?'

'There's no safety in this house,' he agreed sombrely. 'You are in mortal danger every day you spend here. If he should discover what you have done, who you are…'

All at once the stark reality of their situation came flooding in on her. 'I've been very foolish,' she said, stepping away from him and shaking out her crumpled skirts, reaching up with hands that trembled slightly and attempting to smooth down her disordered hair. 'And it must stop now, you're quite correct. You know I am attracted to you – it would be ridiculous to deny it after what has already passed between us. But we are the last two people in the world who should have anything to do with each other.'

'Yes,' he said, his face a mask now, its strong planes hard, uncompromising, almost stern. 'I cannot and should not forget what Wyverne did to your father, and to your whole family. I know you will never forget it or forgive it, and I could not dream of asking you to do so.'

Her tone matched his in bleakness. 'I'm glad you realise that – it means I don't have to say it. I need to be ruthless now, and make sure I get away safely, with everything I came for.'

'I want that too,' he said more gently. 'If I cannot have you, and I know I cannot, because I fear that too much lies between us to keep us apart, I need to know that you are safe and well, some-where in the world.'

His tender words brought unexpected moisture to her eyes, but she refused to give in to them. 'I should go. My place is with your grandmother, carrying out my duties, in case anyone comes looking for me.'

'It will be a while before you can get away from this house,' he warned her. 'Anyone who tries to leave in the coming days will have their luggage searched, I'm sure.'

'I'm in no particular rush. I will be cautious. I have waited too long to ruin everything at this late date.'

He kissed her, a brief sad kiss, and strode towards the door. 'I'll go first,' he said. 'I'll make sure the passageway is deserted. I could find an excuse for being in this part of the house, where you could not. Wait a while before you follow me. And I'll be here, as much as I can. In case you need me.'

And then he was gone and she was alone.

## 24

The next week was terribly difficult for everyone living at Wyverne Hall. The Marquess's guests left the next day, but Sophie did not know if this had been the plan all along, and wasn't even sure if they were aware of what had happened. It was possible that they remained in complete ignorance of the great loss that Lord Wyverne had suffered, since they at least had not been interrogated along with the household staff. She was sure that their luggage, and that of their servants if they had brought any, had been very thoroughly searched before they were permitted to depart – but again, it might be that this had been done discreetly and that they were ignorant of it.

Their departure brought no easing of the tension. Sophie saw nothing of Lord Wyverne for several days, but his fury pervaded the whole enormous building from cellars to attics. If the servants whispered together, speculating on the identity of the criminal, they did not do so in Sophie's hearing, and if Marchand reported back to the Dowager with news from the servants' hall, she wasn't made privy to it. They didn't discuss the matter as they sat together each day – the old lady asked her no questions and she volunteered no information. Whatever the reason for it, she was glad not to burden Delphine with her guilty knowledge. They seemed to have come to a tacit agreement: silence was safer for them both. So they knew nothing, they discussed nothing. Along with everyone else, they waited.

Sophie did not visit her hoard. She tried not to think about it, even, lest she be tempted at last to check on it and thus court disaster. She knew it was most likely safe – Lord Wyverne had not found it, of that she was certain, or she should have heard of it. The whole household would have heard of it. Perhaps the story of the intrepid burglar had been believed – she hoped so. At any rate, there was no hint that any sort of search of the mansion was under way. As far as she could see, nothing was happening. But she was aware that she could not know what went on downstairs, or in the Wyvernes' private chambers.

Lord Drake was spending a great deal of time at the Hall, as he had promised, but still she saw little of him. When he was with his grandmother, she was not. They sometimes encountered each other briefly when he or she was arriving or leaving, but exchanged few words; she curtseyed very correctly, he made her a slight, indifferent bow. If either of them felt an almost irresistible compulsion to push the other up against a wall and ravage their face with hot, urgent kisses – and Sophie had no means of knowing if His Lordship experienced such a compulsion – at any rate they did not give in to it.

Sophie knew that she must be constantly alert, for if discovery or some other less obvious disaster hit, she needed to be ready for it. She'd spent a great deal of time discussing with Nate the best way to get the jewels out of the house once she had gained possession of them, and they had come up with several alternatives, presuming that simply walking boldly out of the door with them in her luggage would not be feasible. And she did not dare do that, not now at least. Lord Wyverne might be many things, but she did not take him for a fool, not where his own advantage was concerned. She had no sense of being watched, but that was probably because she never went anywhere but the Dowager's chamber, or her own.

One fine spring day she could bear it no longer and ventured outside, as if to take the air. It was a reasonable sort of thing to do, she thought, after being cooped up in the house for so long. As she strolled with elaborate casualness towards the elegant, pillared Palladian Bridge that spanned the river between the lakes, her quick eyes spotted men, strangers to her, stationed in the trees. They were well enough concealed, and perhaps an ordinary person might not have noticed them – but she was not an ordinary person. She saw one, and then another, and thought there must be more that she had not seen. She had nothing in her hands, not so much as a reticule, and met nobody on her promenade, returning to the house after half an hour or so entirely unmolested. But it served as a warning – she was sure that if she'd been carrying anything, especially something as large and conspicuous as her portmanteau, or had attempted to go further afield, she'd have been stopped, searched, and if they'd found anything, or perhaps even if they hadn't, she'd have been dragged back to face Lord Wyverne's wrath.

Her discovery also meant, of course, that one of her other possible solutions – dropping the bag very carefully out of a window at night to Nate's men, who'd be waiting by arrangement below – must be set aside too. She had a method that she and Nate had devised by which she might contact him and summon him, by writing a letter that appeared entirely innocent but contained an ingenious code, but it would do her no good now, for she could not doubt that any stranger who approached the house would be seen and apprehended. She could write, though, and warn him of what she had seen – the possibility that guards would be set about the mansion after the theft was one of the things that they had considered.

When she returned sedately to the Hall from her stroll and was next able to be alone in her room, she took up the quill and ink that she had brought with her for this very purpose and wrote to her dear cousin and regular correspondent Fanny. This person was entirely mythical, but nonetheless resided at a respectable address in Bloomsbury provided by Mr Smith. It would be plain to anyone who intercepted the letter – and she was reasonably sure someone would, given Lord Wyverne's growing desperation – that Fanny, Mrs Olivier, was an English lady married to Mlle Delavallois's cousin, and mother of a large and ever-expanding family. Sophie had had some fun with Nate over a bottle of fine smuggled French wine, listing all the possible eventualities that might arise and devising the secret code that applied to each. And so now, after giving her fictitious correspondent her reassurances that she was well and happy in her new position, and that Wyverne Hall was a perfectly lovely spot, she enquired with great anxiety about the baby, and hoped that the painful attack of croup from which he had been suffering had vanished now that the weather was better. She had not the least idea what croup might be, and Nate had confessed that he didn't either, but it seemed like an appropriately childish ailment, and in this context it meant that the Hall was being carefully watched and that it was impossible therefore to remove the jewels under current conditions. She wrote in English to make things easier for anyone who might be spying on her – she thought that using French might raise suspicion and draw attention to her, which was the last thing she desired. That done, she was powerless to do any more and could only continue with her waiting.

## 25

Coming into the house from the stables one morning, Rafe heard a commotion, hurrying feet, raised voices. The great building thrummed with tension, of a quite different order from the oppressive atmosphere that had pervaded it since the theft of the jewels had come to light. Something had happened.

A sudden shock of fear ran through him: had the jewels been discovered? Had Sophie been captured? What could he do to rescue her? He was experiencing the severest anxiety as Kemp, the butler, came bustling towards him down the corridor, with Marchand at his heels, both of them imperfectly concealing extreme agitation. 'My lord!' the man said in tones of profound relief. 'I am very glad to see you. Lord Wyverne has reason to believe... That is, he suspects Mademoiselle Delavallois of the theft. There is no time to explain why, but he is most exercised. He has set all the footmen and maids on to search the house for her; I am supposed to be supervising them, but I came to look for you instead, and thank heaven I have found you. You are surely the only one who can help the poor young lady escape.'

'She's not with my grandmother?'

'I am happy to say she is not, sir, or she would have been taken up long since. It was the first place they were told to look.'

Marchand broke in, 'The young lady has the habit of walking down by the lakes sometimes, milord, when she is at liberty, to take a little air. I am sure she must be there, but I dare not look for her. They will begin searching the grounds soon enough, if they do not find her in the house, but if His Lordship or anyone else should see me, and think I had come to warn her...'

'No, you are quite right; I will go. No one will dare challenge me; how should they? If you wait for me by the side door under the colonnade, I will bring her to you there.' He took a key out of his pocket and passed it to her. 'Take her up to my chamber – will you do that, Madame Marchand?' She nodded resolutely. 'Thank you! I'll go and find her directly.'

It took every scrap of self-control he possessed to stroll casually out of the house and down the steps towards the lakes, quite as if nothing in the world could possibly be amiss. He dare not hurry even when he was among the trees, out of sight of the house, in case any of his father's watchers should be about. He was glad not to see any of them, though he was on high alert, and gladder still when he came across Sophie a moment later, making her way back towards the Hall. Her face lit up at the sight of him, then fell when he came closer and she observed his expression. But she did not panic. 'What has happened?' she said steadily. 'I perceive that something has.'

She was so brave. He drew her into the shade of a great willow tree, where they could not be observed. 'I don't know precisely, only that something has occurred that places you under suspicion. The house is being searched – for you, not for the jewels – at my father's instigation. It is only the merest chance that you are not already taken. Marchand is waiting by the side door in the colonnade, to take you up to my chamber. It's the only place where you will be safe for a time, and she has the key so that you may lock yourself in. I don't believe anyone would think of looking for you there unless they had good reason to. My father has not the least suspicion of any connection between us, I am confident.'

'I suppose I have no option,' she said steadily. 'I cannot leave while the jewels are still in the house, and if I run away, I risk been seen and taken. And flight will make my position still worse – it will be taken as a sign of guilt.'

'I believe so. But if you hide yourself away in the house, at least for a short while, it gives us a chance to plan.'

'Very well. Like you, I can see no other alternative. Let us go.'

There was no time to say more, no time for any expressions of reassurance or any other show of emotion; they slipped stealthily through the trees, using their cover to reach a point close to the great curving front of the house, where Marchand would be waiting. 'Don't accompany me,' she told him with a little smile. 'I will be much more inconspicuous alone.'

'I'll try to find out what exactly has happened – I'll come to you as soon as I can. Good luck, Sophie!'

He watched her as she walked at an easy pace across the short stretch of lawn, a small, drab figure against the grass and golden stone, not hurrying or dawdling, as if she had not a care in the world. If she were seen, she would be captured and placed in the greatest peril, and she knew it, but her back was straight and she reached the shadow of the tall row of columns without incident, so that he was able to breathe again.

But of course he had no idea what might happen to her once she re-entered the house. Once in his room, she should be safe, but she first had to get there. Marchand would not betray him, but she might easily be prevented from coming, or they might be intercepted. A thousand things could go wrong. He needed a share of Sophie's cool courage, to get through the next few hours. He squared his shoulders and went after her.

## 26

Sophie's heart was pounding as she walked sedately across the grass. She was aware of being horribly exposed and vulnerable out here in the open; she'd have felt infinitely safer in a crowd in the worst back alley of London. But she reached the stone steps and climbed them, then struggled not to run along the curving colonnade towards the little hidden door. If Marchand was not waiting... But she was. The abigail did not speak, but took her hand and whisked her up a narrow staircase she did not remember seeing before, and into a maze of rooms that mirrored, Sophie thought, the part of the house in which she had hidden her treasure. At last they came to a chamber which appeared to be their destination. Marchand produced a key from somewhere about her person with brisk efficiency, opened the door and shoved her companion firmly inside, placing the key in her hand and saying, 'Lock it behind me! Lord Drake will come when he is able.' And then she hurried away.

In the sudden stillness, Sophie did as she had been commanded and then turned and looked about her. She found herself in a medium-sized chamber, and she had been right – it had two tall sash windows which opened onto the roof walk behind the parapet, where she had encountered Rafe and where he had first kissed her. Where he had gone on his knees to her, and she to him, in the moonlight. They'd come up here another way, by a different stair and across the leads from the centre of the house, that night after the disastrous dinner party. For whatever reason, he hadn't taken her to his room, as he so easily could have done, and nor had he suggested they go there and spend the night in his bed. Perhaps he hadn't wanted her there, in his private space. If that was so, she could have no cause to object: he owed her nothing. And she wasn't sure at this distance of time if she'd have agreed to stay with him, if he'd proposed it – but she was here now.

It was a comfortably shabby room, with mismatched furniture that had plainly been taken from other parts of the house and assembled without the least concern for style or period. There were a couple of low bookcases – anything larger would never have fitted round the curve of the stair – which were crammed and yet quite inadequate for the many volumes they supported, so that by necessity yet more books were piled on top and lay in heaps on the floor besides. The bed was low and had once been elegant, with tall, tapering pillars at each corner of the frame, and was neatly made up with a faded, patched coverlet. A cracked old leather chair sat beside the fireplace, and the mantel supported yet more books, as well as various oddly assorted items: a cricket ball, some chipped Dresden ornaments, a little model ship. The walls were lined with more of the old Chinese paper she'd seen elsewhere, and now she looked more closely she saw the fine detail: tiny, exquisitely rendered people in rich, flowing robes went about their mysterious business in a landscape of contorted trees and strangely shaped sugarloaf mountains. To complete the decoration, a few small pictures hung here and there – she saw when she moved closer to examine them that they were mostly landscapes, old views of the estate. Under one window sat a battered trunk, the kind boys took away to school; the other had been left clear of any obstruction so that it would be easy to climb out onto the roof. She felt no impulse to open the trunk or otherwise pry into Lord Drake's possessions; she knew how precious privacy could be, having so little of it herself.

It was a lovely room, she thought. Nothing in it was fine or new, nothing matched, but everything was somehow harmonious – much more so than in the grand, oppressive public rooms downstairs. She was quite calm, and felt safer here than she should, since she knew that Lord Wyverne was scouring the house for her. She was, looking at matters dispassionately, trapped here now. They had been excessively lucky to escape the attention of Lord Wyverne's watchers just now, and she could not look to be so fortunate again, so she certainly could not escape, and if the building was searched thoroughly she'd surely be found in the end, even if the jewels weren't. *She* couldn't hide herself in a dark, dusty storeroom for very long, if it should come to that. Even if with Drake's help she managed to evade capture for a while, even if his quarters were as sacrosanct as he believed them to be, she couldn't stay in this room indefinitely. She ought to be panicking, but she wasn't, and this was good, because panic prevented one from thinking clearly.

She didn't have enough information to allow her to plan – she had no idea *why* she had so suddenly fallen under suspicion, and how Lord Drake and Marchand had learned of it, so there was at this moment little she could do. Nothing, really. She might as well be comfortable. She was not hungry, and there was a jug of slightly stale water she could drink, and, behind a cracked old screen in one corner of the room, a chamber pot if she should

need it – currently empty, she was pleased to say. Very well; she'd
spent time in many less pleasant places over the last few years.

After browsing carefully among the books, which were in
both French and English, she chose one, an old favourite, and
settled into the big chair to read it. She'd not had a great deal of
leisure for reading for her own pleasure in recent years, nor
money to spare for such frivolous purchases, and so she was soon,
despite her plight, deeply absorbed in the familiar adventures of
Evelina, and started when she heard tapping at the door.

'It's Drake,' she heard through the panel. 'Let me in – you have
my only key.'

She'd taken it from the lock, habits of caution being deeply
ingrained in her, and hastened to open the door now and admit
him. He was immaculate as ever, but it was no surprise that he
looked sombre as he secured the door behind him and turned to
face her.

'Have you discovered what has happened?' she said steadily. 'I
thought I'd been so careful – why am I suspected? Or am I in fact
not particularly under suspicion, and perhaps there has been
some misunderstanding?'

'Oh, no,' he answered grimly. 'It's true that Wyverne has no
especial reason to think you guilty of the theft, but he has most
unluckily become aware that you are not precisely who you
pretend to be, and therefore that your recommendations were
probably forged. This leads him not unnaturally to think that you
may also be guilty of the theft – I understand that he leapt at the
idea with great enthusiasm and no doubt would be glad if it were
so. Apart from anything else, it would enable him to blame Lady
Wyverne, who employed you, and my grandmother, who has
spent so much time with you. That sort of thing is always a
consideration with him: he so enjoys putting others in the wrong.'

'I understand that, but still I do not see how he has come to such a conclusion.'

'He has not the least idea of your true identity – things are not quite so bad as that – but he is reasonably confident you are not the sedate lady's companion that your references assert. This conclusion came to him, so the butler Kemp tells me, when he was sitting in his study, idly contemplating the pictures on the walls. You have met him, so I am sure you can imagine the sort of images he chooses to decorate his chamber. As he sat there, brooding over his loss, he realised to his enormous surprise that one of his more recent purchases, a most striking, quite lately painted representation of Danae in her shower of gold...'

'Was me,' she finished for him.

## 27

Sophie could not help herself; in reaction to the most unexpected news, she began to laugh, and after a moment Lord Drake joined her. After a while he sobered a little and said, 'You have been an artist's model, I assume. I do not know why I should be surprised.'

He didn't seem to be angry – or not at her, at any rate. Anger with Lord Wyverne was always simmering just beneath the surface. She would have thought less of Rafe if she'd felt he was judging her, since, thanks to his father, she had not had the luxury of living a respectable life. But she didn't see any judgement in his face, just interest. And if there were things she'd done that she regretted, and there were, her time with Bart was not one of them. 'I did pose for an artist several times a few years ago,' she said. 'He was my lover.'

'No longer?'

'No.'

A little silence grew and stretched between them. He said abruptly, 'I didn't have Marchand bring you here in order that I could take advantage of your situation. I hope you know that. It was simply the only solution that presented itself as soon as

Kemp came to me. I have a great deal of respect for your ingenuity, but I feared that once you had fallen into Wyverne's grasp there would be no getting you out.'

'I would have brazened it out – said yes, that was me, but I am guilty only of trying to earn a living. But you know him far better than I. You think he would have seized on me as the culprit regardless of anything I said?'

'He is not a man who cares for being made to look foolish or ignorant, and his love for his collection amounts almost to a mania. Once he had decided that you were not a respectable female, I fear he would have no compunction whatsoever in his dealings with you.'

'I can see that. I fear I have now confirmed his suspicions by running away, though.'

'Perhaps so, but anything is better than being in his power, as you would have been. There must be a way out of this coil, which we can devise together. And now you are safe here for a little time – once the initial search does not find you, he'll think you've run out of the house, and will waste time searching for you and berating his men for incompetence. I have not had speech with him – it seemed unwise – but there is currently a great deal of shouting and blustering going on downstairs. Your composure astonishes me – you're not frightened?'

She sank back into the chair, looking up at him. It suddenly seemed important to try to make him understand. 'Fear does no good, I have learned. It merely paralyses. I've been powerless and frightened, and I hated it. I have resolved that I will always struggle against what seems like fate. I've come so far – I'm a long way from being defeated, and I will not cower before him, of all people. He doesn't know who I am, you say, and he can have no idea of where I have concealed the jewels. That is a great deal, I think.'

'I do admire you,' he said quietly, sitting on the bed and leaning forward to regard her intently, hands on his knees. 'I have never met anyone so indomitable.'

'I find that hard to believe, since for my part I have made your grandmother's acquaintance.'

He smiled. 'That's true. But even she finds it impossible to deal with Wyverne on occasion.' And then he made a palpable effort to change the subject, and said, 'I'm sorry for the disorder of my chamber. I wasn't expecting a visitor, or I would have tidied it.'

'Books do not count as disorder, in my opinion. It is excessively cosy, I think. Was it your room as a child?'

'When I was very small I slept in the nursery, of course, but as soon as I was able to I spent hours exploring, and claimed this place for my own, furnishing it slowly with things I found neglected about the house. I particularly loved the wallpaper and made up all sorts of stories about the people in it to entertain myself. I was... a rather solitary child, and my half-siblings are much younger, so we scarcely played together. And once my step-mother died and the children were taken away by their uncle, I found I needed the refuge even more. It's not clear to me if Wyverne knows about this place. I make sure never to leave anything particularly precious here, so that if he should find it and destroy it I should be sorry, but there would be no great harm done. I've removed the miniatures of my mother, my grand-mother and the children, for example, to keep them safe.'

'Why would he do such a thing?'

He shrugged and said, 'I don't claim fully to understand what drives him. Perhaps I do him an injustice and he is entirely indifferent to me; I cannot say. But I can imagine Rosanna finding my refuge and deciding to wreck it out of malice. I don't think for a second that he would stop her – he'd merely laugh.'

'She hates you that much?'

'She does. She cannot endure that I rejected her. And that is why, I suppose, she spread the vicious rumour that she was my mistress, which all the world now believes.'

'Lord Wyverne at least must know that it is untrue.'

'He has good reason to know that much. Shall I tell you what happened? I have shared this story with very few people.'

'Only if you want to.'

He leaned back against the pillows and said with an unconscious sigh, 'I'd like to. You have seen so much of how things are here – you at least will not be shocked or disbelieve me.' Thinking of the night of Lord Wyverne's Roman orgy, she could only nod her agreement and understanding. He continued in a level tone, 'I was fifteen or sixteen when he married her. She'd been his mistress for a while, I suppose, but he hadn't brought her here, or if he had done so I had been at school and had not been aware of it. She was – even now she still is – very beautiful, and she can be amusing; have you seen any sign of that?'

Sophie thought of Rosanna when she'd first met her, and how she had described the Dowager's previous companions. 'Yes, I have,' she said. 'Just briefly, but yes. She has a clever turn of phrase; she made me smile.'

'She was wittier then, before the years of marriage had worn her down. I was a little shocked that my... that Wyverne had married her so quickly after my stepmother's death, but after all, that wasn't her fault but his. She set out to charm me, and I was happy enough to be charmed, until one day... She'd summoned me to her sitting room and asked me to fetch her some trinket or other – as I passed it innocently to her, she put her hands on me and pulled my face down for a kiss. Not at all the sort of kiss a stepmother should give a boy of sixteen, I need hardly add. I froze for a moment in shock and then pushed her away from me, and as I stood some instinct made me look into the mirror. In it I saw

Lord Wyverne watching me from the half-open door to the next chamber. No emotion in his face, just observing us very intently. He saw that I had seen him, I make no doubt. And then I fled, as far from them both as I could contrive. I've never been alone with her since, and avoid him as much as I am able.'

She digested this slowly. 'You believe she knew he was there.'

'More than that, I believe he set her to seduce me. I'm sure the whole thing was planned out between them. What I don't know, and I'm not sure I ever will know, is whether she is as wicked as he, and glories in it, or simply accedes to his demands – all his demands, you've seen just how far they extend – as part of the devil's bargain she entered into when she became his wife. It is no small thing, for a woman who came from poverty, to be a marchioness, I suppose. And I hardly need tell you how cruel he can be when he is crossed. She may be numbered among his victims too, rather than as an accomplice; even after so many years, I can't say.'

'It would almost be easier to think her wicked. Otherwise she must be terribly unhappy, even perhaps terrified of him. Consider the other night, too, and the horror of what she did so publicly, if she did not do it entirely of her own free will.'

'It does not bear thinking of. But whatever the truth of the matter, I do not believe she would welcome any intervention from me. My friend Simon – he is the rector here, I believe I may have mentioned him to you before – tells me that I have a constant desire to rescue people, to make amends somehow for Wyverne's behaviour. But rescuing Rosanna, even if I could be sure she needs it, is a task far beyond my power.'

'You've been trying to rescue me,' she said with a smile. 'So perhaps your friend is right.'

He sighed. 'I know you want nothing more than to leave this place, and I cannot find it in my heart to blame you. All you said the other day was true, of course it was. We should not be together. It is madness to think otherwise. And yet...'

And yet...

She didn't make any reply, but stood, crossing to the bed, as he moved aside to make room for her to lie by him. He reached out and pulled her close, and said, his big hands warm on her back as he held her, 'Normally when I contemplate Wyverne a great black cloud sinks over me and depresses all my thoughts and feelings. But somehow with you it's different. The effect you have on me is far too powerful to be suppressed. I didn't know such a thing was possible. Even though it would be the height of folly on my part to think it could last, I'm glad you're here with me, no matter how it's come about.'

'So am I,' she said, and kissed him.

## 28

It was a sweet kiss, as much a reaction to the shock they had both suffered as anything else, and as she kissed him Sophie relaxed into the knowledge of his decency, his openness; how much he had shared with her, and how little she had told him in return. He knew what she had been once, and what she was now, but he did not know who she was, not really, and she was possessed of a great desire to tell him. She was teasing him with little kisses, he was letting her set the pace, and she moved away to put her head on his shoulder, saying against the comforting warmth of him, 'You didn't seem shocked when I told you I had had a lover.'

'Well, I assumed you must have.' He was choosing his words carefully, she thought. It was a delicate topic, after all, her past, with many traps, both obvious and hidden, that they could easily fall into. 'I didn't want to assume anything else. If it was a happy experience – and I thought it must be, given your confidence when you were with me out there on the roof – then I can only be glad for you. I know nothing of your life, but I would be honoured to know, Sophie, if you care to tell me.'

'I would like to. I don't want to dwell too long on the bad

things that happened to me, though I cannot help but mention them if I am to make you understand. I was lucky, really – I could very easily be dead. I was destitute, alone, and faced with only one way of making a living. My landlord had already made it clear to me precisely how my arrears of rent could be paid. I was frightened, grieving, but most of all I was angry, like a cornered animal. I knew that sooner or later I would have only one choice, which is no choice at all, or some man would overpower me without even the illusion of choosing. It seemed inevitable, but I resolved at least to make that man pay for it. It was probably foolish and dangerous, but I wouldn't submit willingly and accept the value they all placed on me.

'And then a stranger came to me and said that he had heard of my plight – people tell him things, to win his favour, I found out later – and that we might help each other. I thought he wanted what they all seemed to want, but I was wrong, he didn't. He still wanted to use me, but in a different way – to make me into a thief, a weapon of sorts – and that seemed better to me. It *was* better.'

She saw his expression and said, 'He's not my lover, he never has been. His name is Nate Smith, and though I'm sure you've never heard of him he is a very dangerous man, but we're friends, or something of that kind, as far as that is possible in his world. I know after all these years together and the way he treats me, people think I'm his mistress. That's useful in a way, because it makes them frightened of me, because they're so frightened of him, and I have sometimes thought that he quite likes them to believe it too. For his own complicated reasons, he has protected me. No one who knows him would ever dare lay a finger on me to hurt me. We've been so close for so long, people fear he might kill them for harming me, though I don't know if that's true or not. He has shared some of his secrets, but not all of them. He hates your father, I am certain of that, though I have no idea why.'

'After all, lots of people do,' he said drily. 'It would be much harder in all honesty to find people who are even slightly acquainted with him and don't loathe him. But go on.'

'I felt safer, you see, under Nate's protection, and I was learning all sorts of things, good and bad, that I'd never have dreamed of in my previous life. Doing things Clemence de Montfaucon would never have done in a thousand years. After a while I realised how much I had changed, and I thought that I should take a lover.'

He smiled, though she could not tell exactly what he was thinking of what he had heard. 'And why should you not?'

'Perhaps you're teasing me, but really it was a sensible decision. I wanted to give my body to someone I chose, rather than be taken against my will as could so easily have happened, and also, I suppose, I needed to remind myself that I was no longer Clemence de Montfaucon, and never would be again. My virginity began to seem – a useless sort of a thing. A mockery, almost. I thought, if by some miracle my old life was restored, nobody would ever believe that I was still an innocent, given the way I had been living. So I might as well not be, in practice as well as in theory. I wanted some pleasure for myself – I understood from all that I had seen around me that it could be pleasure – and some company, some comfort, I must admit that too. And I chose Bart.'

'The artist.'

'Yes. He was very poor – he's richer now, I hear – living in cheap lodgings and drinking in Nate's tavern. This was some years ago. Bart told me he wanted to paint me, and I thought, That's not all he wants. I'd been saying no to everyone for a long time, and then I decided to say yes. I liked his looks, and let him know I did.'

'You seduced him.'

'It wasn't very difficult.'

'I don't suppose it was. But you aren't together any longer.'

'We were happy for a while, for a year or more, but in the end he wanted to marry me. Or thought he did. He was from a good family, just playing at being a romantic starving artist, and he was getting tired of the cheap lodgings and the cheap wine and living like a pauper. He wanted to be respectable. He was very talented, and people were starting to buy his pictures, to pay more for them. If he knows your father has one, he'll be delighted. He's very ambitious.

'He had some idea, because I'd carelessly let something slip, that I am – I was – of noble birth, and he thought we could be respectable together. He liked the idea that I was a French aristocrat's daughter, and so he was prepared to be very generous and forget I'd been his mistress, and that I'd chosen him as my first lover. But I thought actually he never would quite forget it. And I didn't want to be forgiven. Why should there be one rule for him and another for me? He wasn't a cruel person, and I don't regret what I did. We enjoyed each other. But I'd lost sight of my purpose for a while, and as we started to argue and grow apart I remembered it again.'

'And here you are.' He might have said, in danger of losing sight of your purpose again.

'And here I am.' They were still lying very close, his arms were still about her, and she was glad she'd told him. There was no future in this, she knew that as well as he did, no more than there had been with Bart, but it was so tempting, here in Rafe's embrace, to relax into the novelty of having someone she could really talk to, even setting aside the other temptations that he offered. She'd never shared half as much with her artist – her body, certainly, but not the details of her past or her deepest thoughts.

'Just one lover?'

'One and a half, counting you.'

'I'd like to be more than a half. You must know that.' He wasn't caressing her, except with his voice. He scarcely needed to.

'I would too, but... I've always been careful – you know women have to be. I can't stop now. I dare not.'

'So have I. I've had an example of appalling irresponsibility set in front of me my whole life, Sophie. Wilfully destructive behaviour, a total lack of concern for others' safety and one's own. And my grandfather was no saint either; it appears to be a family tradition. I was always going to choose one extreme or the other – to become exactly the same and spread chaos all around me, or to be very different. You know that I have made love to just one woman in my life. Perhaps I needed to prove to myself that a Wyverne could be faithful – well, I was. We were together for many years and I would have married her if she hadn't already been tied to another. But we made sure we did not bring a child into the world that I could never give my name to.'

If one was honest, one couldn't complain when receiving honesty in return. 'And is she still...?'

'We parted a year or so ago. Her husband came back into her life unexpectedly after many years of separation, and she felt she needed to accede to his wish to live together again. He spun her some story that she chose to believe. I don't think she'd ever fully recovered from his desertion of her – I was always second choice. And she did desperately want a child. I had begun to think, even before her husband reappeared, that she gave herself to me because when he left her she didn't really care what happened to her. Once such a thought has occurred to you, it makes it rather difficult to continue together with any self-respect – or it did for me. Perhaps that was really why she left me, in the end.'

Sophie had a strong desire to ask him if he'd loved her,

whoever she was, and if his heart was broken still, but was not sure if she truly wanted to know the answer. And what good did it do to talk of love? They shouldn't. It was a foolish indulgence she could not afford. Love was for girls like Clemence de Montfaucon, girls who deserved the best of everything, not for Sophie Delavallois. She'd never spoken of love with Bart, and now she was glad she hadn't. And she wouldn't now. She would not put Rafe under the awkward obligation of pointing out to her that he was a viscount and she was a thief.

'We are both a little bruised, are we not?' she said. She felt as though this room, though it was only a temporary and precarious refuge, was a precious haven, a tiny bubble where the world didn't matter and couldn't intrude. But it wasn't true. She wouldn't let the illusory sense of safety seduce her. 'I'm very tempted to throw caution to the winds. But I won't. I don't want to risk bringing a child into the world either.'

'Never, or just because of our particular circumstances?'

What a question to ask her. She looked up at him, desperate to make him understand the nature of her life, so very alien to all he knew. 'Rafe, I'm a thief. You know I am. More than that, I've stabbed people and told myself they deserved it. I'd do it again if I had to. I'm not an assassin – it's not quite as bad as that – but there have been occasions when I've been cornered by men much bigger and stronger than me, and the only way out has been by means of the blade you know I carry. And I've used it.'

'Were any of these people officers of the law?' The question showed the true size of the gulf between them, she thought.

'No, but if they had been, I can't swear to you I'd have done anything different, if the choice was escape or be taken and hanged. And Rafe, I live – in so far as I live anywhere – in a room above a sordid tavern. How could I even contemplate making a child? Should I get Fancy Fred, Nate's tapster, to mind the baby for me while I go out picking pockets? Or maybe one of the whores – One-Eyed Sally, or Daisy the Dasher? You spoke of appalling irresponsibility earlier – well, I won't live like that either, or inflict it on a helpless child. I won't. There are too many suffering innocents in the world already.'

He didn't try to argue with her. 'Eight years ago,' he said a little sadly, 'Lord Drake might have wooed Mademoiselle de Montfaucon. One dance could have led to more. It would have been an eminently suitable match in anyone's estimation.'

'You know it's far too late for that.'

'It may be. But we can still take comfort from each other. I have been taking comfort, lying here, and I think you have too. I'd never do anything you didn't want, Sophie. If you say I mustn't touch you, I won't, however much I desire you. Need you.'

'What do you want?' She felt weak for asking, but she couldn't help herself. His honesty pierced her to her core.

'I want everything. I want things I can't have. But just now I'd settle for tasting you again.'

She hesitated for a moment, as if she might refuse him, but she was fooling herself, she knew. 'Yes,' she whispered.

'You're sure?'

'I'm not sure of anything. But I do want that too. I'm not strong enough to resist completely.' She'd known when she lay down in his arms that sooner or later passion would flare between them once again.

'May I undress you?'

She could not help but laugh. 'Such a typical man – you say you'll settle for one thing, but then immediately ask for more.'

'It's only a fraction of what I want, but I haven't seen you naked, and I need to. I warn you, Sophie, I want to make this last. I aim to undress you very, very slowly, and then take hours to drive you crazy. I was too eager last time.'

He was irresistible. Wordlessly she offered him the prim cuff of her gown where it closed at the wrist. First he kissed her palm, very gently and softly, and even that innocent caress made her shiver and close her eyes against the sweetness of it. Then he undid one tiny grey button, pressing his lips to the blue vein that was revealed. It was the lightest touch, the merest brush of contact, but her skin was thin and sensitive there, where the pulse beat, and she whimpered. Another button, another tiny kiss. By the time he had undone every fastening on one sleeve and kissed his way with exquisite tenderness up to her elbow, her breath was coming fast and her breasts were heavy and aching for his touch. Heat was uncoiling deep within her, and she moved restlessly on the bed. But he would not be hurried.

He turned his attention to the other cuff, the other sleeve, and worked his way just as slowly, just as carefully up to her elbow. She heard herself moan softly – what was next?

'Turn over,' he said, his voice very deep and low, and she hurried to comply. He started at the nape of her neck, taking his sweet time with the tiny buttons, kissing each inch of her skin as it was bared to him and murmuring soft endearments, and by the time he had reached the edge of her chemise she had half a mind to beg him to rip it off her. In fact, she wasn't sure she had so much as half a mind any more. She was a quivering mass of need. She rolled over and lifted herself eagerly so that he could pull her gown away and discard it, and then he turned his attention to her petticoats and her stays. By the time they'd been peeled from her with tantalising deliberation and she was left in nothing but her chemise and stockings, she was writhing shamelessly and arching her back to present herself to him. The abrasion of the fine fabric upon her sensitised nipples was close to unbearable. He pulled the flimsy garment over her head and she thought, Now! But he occupied himself in unfastening her hair, unravelling each plait and pulling out each pin with a maddening slowness, then combing his fingers through it where it lay across his pillow.

When he shifted down the bed she thought again, Now! But he was engaged in very slowly untying her garters and rolling down each stocking, kissing his way down each leg in turn, heading in entirely the wrong direction as far as she was concerned. He explored her with his lips, his tongue, but hardly at all with his fingers, and how desperately she wanted his hands on her, and firm touches that satisfied instead of tormenting.

And then at last she was naked and exposed to him, and he, fully clothed and booted, immaculate, sat back on his heels and looked at her with smouldering intensity. His dark eyes ran over her body as his lips had, and with much the same effect. His gaze was a caress, and she felt gloriously wanton under it. Her nipples were hard pebbles, and every hair on her body stood on end in delicious, near-painful anticipation; she was shivering with desire. 'Do you want me to beg?' she almost moaned.

He considered the matter seriously, his eyes dark with desire. 'No,' he said at last. 'I want you to be far beyond begging. Beyond speech of any kind. I want you to forget your own name. I want the room to spin around you and the heavens reel.'

'Fine words!' she managed. And then he was working his way up her body again, and she could say no more. His big hands were on her now, holding her just as she needed to be held – how did he know? – and when he reached the junction of her thighs and commanded her to spread herself for him she was trembling, already dizzy, thrusting her hips up at him in mute appeal. When at last the tip of his tongue claimed her swollen nub, she cried out and surrendered to the waves of pleasure that overwhelmed her with shocking suddenness.

He was devouring her suddenly with hungry urgency, all restraint abandoned, and she did forget her name, she forgot everything except the feel of his tongue and his fingers on her, in her. When he moved to worship her breasts with the same fierce focus, she spasmed again, but he was merciless in drawing the last quiver of arousal from her, and when she came back to herself it was dark outside. Hours had passed, or days.

'Good God,' she said weakly. Her own voice sounded foreign to her. He'd destroyed her – if he lays so much as a finger on me again, she thought, anywhere, or blows on my skin like he just did, I'll come again, and then I'll die of it. It's too much. But I don't care. Her body was so relaxed with the aftermath of glorious release that she felt she was melting into the bed. She hadn't known a man could be so ruthless in his determination and so selfless in his disregard of his own physical satisfaction.

'I'd like to please you,' she whispered. 'I really would. God knows you've earned it. And I want to. But I don't think I can move. If I try to sit up, I'll probably faint.'

'Good,' he said, and though the room was shadowy she could hear that he was smiling. He'd done all he promised and more, and he was touchingly pleased with himself. He pulled up the quilt, which had been pushed aside long since, and covered her tenderly with it, tucking it around her. 'Why don't you sleep a little? I'll go and get you some food – you must be ravenous. I'll take the key with me so that you can be sure you will be undisturbed.'

She thought of saying, Your self-control is barely human. But she was fast asleep before he had closed and locked the door behind him.

## 29

When Sophie awoke, Rafe was sitting beside her. He had drawn the curtains and lit a few candles, and the room was even cosier and more intimate in the soft light. He'd brought her a tray with lots of tempting little morsels of food, napkins, and a bottle of rich red wine with just one glass. They would have to share, he told her. She sat up, suddenly as ferociously hungry as he had predicted, and they set about the meal. She was still naked and did not think to cover herself, but found that she was eating in a deliberately provocative manner, sucking her fingers, shaking back the dark cloak of her hair to bare herself to him again. He was sitting beside her, propped against the pillows as she was, and after they had eaten their fill and were merely toying with the food he took the glass from her hand. He sipped, holding her with his eyes, and then dipped his finger in the dark liquid and very deliberately dribbled a trail across the upper slope of her breast, then lowered his head and licked it slowly from her, careful not to miss the smallest drop. Her nipples peaked, pleas-antly sore still from his attentions but eager to be tongued and tweaked and nibbled again. She shuddered with returning desire, and with the sudden knowledge – half enticing, half alarming – that he'd be quite prepared to do it all once more.

'No,' she said. 'It's my turn now. I'm going to do to you just exactly what you did to me – the only difference is there's more of you, and so it will take longer.'

'Do what you will with me,' he said very low. 'Fast or slow, I don't mind.' He swung round and sat up, setting his feet on the floor, and she slid from the bed and knelt between his legs so that she could take off his top boots. 'Stay there a second,' he said. 'Let me look at you. You're so beautiful.'

'I can't linger, my lord. I have a great deal to do. Does your valet generally perform this task for you?' she asked, grasping the shining leather and tugging. He was a gentleman of fashion, not a dandy but a Corinthian, and he must surely have a valet to take care of his clothes.

'I suppose he does, but I can assure you that it's really not the same.'

'I should hope not,' she said, setting one boot aside and commencing on the other; they were tight, and not easy to remove, but at last she had the second one free, and moved to unfasten the buttons at the knees of his breeches. She slipped her fingers under the hem and caressed the skin still hidden there, and then she pulled down his stockings, as slowly as she could manage. It seemed she was more impatient than he by nature. His calves were firm and muscular, and she stroked them apprecia-tively, then bent to kiss his feet, her hair falling in dark curtains about her face.

'Sophie...' he groaned.

'Shush! I'm wondering what to do next. Your coat, I think.' She stood between his thighs – he was still sitting – and began to peel back his tight blue superfine coat from his broad shoulders. He helped her, shrugging out of it, and his plain waistcoat came off much more easily, after she had slowly undone each of its buttons. He had far fewer buttons than she did – it didn't seem fair. But she was tantalising him quite satisfactorily, she thought: he'd plainly been entranced by the sight of her kneeling at his feet, breasts bouncing with the effort of dragging off his boots, and the removal of his coat and waistcoat had presented him with the same prospect, far closer. It was an effort for him not to seize her, she knew instinctively.

She could just pull his shirt over his head in one swift movement and have done with it – but no. Too fast, too easy. She moved to straddle him, her bare thighs and bottom resting on the soft buckskin leather of his breeches, and began inching up the fine lawn of his shirt, untucking it from his waistband and pulling it higher with painstaking slowness until just a glimpse of his sculpted abdomen was revealed. Really, who was tormenting whom here?

Gathering the fullness of the fabric in both hands, she raised it higher, and he lifted his arms obediently so that she could pull it right over his head and discard it. But she didn't. When it was high enough to cover his face and trap his arms, she stopped. She held him there, her prisoner, and pressed her body close against his, glorying in his warmth, the intoxicating masculine scent of him, and the fact that the tables had turned and he was in her power now.

She slid her core against the hot leather that covered his groin, his hardness straining against her, and rubbed her breasts deliberately to and fro over the whorls of dark hair on his muscled chest. 'Sophie,' he said, his voice hoarse and muffled in the folds of material, 'you are pleasuring yourself against me, and I cannot see it! Do you have any idea how unfair that is?'

'Just a little pleasuring, and just a little unfair,' she said breathlessly, her skin sensitised by his rough hair, the hard muscles and the smooth leather. 'But now it is time to move on.' She pushed him firmly back to lie flat upon the bed, but she did not remove his shirt to release him. He could have pulled it over his head and freed himself quite easily – but that would be against the unspoken rules of the game they were playing, and so he did not.

Her hand was on the buttons that closed the fall of his breeches. She gripped one strong thigh between hers as she undid him, and shamelessly she ground herself against him while her fingers worked. They were both panting now, and she thought she might climax again long before she had done with him. She was both sorry and not sorry when it was time to dismount from him and pull down his breeches; when they were cast aside and he had sprung free in all his magnificent erectness, she could only be glad. She wanted to eat him – but again, that would be too easy.

She darted out her tongue and licked the glistening slit at the head of his member, just a fleeting taste, and he groaned, his body bucking under her, but she pulled away. She straddled his thighs and paused to consider. He was hard against her curls, so close to where he needed to be, just a few inches away, but not quite there. She could see and feel him twitching against her. Then she smiled to herself – of course her face was not visible to him – and twisted her locks into a great hank, which she then used to flick and tickle all across his chest, while her thighs gripped him and he thrust involuntarily up against her. Between tantalising flicks of her hair she found one hard, pebbled nipple and sucked on it. When she ventured to nip him a little with her teeth, he jolted so hard that he lifted his body and hers right off the bed.

'Was that pleasure or pain?' she whispered, and as her breath feathered his skin he shuddered.

'I don't know. Does it matter? Do it again!'

She did, and now that she was beginning to understand what he liked she was more confident. She kissed and nipped her way down his body, leaving him gasping, following the line of dark hair that pointed the way – although she was not likely to get lost, she thought, with such a substantial signpost beckoning to her. There was something intoxicating about his responsiveness and the power she had over him. She could do *anything*. She'd never been shy, not since she discovered how to give and receive pleasure, and now she was made bolder by the fact that Rafe could not see her.

God, he was beautiful, with his hard planes of muscle scattered with dark hair. Not like a statue, or no statue of a Greek or Roman god that she had ever seen – no smooth marble perfection here. She lay down between his muscular thighs and amused herself by kissing them, and biting them where she found that he was most sensitive. Each little bite set him writhing with electric intensity upon the sheets. She made teasing forays up to stroke and kiss his silky hardness, and he was so aroused and so far beyond ready for her that after a while she could no longer resist tasting him more fully. She'd wanted to tantalise him longer, but – she couldn't. Her lips were on him, her mouth and her hand. Her world shrank to the pure sensation of tasting him, touching him, pleasing him and herself. He lost himself in her. When at last his body was no longer racked with his intense and prolonged spending, she laid her head on his thigh and closed her own eyes, drinking in the scent of him, sweat and seed and spicy maleness, and the lingering taste. He was still blindfolded, his arms still tangled in his shirt. He'd cried out as he came, but he hadn't spoken and he hadn't been able to embrace her, captive as he was.

Now he said, 'Sophie...' There was a great deal of feeling in the single word.

'Rafe. Yes, I'm still here.'

'I thought you might be.' There was a lazy, satiated smile in his voice. 'May I disentangle myself now? I want to hold you.'

'Of course.'

He was free in an instant, and she moved up his body to lie in his arms, her head on his shoulder. He was, to her delight, no longer immaculate, but as flushed and dishevelled as she must be. 'I think you must know how much I enjoyed that,' he murmured. 'And I believe you did too, but I wonder how much.'

'Very much,' she said. 'But not very, very, very much.'

He was so quick, and understood her instantly. 'Well, that must be rectified.'

She lay back on the tangled sheets, inviting him, and he ran his hand down her body, slipping his fingers into her curls to find them damp, her secret places ready for his touch. 'Mmm...' she said. 'Yes, just there. Oh, you are a man of many talents, Rafe.' She was very aroused, she had been close to climax when he'd spent himself, and his clever fingers took her closer still with their first touch.

'So gloriously wet,' he whispered, sliding his fingers into her. She bit her lip and took one engorged nipple between her fingers, playing with it and arching her back as he pleasured her once more, pushing herself up against his hand, convulsing as he worked her, surrendering to the delicious waves of oblivion.

Afterwards she lay in his arms, dazed, and he pulled up the covers over them both. 'Is it late?' she said languidly. 'I've lost all sense of time.'

'I think it must be.' The house was very quiet; it felt as though they were the only two people awake in the world.

'Will you stay here tonight? I think you don't normally sleep here.'

'I never do, but I will tonight. I took a foolish vow long ago never to spend another night under Wyverne's roof. But this is the time to break it, I think.'

She stirred restlessly. 'I don't want you to do violence to your feelings on my account.'

'My feelings are different now. I'm not leaving you. Even if I could tear myself away from the warmth of your embrace, which I don't think I could, I wouldn't rest easy knowing you were here alone.'

'I must admit I don't want you to go. But I do need to leave your arms for a moment. It would be most romantic to fall asleep like this, but I am not entirely comfortable.'

He understood her instantly, and told her that there was a necessary behind the screen, which she had known already.

When it was his turn to use it, she returned to the bed. She was damp with perspiration, and so was he, and the room smelled inescapably of sex. There could be no mistaking... And with that thought, the clever, calculating part of her brain, the part that had seized on the chance to stay alive and thrive when it had been offered her by Nate, clicked into operation and gave her the solution.

He came back to her and joined her in the warm bed, and as she relaxed into his arms once more she said, 'Rafe, I think I know how we can ensure that I escape suspicion, and no longer need to hide away here.' She felt his body stiffen, and added hastily, 'Don't misunderstand me. There's a large part of me that would like to stay here forever. It's so tempting to feel safe in your embrace, and God knows I don't *want* to leave you. But I must. You know as well as I do that my situation is desperate, and to think that I can stay concealed here for long enough to escape discovery is simply unrealistic. You can't stay here all the time or guarantee my safety when you must be absent. Someone will realise eventually that I'm here, even if it takes days or weeks. And then I'll be in a desperate case.'

'I know,' he said a little bleakly. 'Everything you say is entirely correct. I collect that you have a plan?'

'I do. And I do believe it could work. But I don't think you're going to like it.'

## 30

Rafe wasn't happy about Sophie's scheme. It was ingenious – there was no denying that – but it was also extremely risky. She was so brave, and she was prepared to accept that risk, so he must be too. If it worked, her plan would release her from concealment and give her a great deal more latitude to move about the house and the estate than she'd had even before she'd fallen under suspicion. She wouldn't be a servant any more, and so, presumably, she couldn't be detained here by Lord Wyverne. He might, he surely would, want to search her luggage before she was permitted to leave – that was an obstacle they still needed to overcome – but it was still a step towards setting her free. He'd been horrified when she'd first suggested it, worried most of all about her safety, but she'd been so emphatic in her disregard of herself that he'd been obliged at last to accept that it might be the only solution.

It wasn't as if he wanted to keep her here in his room. Well, he did, but it was selfish and unfair to dwell on the idea. Of course he wasn't a man to keep a woman prisoner. He might wish she had a stronger desire to stay, but he dismissed that unworthy feeling and tried very hard not to show her the least hint of it. She was that strange paradox, an honest thief. She'd never claimed to be able to imagine any world in which they could be together forever. For his part he could imagine it, quite easily, but he knew it was no more than a self-indulgent dream.

The truth was, he was torn, and in a state of sad confusion. He was a man who'd lived his whole life up to his current age of one and thirty in the fixed determination not to be anything like his scandalous father. He'd always known this gave him a dilemma that might have been devised by some ingenious demon to torment him. No innocent woman could be brought into his family as his wife while Wyverne lived and Rosanna stood at his side, but if he had any hope of restoring some honour to the family name, which was vital for the sake of his sister and brother and the secure, happy future they deserved, he must marry someone with a far better reputation than his. Only a woman far above reproach, famously virtuous, could help him reverse the damage Wyverne had done. It would be hard enough to persuade such a woman to take him, Rafe; impossible, until his father and Rosanna were gone for good. He'd never found a solution to this problem, other than to wish for Wyverne's speedy death. Amelia was still young, he'd told himself – she need not think of marriage for a few years yet, and by then, he hoped, the family name would be restored so that she might be free to pair with the sort of man she deserved. As for him, he was lonely while he waited in this limbo, but he could bear it.

But now Sophie had come into his life, and his previous predicament took on the aspect of a child's puzzle, compared with the tangle he found himself in now. It was quite easy to picture the sort of woman who might take on the Herculean task of reclaiming the Wyverne name; she would most likely be socially ambitious, highly interested in his fortune and conspicuously devoted to the outward show of morality and piety. She probably wouldn't be enormously enjoyable to live with unless he was luckier than he could hope to be, but one thing was certain: she'd look nothing like Sophie. She would have no sort of a past, let alone a past like Sophie's. What hurt him was that Clemence de Montfaucon could have been a much more palatable version of that woman, she could have helped him build a better future *and* they could have shared so much more, they could have made each other happy beyond all his current expectations. Again the vicious elegance of the trap revealed itself, for whose fault was it that Sophie was no longer Clemence? Not hers. He was not the man to blame her for surviving. It was Wyverne, spreading his poison wherever he went.

No, she had to be free to leave, for his sake as well as her own, and he had to do everything in his power to help her, however much it went against his own deepest wishes. He knew he should tell himself it was for the best; at present, he couldn't quite manage it.

The audacious nature of the plan required that they'd both have to endure a certain amount of discomfort and humiliation – inevitably, she more than he. It would also mean that they'd both be brought into direct and unpleasant contact with Lord Wyverne, and likely with his wife too. Sophie had been worried about that, worried about him, and if he'd said he couldn't countenance it, he believed she'd have been perfectly prepared to abandon the idea. But it was quite clear to Rafe that as far as she was concerned that was the only flaw in the scheme. And so he'd realised that it would be wrong to refuse. It wasn't as though his relationship with his father and stepmother could well be much worse. If Rosanna realised at long last that he would never have any sexual interest in her, that would be a relief. And Sophie's idea had the further advantage that it wasn't at all likely to cause some final rift with Wyverne, which she knew he could not afford. He'd gladly endure a little unpleasantness for her sake. Look what *she* was prepared to do.

The stage was set late in the morning. Sophie had now been confined to Rafe's chamber for some twenty-four hours, while, he understood from what his many allies among the servants had told him when he went to get food, Lord Wyverne searched for any trace of her around his estate with increasing desperation.

When at last the mechanics of the plan began to unfold and the door of his private chamber crashed open – finding another key and ensuring others could plausibly find it too had been ridiculously complicated and caused some delay – Rafe hoped that his own face was a convincing mixture of consternation and anger. But he doubted anyone was sparing him more than a glance.

Sophie was the focus of attention. It could hardly be otherwise. She was clad only in her chemise and covered by a rumpled sheet. Her hair lay spread across the pillows in wild disorder and her eyelids were sultry with satiated passion, her lips red and swollen where Rafe's unshaven cheeks had abraded her pale skin. She gave the most convincing impression of a woman who'd been most thoroughly pleasured in a manner that she'd very much enjoyed. The room was redolent with the heavy scent of sex, and the rest of Sophie's clothes, and Rafe's, were discarded here and there.

Lord Drake himself was clothed in a loose banyan of magnificent dark blue silk – he'd drawn the line at nakedness, given the audience for their little play. There was a large, unmissable love mark on his neck and his hair was in a state of great disarray. Lord and Lady Wyverne had burst into the room in a flurry of movement and stood staring in blank astonishment at the picture thus presented to them. It plainly wasn't in the least what they had expected to find.

The Marquess's butler, Kemp, had gone to his master a short while ago with a report that he and Rafe had concocted together. Kemp was obliged to tell Lord Wyverne that he had overheard some of the maids whispering, and compelled them to tell him what they were gossiping about: it was their belief that the fugitive French-woman was concealing herself in one of the attic rooms. A light had been seen there late in the evening, and while it was widely known among the staff that Lord Drake kept a chamber high up in the house, they also knew that he didn't usually spend the night in it. It was all most suspicious, even suggestive. Kemp had not presumed to verify the truth of the rumours himself, but he'd found after some trouble the key to the room in question and brought it straight to his master. It had a rather helpful label on it which said in a bold clear hand 'Lord Drake's Chamber', so there could be no mistake.

When Sophie had proposed the whole misbegotten idea, Rafe had been forced to agree with her main point: it was quite impos-sible that Lord Wyverne would be able to resist coming to see for himself. If the fugitive should indeed be cowering guiltily in the attic, and if, even better, she should have the jewels with her and be caught red-handed... Rafe supposed that his parent had never climbed a set of stairs so fast in his life. He was flushed and panting now, as was Rosanna, but there was no triumph in either of their faces, only confusion.

It was time for him to speak. It wasn't at all hard to achieve the appropriate level of incredulous fury for the occasion. 'I confess, as you can see, we were not expecting visitors. I will not apologise for our deshabille, for after all, this is my private chamber. I don't come bursting into yours, sir, to interrupt your... activities. What do you want?'

Lord Wyverne was purple in the face, his eyes bulging in a most unhealthy manner, and all but gobbling with baffled rage. But he was not a man to admit defeat, nor one who changed his mind readily. It must be obvious to him that matters were not as he had hoped, but he was hardly about to admit this and slink meekly away with his tail between his legs. 'What do I want, sirrah? I came to find the impudent doxy who has stolen my jewels! And I have found her, and you with her! I knew you had played some part in this!'

Rafe had to admire Sophie's perfect composure under this verbal attack, though he doubted this was an emotion shared by anyone else in the room. 'I haven't stolen anything, my lord,' she said coolly, to all appearances entirely unembarrassed by her condition. If anything, she seemed to be quite enjoying herself. 'If we are to speak of theft, Lord Drake has stolen me and kept me here.'

'My dear...' Rafe said indulgently, his tone an enormous contrast with the one he'd used to address his parent. His deep voice was charged with a sort of heavy concupiscence that was most unlike his ordinary mode of speech. He was quite proud of how he sounded: like a man entirely in thrall to the sexual allure of a woman, and uncaring who knew it. Perhaps it was so convincing because there was more than a grain of truth in it.

'You know I'm right, you wicked creature,' she said, pouting seductively. 'You quite overcame me when you encountered me yesterday, and have kept me captive here ever since while you used me at your pleasure.'

'My pleasure, and yours, wench,' he growled. 'Don't try to deny that.'

'Oh, Rafe...' she sighed. 'I do declare you put me to the blush!' Despite her words, she didn't, in that moment, give the appearance of a woman who would be embarrassed by anything in the world.

There was no question that Lord and Lady Wyverne were not in the least accustomed to being ignored in such a manner, and that they did not care for it. 'You lied to me, girl!' said Rosanna, her voice high and indignant, determined to take her part in the farce that was playing out. 'You told me you were a respectable lady companion! But my husband has discovered that you have posed for indecent pictures, and now this! You have betrayed our trust, and you should be whipped for your deception!'

Perhaps fortunately, Sophie had no time to reply to this; Rafe could all too easily imagine what she might have felt impelled to say.

'Enough of this nonsense!' grated Lord Wyverne. 'I don't give a damn if my mother's latest companion turns out to be a whore. It makes a change from shrivelled-up old maids. But when I hear she's a liar and not who she pretended to be, and my most valued possessions disappear within a few weeks of her arrival, then I'm interested.'

'Sophie didn't take your blasted jewels,' Rafe said impatiently. He'd had quite enough of his father's company, and every reason for showing as much. 'You suspected her because she vanished – well, she vanished because I got tired of sneaking around with her and wanted her here at my convenience. She didn't steal anything; she's had other fish to fry and plenty to keep her occupied. She's still here, and she's not leaving anytime soon.'

'So masterful...' sighed Sophie soulfully. 'But to be serious,' she went on in quite another tone, 'I didn't need to steal anything. If I play my hand cleverly, I could end up owning it all, and much more besides. As you did, my lady. I'm only following your excellent example.'

'Why, you insolent little bitch!' Rosanna made a lunge towards her, but Rafe reached out one long arm and held her back without the least appearance of effort.

'I think it's past time you both left,' he said. 'You can search the room if you like, tear it apart if you must, but you must know you won't find anything. And it seems like a good moment to say that if either of you lays a finger on Sophie, I promise I will make you sorry for it.'

'I won't take threats from you, boy!' Wyverne managed.

'In this instance, sir, you will. And I don't wish to hear the word "whore" again in relation to Sophie. After all, you must both know the saying about people who live in glass houses.'

He was still restraining Rosanna, who showed every sign of a continuing determination to lay violent hands on Sophie if he relaxed his vigilance for a second, but when she heard his final words she rounded on him in fury instead, and was still protesting shrilly as Lord Wyverne, his patience clearly at an end, pulled her from the room. Rafe knew him well enough to expect that he would seek to have the last word, and so was unsurprised when his father turned and said, his colour still high and his voice menacing in its conviction, 'I'm watching you – both of you! Don't imagine for a second that you can pull the wool over my eyes! If you try to cross me, I will make very sure that you pay for it!'

And then he slammed the door behind him.

# 31

Rafe locked the door again – Wyverne had in his bafflement most usefully left the spare key behind – and then sank down on the crumpled bed beside Sophie.

'Rafe, that worked out splendidly! Much better than I could ever have hoped.' She sat up, hugging her knees, triumphant, her dark eyes sparkling. He'd never seen this mischievous side to her before today, and he was enchanted by it. Would she never cease surprising him? But with a sharp little stab of pain he realised she'd be gone soon, and he'd likely never see her again. There'd be no time for him to discover any more enchanting things about her. He'd have to live on these memories.

'You were magnificent,' he said seriously. 'Entirely convincing in the role you had chosen. It's plain to me that the stage has lost a great actress in you. You might even have been too good – I thought Rosanna was about to scratch your eyes out when you commenced taunting her.'

'She wanted to, but with great presence of mind you stopped her. It doesn't matter, as she was always sure to hate me once she knew you and I were involved. You were excessively good too –

the very picture of a man driven half out of his senses by lust. I'm sure they believed it all completely, and it was wonderful to see them so confounded.'

'It was, and there's no denying it went well.' He gathered her up in his arms and looked down at her, his face still somewhat troubled. 'But he will still be watching us – you heard him. We mustn't be lulled into thinking that everything will be plain sailing now. You no longer need to hide away here, and you're in no immediate danger – very well. But let us not forget that he remains a dangerous man, and escape will not be easy.'

'I know it,' she said. 'Believe me, I do. I am not underestimating what is still to be achieved, nor letting down my guard for an instant, except when I'm alone with you. But it is important to celebrate a win, you know, when life is so uncertain. We bested them, Rafe! We did it together. And I do like you in this banyan – it brings out the blue of your eyes. It is most becoming, and besides I enjoy the knowledge that you are naked beneath it.' She slid her hand between the fastenings to find the warmth of his bare skin. He closed his eyes for a moment and enjoyed her caress. He could see that she was in alt, quite intoxicated by their success, and he found it impossible to resist her, in this mood or any other. She had earned this moment of victory, however brief it might be. They both had.

He claimed her lips in a deep kiss, and she pulled him down to lie close by her, tugging persistently at the braid loops until she had undone as many of his buttons as she could easily reach and had free access to his nakedness beneath it.

'I almost laughed aloud when you called me wench,' she murmured against his mouth, her hands busy stroking him to excellent effect.

'I struggled to keep a straight countenance myself at times. If I'd known deceiving Wyverne would be so enjoyable, I'd have done it years ago,' he said between increasingly passionate kisses, and then as their mutual hunger grew he seized her ruined chemise and ripped it from neck to hem, pulling aside the rags that remained, impatient to see her in all her glory once more.

'Oh, it's just as I said!' she purred. 'You are so masterful, my lord! What is a poor girl to do but submit?'

He reached out and ran his hands slowly down her body, affection and amusement as well as desire written plainly on his face. 'And you have the ability to be so deliciously vulgar, my most wicked creature. I was quite astonished by what had been unleashed in you.'

'I know!' she said gleefully, returning to her diligent exploration beneath the loose robe. 'I can't remember when I've enjoyed myself so much. I warn you, I'm going to be horribly, horribly vulgar over the next few days. It's too much fun to stop now. I may have to think of an appalling nickname for you, and use it widely in front of others.'

'I hate to think,' he murmured distractedly as she began to wreak further havoc on him.

'Stallion!' she suggested, her fingers caressing his silky hardness. 'My proud stallion!'

'Call me what you like, in any language you choose, as long as you continue to do that!' he groaned.

'You'll be sorry you said that. My vocabulary is extremely extensive!'

Lord Drake, just then, could not have said the same. His vocabulary seemed to consist entirely of moans and gasps, and half-muffled cries of, 'Sophie!' But he resolved, in his last coherent thought for some time, to be revenged on her by reducing her to the same state as soon as she had done with him.

A good while later they lay in each other's arms, both drugged with pleasure, and he roused himself to say, 'Thank you, Sophie.'

'For what?' she said with drowsy contentment. 'You've done a great deal to help me, I'd have thought it obvious, rather than the other way around, if we are to talk of gratitude. I should be thanking you, and I have not properly done so. I'm the one with the portmanteau full of stolen jewels, after all. You didn't have to concern yourself with the matter.'

'No,' he said, stroking her hair and trying to put into words what he wanted to say to her. He felt such happiness, holding her, and it would have been easier just to let it carry him away. But he wanted to tell her, if he could, while there was still time. 'That's true, as far as it goes, but that's not what I mean. You've done far more for me than I could ever do for you. Sophie, I am quite serious.' She let out an adorable little snort and caressed his cheek with lazy affection, which he chose to take as permission to continue with his explanation. These things were not easy to speak of, he found.

'I've spent my whole life struggling with my feelings for my father. I often take myself to task for how little I have done to oppose him, but I've not been passive. What small measure of good I could perform, I have. I've kept a foothold here, for the sake of the staff and the estate as well as for my grandmother. When tenants or servants have been carelessly treated, I have heard of it, and tried to mend matters. I have a certain status as his heir which he is obliged to accept. The estate is not half so badly managed as it might be, and that is important to me. I've always known I couldn't afford an open breach with him, because of Grand-mère, and now because of the children, whom he could take from my care in a moment if he chose to. He could overset their whole lives just to punish me, so I've always felt I was walking a tightrope. It's been necessary, I can't forget that, however hard it's been. But I've never found a way to go on the offensive, and I realise now how bad that's been for me. It's almost as though I've been waiting for him to die so my own life could begin.'

He hesitated for a moment and then went on slowly, 'I've never been able to laugh at him before today, to see him as preposterous. I've always been a little frightened of him, though since I reached manhood I'd never have admitted it to myself. But you're not scared of him, though you have far more reason to be, considering all he's done to you. You've given me a wiser perspective: he is a monster, and a wicked man, but he is also ridiculous, because he is so utterly predictable. I don't understand exactly *why* he does things, though I see the greed and hatred that drive him, but I don't need to. And therefore he can be defeated. I needed you to show me that.'

'I'm glad,' she said warmly. 'I truly am. I came here thinking only of myself, and what I was owed, but I can see now that I should have realised just how many others he must have damaged. That's been good for me too, I think. I'm very far from being the only person in the world with a valid grudge. Suffering can make one selfish.'

Rafe thought this was far truer of him than of Sophie, but he feared that if they continue to converse at this high emotional pitch he would be bound to say things he must later regret. 'Are you hungry?' he asked her with an effort at lightness. 'I should think you must be. I can obtain more clothes for you, and we can eat where we please. You're an acknowledged member of the household now.'

'Lord Drake's mistress,' she said, and he couldn't tell whether she was glad or sorry to be so known. 'I do not care what your father and his wife think of me – I imagine I have demonstrated that to you quite adequately today – but I confess it would distress me if your grandmother turned a cold face to me. Do you believe she will?'

He laughed. 'With her own history? Hardly! I think you underestimate her. That a man should take a mistress, or a woman a lover, is of little importance to her. If you feel a little awkwardness in her company, I assure you, it will be on your side only, never hers. And do not forget that she likes you, which counts for a great deal.'

'If you say so, I must trust your better knowledge of her. But would it not be expected that you should remove me to your own home, rather than keeping me here under your father's roof? Because you know I can't leave until I've found a safe way to extract the jewels.'

'I doubt Wyverne thinks of such things; he has very little curiosity about others unless their actions impact on him directly. And if he charges me with the matter – which he won't – I'll merely say that I am setting about finding a house for you where I can establish you, and that you will be gone soon. I have two young wards at home, my half-siblings; they're not there now, but I'm sure he doesn't know of their absence. It is hardly usual to bring one's mistress into such a respectable household, where legitimate children are living. Even he didn't do such a thing to me when I was a boy – Rosanna didn't reside here until they were married.'

As he had expected, she changed the subject, moving it skilfully away from these dangerous topics. 'How old are they, Rafe? I remember you said that they were much younger than you.'

'Charlie is nineteen, currently at Oxford, and Amelia is seventeen, and staying with her mother's family for a while; one of her cousins is to be married in a couple of weeks and she is to be her attendant. I've never seen her so excited. They lived with another aunt and uncle for many years, but their aunt died a couple of years ago and they came to me. I'd always visited them as much as I could, but they've never lived here at Wyverne Hall, not since they were tiny, and it is my earnest hope that they never will while my father is alive.'

'I can understand that. Your lover did not live with you, then? I suppose that's a foolish question – it would not have been possible.'

'Sarah? No. I took a house for her in Oxford, and visited her there; her servants believed that I was her husband, and were ignorant of my true identity. The city was where we met, when I was visiting friends, and she was comfortable there. Since I was unable to live with her at my own home, it would scarcely have been fair to hide her away alone in one of the villages or small towns here, where everyone would soon have known her situation and made her suffer for it.'

'It is always the woman who suffers in such a circumstance,' she acknowledged. This was a fact of life that could not be denied, and he did not attempt to do so.

'I hope nothing that we have set in motion today causes you any distress or difficulty, Sophie,' he said gravely.

'You don't need to worry about me,' she replied a trifle bleakly. 'I have no reputation to lose. And neither do you, I suppose, since all the world believes that Lady Wyverne is your mistress. So there can be no damage done to either of us. We must be grateful that your brother and sister are not here to be dragged into all this. I must suppose that the servants will think the worse of me, but I cannot allow myself to regard that, when there is so much more at stake. Will you find us some food now, Rafe? I really am excessively hungry, and I think I would prefer to eat here.'

'I cannot have you starving. I will be back soon!'

## 32

The next few days were a curious time, a sort of limbo. Sophie was free now to go where she pleased about the house, but she had no desire to spend any time in Lord or Lady Wyverne's company, and carefully avoided places they might be. Unsurprisingly, she wasn't invited to dine with them or otherwise forced into their society, and was glad of it.

She'd been, despite her careless words to Rafe, a little nervous of the Dowager's reaction to recent events. It had already been obvious to her that Marchand knew everything that happened in the house, so she could hardly expect Delphine to remain ignorant of what had passed upstairs and the change in her own status that it had brought about. She was still aware of an odd, irrational little fear that the old lady would be disappointed in her, would judge her and find her wanting, but if this was indeed so she displayed no outward sign of it.

'I am glad to see you once more, my dear child, and to know that you are no longer under suspicion,' was all the Dowager said when Sophie next presented herself in her chamber. Sophie

looked at her tranquil face and understood that that was all she
intended to say upon the subject at present. Since she had no real
desire to engage in any sort of more detailed discussion with her
lover's grandmother, and even less did she desire to reveal the sad
confusion of her own feelings, she was quite happy to comply.

They resumed their novel-reading and their afternoons of
conversation, and this, Sophie knew, was the only time Rafe felt
able to leave the house and ride off to his home to perform his
duties there. It was strange to think that he had another life that
she could never be a part of – he had his friends Simon and Elizabeth at the rectory, his wards, his house and lands and servants,
and she would never set eyes on any of them. If this seemed to her
a melancholy notion, she refused to consider the implications of
it. She was here for a purpose, after all, and was no green girl to
moon after a man and wonder how he spent his time when he
could not be with her, and whether he thought of her when they
were separated, as – she was obliged to admit – she thought of
him. That would be perfectly ridiculous. It was the sort of thing
silly little Clemence de Montfaucon would have done, not Sophie
Delavallois.

They otherwise spent a great deal of time together, at night
and in the daytime. Rafe felt protective of her, she knew, and
though she did not in the least need his solicitude she welcomed
it. She was no longer accustomed to anyone showing themselves
concerned for her safety with no thought of advantage for themselves. She experienced this unfamiliar sensation of being cared
for with him, and with his grandmother, and though she was too
strong to need it, and would soon be gone from their lives forever
and out of reach of their concern, she couldn't deny that it gave
her a warm feeling, as if something that had been frozen inside
her was beginning slowly to thaw out. She did not ask herself

whether it was safe to let it thaw – she knew the answer to that already. When one was frozen, one could not feel pain.

She spent each night in Rafe's bed, and in his arms, and in the day they sat and read and ate together, always alone, or he showed her the wonders of the house. They also began to take casual strolls about the estate, close to the mansion at first and then further afield. Sophie, on high alert, spotted the watchers Lord Wyverne had set almost as soon as she and her escort had left the building, and was aware that Rafe had noticed them too; the pair exchanged significant glances though they said nothing. But the men who observed them from the woods did not presume to challenge the Marquess's heir or his companion, and as she and Rafe began to venture further in their promenades she began to entertain the hope that the surveillance might be evaded.

She wrote again to her fictitious correspondent Mrs Fanny Olivier, saying that she was worried that she had had no response to her last letter and hoping that the baby's croup was no worse. This code was the only means at her disposal to convey to Nate the fact that she remained at Wyverne Hall and that the grounds were still patrolled so that the jewels could not be retrieved. She added, in a natural sort of way, that she was very much enjoying the many healthful spring walks that the estate provided. After some further thought she appended coyly the interesting fact that Lord Drake, a most gracious gentleman, was often good enough to accompany her and offer her his arm. They were spending a great deal of time together, she added, *unchaperoned*. It would present an odd appearance, she thought, not to mention Rafe at all, presuming that Lord Wyverne was still opening her letters.

She hadn't so far pictured her imaginary correspondent as to be able to say whether she would approve or disapprove of Sophie's throwing caution to the wind and becoming the

Viscount's acknowledged mistress. Her surrender to his improper advances was all very shocking, no doubt – but on the other hand, he *was* a viscount, heir to a marquessate, and Sophie could scarcely expect any more respectable sort of offer in her supposed station in life.

Rafe, when applied to in the matter, sketched in the imaginary lady's character in such an effective manner that he soon had his audience of one crying with laughter. Mrs Olivier, he decided, had had her own adventures before her marriage, and was disposed to give Sophie all sorts of frank advice along with rather startling reminiscences of her hitherto unsuspected past life.

It was all the more amusing, then, when a letter of reply did appear, bearing the superscription of Mrs Olivier's respectable address in Bloomsbury. 'It must be from Nate!' Sophie exclaimed when they were alone, tearing it open.

It was, in his own neat hand, and it contained a thundering scold, a positive homily, in which Nate's version of Fanny proved to be a stern moralist who hoped that her young relative would not be led astray, as so many foolish girls had before, by the honeyed words and practised seductions of a member of the dissolute nobility. 'It's very funny,' Sophie said at last when she had finished reading it aloud, 'and he obviously enjoyed writing it, but I have no idea what it means. Apart from the fact that she – he – says in a postscript that I'm not to worry about the baby's croup, which I assume signifies that Nate is aware of the men watching us, and has a solution to the problem in mind.'

'What could that be?' Rafe asked doubtfully.

'He might bribe some of them, or threaten them, or otherwise arrange for them to disappear.'

'Surely he won't want his name appearing in the matter?'

'He's a very powerful man. People are frightened of him, Rafe, and his reach extends very far. He's certainly not afraid of being blackmailed – a person would have to be out of their wits to try it. So there is no knowing what he might do. We must be prepared.'

It was not, then, as much of a surprise as it might have been to encounter a solitary walker when next they set out on one of their expeditions. They'd already come some distance, having passed through the triumphal arch to make their way down one side of the tree-lined avenue that led in the direction of the village. About halfway down the long, straight road, an individual stepped suddenly out from where he had been concealed in the shadow of the branches and said in level tones, 'Miss Delavallois, Lord Drake. Good day to you.'

It was Nate Smith himself. He was as usual dressed as a slightly old-fashioned but respectable person of the middling rank, and had removed his Joliffe shallow and made a neat bow to do obeisance to the Viscount and his companion. Rafe nodded warily, since he could not yet be sure of the man's identity and plainly did not wish to compromise himself or Sophie by any more positive gesture or speech.

Sophie said urgently, 'Nate, I am glad to see you, of course, but is it not terribly dangerous for you to appear here in person?'

'If we are to talk of danger, my dear, what of your behaviour?' Mr Smith said drily. 'I confess that I was surprised to receive your letter and learn of the company you have been keeping, and now here you are, confirming my worst fears. You can't be astonished that I have a great desire to know what in the seven hells is going on.'

There was an edge to his urbane voice on his final words, and Rafe stepped forward when he heard it, his tall frame tense, but Sophie put her hand on his arm soothingly, holding him back. 'It's a reasonable question – yes, it is, Rafe. There's no need to worry, Nate, I haven't gone over to the enemy. Lord Drake knows that I have taken the jewels. In fact, he knew before I did it, and had no notion of stopping me. When I fell under suspicion, he rescued me, and he is very well aware that I mean to smuggle them out of the house just as soon as I am able. He will help me, if he can.'

'Will he now? That's one of the unlikeliest tales I ever heard in my life.'

The two men regarded each other measuringly, distrust and suspicion plain on both their faces, lending them an odd and surely illusory moment of resemblance. Rafe broke the silence. 'Miss Delavallois tells me that you are somehow acquainted with Lord Wyverne, Smith, and dislike him greatly,' he said.

'That's true, if something of an understatement,' Nate replied shortly.

'Nevertheless, if that is so, you will perhaps be able to comprehend why my sentiments towards him fall far short of filial devotion.'

'I can well believe it, but I have never met a man before who'd willingly deprive himself of thousands and thousands of pounds of property. Perhaps Sophie has enchanted you, which is perfectly understandable, but even so, you'll forgive me for displaying a certain healthy scepticism.'

Sophie looked anxiously up at Rafe, but he merely said levelly, 'I don't want any part of his ill-gotten gains. I hadn't realised, in fact, just how ill-gotten they were until very recently. Wyverne will be mine one day, and I will defend it and its people with all my might, but I desire no such tainted inheritance. I'd prefer that everything he's stolen and tricked away from its rightful owners went back to them, but I realise that is scarcely possible, and I presume I'm not addressing some modern incarnation of Robin Hood. Take it all, with my blessing, Smith. All I care about – and I really do mean this, so mark it well – is ensuring that Miss Delavallois is not harmed in the process.'

'By God,' Nate breathed, more affected by some powerful emotion than Sophie had ever seen him, 'now that I look at you, you have such a look of the old Marquess, your grandfather, about you, that I could almost bring myself to believe you don't give a damn for the jewels, and I'm not by any means a credulous man.'

'Believe me or not, as you choose,' said Rafe. 'Why should I care? As long as you understand that I am deadly serious in my concern for Sophie's safety.'

'If that is true, you really are nothing like your father.'

'I devoutly hope not.'

A fourth person suddenly joined the conversation, making Rafe and Sophie start at the unexpected interruption. 'Time to go, Nate,' said a deep, calm voice from close by. 'Don't want to be hanging around here too long today. Might be seen by someone as shouldn't.'

'I know, Fred,' Mr Smith responded. 'Just a moment longer. Fetch me the jewels, Sophie. Let me worry about whether you're watched or not. Bring them tomorrow – not here, but to the Gothic Tower. It is such a striking landmark, up there on its hill in all its peculiar glory, that we cannot possibly miss each other. You can be sure I'll be waiting.'

'*We'll* be waiting,' Fred amended. He stepped out of the shadows of the overhanging trees, and Sophie smiled at him. She'd always liked the ex-prizefighter, who was a much gentler man (except when violence was most definitely required) than his menacing appearance and huge stature would lead one to imagine. She should have realised that where Nate was, he wouldn't be far away.

Nate smiled, the first sign of amusement he'd shown throughout this tense interview. 'Of course. *We* will be waiting.'

'I don't like any part of it,' Rafe said. 'If Sophie and I walk out of the house carrying a heavy bag, you can't possibly guarantee that we won't be stopped. The watchers can't be utter fools. They'll see us and drag us to Lord Wyverne before we get fifty paces from the door.'

'We? You mean to go so far as actually to assist in this?' asked Nate incredulously.

'Of course,' Rafe replied. 'You don't suppose, after all I've said, that I will allow Sophie to put herself at such risk alone? You show a touching confidence that we will achieve the thing unmolested, Mr Smith, but then, you won't be the one risking your neck. I doubt we'll get anywhere near the Gothic Tower to meet you.'

'I wouldn't be so sure of that,' rumbled Fred. 'If it came to a mill, I'd wager you could give a decent account of yourself. Well known at Jackson's Saloon, you are, my lord. Seen you there on more than once occasion myself, and I must say you do peel to remarkable advantage. Wouldn't mind at all seeing how you display in a proper bust-up.'

'I dare say,' Lord Drake said with a touch of impatience. 'I believe I saw you fight Jem Belcher in '03, which would be a fine subject for cosy reminiscences in other circumstances, but we're not in the prize ring now. Those men of Wyverne's may have pistols, and if they don't I can assure you that he does. Sophie, I know I've said that I admire the fact that you're not frightened of him, but on this occasion I assure you, you should be. He'd put a bullet in you without blinking, or order it done without so much as breaking sweat.'

'Leave that to me,' said Nate with superb assurance. 'Nobody will be shot. Nobody will punch anybody, unless you really feel you must, Fred. Do you trust me, Sophie?'

'I do,' she said steadily. 'Having come so far and done so much, I must. I'll bring the jewels out to you – reserving only the

Stella Rosa for myself, of course, as we agreed. What time would suit you best, Nate?'

'Dammit, Sophie, we're not arranging to take tea here!' Drake objected. 'This is a life and death matter!'

'If Nate says all will go smoothly, I believe it will,' she said serenely. And nothing he could say would weaken her resolve, so that at length, much against his will, he was obliged to agree to all that was proposed. They parted from their companions then, after having arranged to meet them by the Gothic Tower at eleven in the forenoon of the next day. The die was cast.

Sophie and Rafe thought it wise to continue with their walk, as if nothing of any particular significance had happened, rather than turning back immediately and lending importance to the meeting to anyone who might be watching. 'We must suppose that Nate has somehow suborned some of Lord Wyverne's men,' Sophie mused as they strolled up the avenue of trees, 'but we can't assume it's all of them.'

Lord Drake seemed lost in a brown study. At length he said tersely, 'And what of you, Sophie? Once your purpose is achieved tomorrow, if indeed it is, will you go?'

'I hadn't thought past smuggling out the jewels,' she confessed with studied lightness. 'If we manage that without attracting any attention, it will be a great weight off my mind. I'll be safe then – Lord Wyverne will have no reason to suspect me, and no reason to think that anything has changed. Indeed, he may never know what's happened to his jewels, and always live in doubt and uncertainty for the rest of his life. I like that thought.'

Rafe did not seem to share her apparent optimism. 'You'll still have the Stella. If he found that, you'd be very far from safe.'

'That's easy enough to hide,' she dismissed. 'I can sew it in my bonnet, or conceal it in any of a dozen places.'

'Very well. What then? I know you haven't thought about it,

and I understand why, but think about it now, if you please. What will you do?'

She was silent for a moment in turn. Then she said with a little effort, 'I can't stay here. You must know that. These past few days have been... magical. A moment out of time, for both of us. But we don't inhabit a world where magic can last, Rafe. You have your life, and I have mine, and they're very far apart.' She saw that he was about to speak, and shook her head. 'Perhaps you're going to suggest that you carry out the plan you mentioned a few days ago and set me up in a house somewhere as your mistress. As you did before. But I don't want to exist like that, as a dirty secret, a kept woman, always waiting for someone who can't truly share himself with me. I need a life of my own, whatever it may turn out to be. And I don't think you want that sort of clandestine existence either. Not really. You deserve better, even if I don't any more.'

'You're so far right,' he said heavily, 'that I don't have the slightest desire to live in that manner. And as to what you deserve, my God... You are fair and far off in your supposition, Sophie.'

She swung round and looked at him incredulously. What she saw in his face made tears spring to her eyes, but she dashed them away angrily. 'No!' she exclaimed. 'No! Don't say it. I don't want to hear it.'

'I don't think I've ever seen you cry before,' he said rather unsteadily. 'And I haven't even said what I meant to say. Will you not hear me out, my love?'

'I won't!' she said fiercely, tears streaming down her cheeks unregarded now. 'You're deluding yourself. And don't call me that. I can't bear it. What you think you want is impossible. It's nothing but a fantasy. It's cruel! I know how hard you have struggled all your life to be different from your father – to prove it to yourself as much as to others. I know what the future of your family means to you. So how could you and I ever have any kind of life together? You must know in your heart that we cannot!'

And, picking up her skirts, she ran from him, back towards the house, and though he could easily have overtaken her, could have forced a further scene, Lord Drake did not do so, but followed her more slowly, his face sombre, his manner dejected.

## 33

The rest of the day dragged by. Lord Drake did not attempt to reopen the conversation that Sophie had so emphatically refused to engage in, and there was inevitably a certain amount of constraint between them. They sat together in the library as night fell, and she tried to pretend that everything was as it had been before, though it was not. Eventually he said rather sadly, 'I will not say what you don't wish me to say, my dear. The last thing in the world I want is to make you unhappy, and yet I have done that, and I regret it bitterly. Let's go to bed, and hold each other, and take comfort from that if we can. We must get past tomorrow. I can't believe matters will go as smoothly as you seem to think. I have all sorts of fears that I can't put into words. Anything might happen. We should not be at odds, then, tonight of all nights, in case it is our last.'

She did not answer him in words, but rose and put her hand in his, and went up the stairs with him in silence, through the big, quiet house. They caressed each other with a sort of fierce desperation that was new to them, and their pleasure was intense and mutual, but afterwards when he held her and felt her cold tears trickling down her face onto his bare chest he whispered, 'You have the right to refuse to hear me, and I respect that, as I must, but one thing you cannot ask of me.'

'What, Rafe?' She could not see his face in the darkness.

'I will not cease calling you my love. You are that and you always will be. If you leave tomorrow and I never see you again, or if one of us does not survive the day that is coming, you'll still be my love. I won't pretend that isn't true. Not even for you.'

'I can't...' she said brokenly.

He sighed, and kissed her hair. 'I know. Go to sleep, Sophie. You need your strength, and so do I.'

She couldn't sleep, and didn't think he was sleeping either, though he stayed still and feigned slumber. She lay in the darkness, feeling the warmth of his body, so close and yet so far away, and wishing, for the first time in years, that things could be different. She'd come here with a very clear plan in mind, and she'd succeeded in carrying it out against all the odds. A few weeks ago, she'd known she was a honed weapon, a dangerous woman with depths nobody would suspect until it was too late, and she'd gloried in that – felt strong and powerful. Nothing that could happen at Wyverne Hall could possibly overset her, she'd thought. She was prepared for anything.

But she hadn't been prepared for Rafe. The place would likely be full of predatory males, she'd known, indiscriminate in their attentions, entirely prepared to use force, and so she'd had her sharp knife at the ready. But she'd been wrong to think him one of them. He'd distrusted her, with good reason, but he'd never taken advantage of her, and that first kiss had been a mutual acknowledgement of a growing bond between them, beyond all sense or reason. Every meeting after that had shown her, little by little, that he wasn't the man she'd thought he must be, and certainly he was nothing like his father. She'd made so many assumptions, and they'd all been wrong.

Her certainties had been shaken to pieces. She'd built a life and an identity for herself that had been based on hatred and revenge, and she'd never imagined that coming to Wyverne Hall – the seat of all that was evil in the world – would rock all that she had so painstakingly constructed to its foundations. She hadn't cried in years before arriving here, had refused to, and here she was weeping like a lost child again. Like Clemence.

He'd destroyed her with his declaration of love. She'd told him that there was no world in which they could be together, and it must be true, so what use was it for him to tell her that he loved her? Though he did not mean to be cruel, he hurt her by it. She felt in this moment that she didn't know anything, not even who she was any more. Her revenge had so possessed her that she'd had no idea what she would do when it was fully executed. It was impossible to consider becoming Clemence de Montfaucon again, but was she then Sophie Delavallois? Might there be a third identity lying in wait for her? It surely, surely, couldn't be Lady Drake, and then in the course of time Lady Wyverne. A country lady, wife, mother. A member of the haut ton – a paragon of respectability. The idea was preposterous, grotesque, impossible. Even if Rafe overcame his doubts and decided to set aside all his plans for his family's respectable future, it would be wrong and wicked to let him do so. The next Lady Wyverne must be nothing at all like the present one; she must be a woman of unimpeachable background and reputation.

Sophie fell into an uneasy sleep at last, made all the more unrestful by strange dreams. She was wearing the gown she'd worn at the ball eight years ago, the ridiculous pink and green confection that she'd sold to pay the doctor who had failed to save her mother and her brother. About her neck, heavy, was the Stella

Rosa. She was being presented to Queen Charlotte. She'd never met the lady, never experienced a costly court presentation, she'd only seen prints of her likeness, but the fact that the old lady was seated on a throne and wearing an enormous crown made the identification fairly certain. The event was taking place in a large room, thronged with people, though she couldn't see any of them clearly. Sophie – perhaps in these circumstances she was Clemence again – advanced in a dignified manner, head held high, but when she sank into her deep curtsy the knife she carried in her garter fell out and clattered across the floor to the Queen's feet, shockingly loud in the silent chamber. The expression of outrage on the illustrious lady's face might have been amusing in other circumstances, if Sophie hadn't been the cause of it. The whispers from the crowd began then, the taunts, the slaps, the spitting...

The vision dissolved into a familiar nightmare of pursuit and frantic evasion, of leering faces looming over her, Lord Wyverne's and his wife's among them. She was glad when she awoke at last to see morning light creeping though the worn patches in the old curtains.

Rafe was no longer beside her, but before she had a chance to untangle the complicated feelings this evoked in her, he was shouldering his way into the room bearing a heavy tray. 'Breakfast,' he said with an attempt at cheerfulness that fell sadly short of being convincing.

She didn't think she'd have much appetite for it, but the coffee at least would be welcome. 'You're too good to me,' she said with a wan little smile, and then wished she had not when he replied, his voice rich with emotion.

'I couldn't be.'

This seemed likely to set her weeping again, but he said no more, and after making a show of eating she was able to regain her precarious composure and maintain it though the long morning. She sat with the Dowager as usual and read to her, and if the old lady noticed that she was sadly distracted and kept breaking off because she'd lost her place, she made no comment on it, for which Sophie was grateful. She didn't want to lie to someone she had come to care for, but it would be most unwise to tell her the truth, not least because if Delphine remained in ignorance she would be safer.

She retrieved the heavy little bag from its hiding place at the last possible moment, and spent a while dusting the grime of decades from it and from her gown so that she didn't present a suspicious appearance. A more suspicious appearance. Rafe had by agreement waited for her where the staircase led out onto the corridor of unused bedrooms, and stopped her as she descended. 'You have cobwebs in your hair again,' he told her, brushing them away with the gentlest of touches. The lump in her throat prevented her from replying, and though she felt a strong impulse to reach up and kiss him, she resisted it, even though she was painfully aware that it might be their last kiss. It was time. She fetched her pelisse and plain bonnet, and they set off.

She hadn't sewn the Stella into her clothing to conceal it. She'd thought of it, but some impulse she didn't fully understand had led to her to wear it as she had not done for so long, though she tucked it inside the neck of her gown so that it could not be seen, and buttoned up her pelisse securely over it. Though it was undeniably rash to have it on her person, it seemed fitting. The precious thing was hers by right, and it would give her courage. If it was cursed, let the curse fall on Lord Wyverne.

There was no point sneaking out of the house. They would be seen and apprehended immediately, or they would not. Sophie and Rafe set out boldly down the steps that led out from the Marble Saloon – she had a fleeting thought of that night when she had taken the jewels from Lady Wyverne, which seemed like months ago now – and made their way, Lord Drake carrying the bag, down towards the lakes, from which the path led up to the Gothic Tower.

'I have a sensation,' said Sophie as they walked, 'a most disagreeable sensation, of being watched. As though unfriendly eyes were boring into my back between my shoulder blades.'

'So do I,' said her companion grimly. 'But nobody has tried to stop us yet. We must be slow, and casual, or as casual as two people can be when carrying a travelling bag for no obvious reason. Has it occurred to you that this could be a trap?'

'Yes,' said Sophie. 'Of course it has, for all my trust in Nate. But to what purpose? He wouldn't gain anything from us being captured by Lord Wyverne and his men – he certainly couldn't guarantee to get away with the jewels.'

'I know. But did you notice how very familiar your friend was with the estate? He spoke as easily of the Gothic Tower and its setting as I might, or anyone else who's lived here all his life. I don't know what's going on, Sophie, but I am very sure that something is, and we neither of us have the least idea what it might be.'

As he spoke they passed among the trees, and Sophie breathed a little easier, though she knew it was irrational – this was where she'd first seen the men concealed, and they could very well be hidden here now, lying in wait. She darted anxious little glances about, and said distractedly, 'I did notice that, but I have no idea what it signifies. Nate has never mentioned to me that he has any familiarity with Wyverne Hall. It had never occurred to me before yesterday that such a thing was possible. Perhaps it isn't that at all – perhaps he was just very well prepared. He usually is.'

It was a few long minutes' walk to their destination, and they completed the rest of the journey in tense silence. The folly was set atop a hill, and though it was not terribly steep they were both breathing hard when they reached the top and stood looking at each other with a ridiculous sense of anticlimax. They were quite alone, and Sophie found herself struggling with a desire to burst into hysterical laughter.

'This is a preposterous building,' said Rafe conversationally, setting down the bag upon the ground at his feet and leaning back against the wall as he scanned the landscape around them. 'I can't imagine what my grandfather was thinking. It's quite out of keeping with everything else here.'

'What was it built for?' Sophie asked, looking up at the battlemented tower, embellished with leering dragon gargoyles, that crowned one side of the edifice, and the curious domed steeple that topped the other. 'It looks like a church designed by a madman. Can it really be triangular, as it appears to be from this angle? I don't feel greatly inclined to go and inspect the rest of it at the moment.'

'It is triangular,' said Nate, stepping out from around one of the corners, Fred close on his heels. 'I believe I'm right in thinking it's a temple to your illustrious ancestors, am I not, Lord Drake? Such arrogance, such pride of lineage! Which makes it entirely appropriate that you should here hand over the ill-gotten jewels to me.'

'Gladly,' said Rafe shortly, picking up the bag and swinging it in Mr Smith's direction. Nate took it from his hand, but what he had been about to say next was destined never to be heard, for at that moment Lord Wyverne appeared from behind the other corner of the façade, and stood, chest heaving, confronting them. He had a silver-mounted duelling pistol in his hand, and he was pointing it at his son.

## 34

'I knew it!' gloated the Marquess, the barrel of the pistol he held waving about from one target to another in a most alarming manner. 'I knew the bitch took the jewels and you were caught up in it, Drake! That's why I set a reliable man to watch you, and to bring me word of your movements. I knew you had betrayed me—'

'You've given me no cause to feel the least scrap of love or loyalty for you,' said Rafe steadily. 'If I'm betraying you, I'm only repaying the favour with interest. I have always been well aware you never gave a damn about me, or anyone but yourself, so to be expecting filial concern from me at this late stage is ridiculous. I hate you, and with good reason. And I don't know how you have the gall to call Sophie a bitch – what does that make the woman you married, and set on to seduce me when I was only a boy? While you watched!'

'By Christ, Drake, I'll shoot you myself before I let those jewels leave my sight!' said the Marquess, his face quite purple with fury and exertion. If he heard his son's accusations, he had no response to make to them. It seemed that all he cared about was the possessions he'd lost and thought he had a chance of regaining now.

'It's very lowering to see how little you have changed, Gervais,' said Nate, stepping forward in a manner, Sophie thought as she watched in silent incomprehension, that seemed calculated to draw Wyverne's attention, and the aim of his pistol, away from his son. 'I knew, of course, of your reputation – as does everyone in England, I expect – but here I see it confirmed in every unpleasant detail. What a nasty bully you have always been, and how I shall enjoy besting you at last.'

'You!' said the Marquess blankly. And then, 'How dare you set foot on my land after all these years, you trespassing bastard? Have you forgotten the beating I gave you the last time I set eyes on you? Are you in league with the treacherous cub, eh?'

'I never met my nephew before yesterday, nor had any contact with him,' said Nate deliberately. 'For all I knew, he was as vicious as you are. And yes, I am a bastard, as you so often reminded me when I was a boy, but those ancestors our father built his ridiculous temple to are mine also, which is why I arranged for us all to have our little encounter here. And don't think of calling for assistance – some of the ruffians you think you've bought are in my pay now, and you don't know which. They're as likely to knock you over the head as help you.'

Sophie realised now why Lord Wyverne had always seemed oddly familiar to her, and how the unmistakeable resemblance between the two men had come about. A great deal that had been unclear now made perfect sense. She darted a glance at Rafe to see if this revelation had shocked him equally, but was surprised to see that his expression had not changed. He smiled at her, a strange moment of lightness in such a tense scene, and said softly, 'There are others. I really should have made the connection myself. Many others. My grandmother had a great deal to bear in her marriage.'

Before Lord Wyverne could gather his wits to respond, Nate went on, 'I'm not the only person here with good reason to hold a grudge against you. Tell him who you are, Sophie, and why exactly you did what you did. This is a morning for revelations, I think.'

'I'd be delighted,' she said, unbuttoning her pelisse and pulling the chain that held the Stella Rosa out of the neckline of her gown. She held it up, and the huge jewel sparkled with pink fire in the spring sunshine. 'I'm Clemence de Montfaucon, and this is mine,' she told him fearlessly. 'And I've taken it back. You destroyed my family, but you didn't destroy me. My father was shamed, and took his own life, and when you heard about it you laughed. You thought, if you thought about the matter at all, that you could tear down my reputation, and my mother's, steal this from us, and just walk away, because I was a mere woman and too weak to fight you. But you were wrong, because you're stupid as well as wicked. You're a common thief – much worse than that, in fact, because common thieves steal to live, and you just do it because you enjoy it. When you're in the ground nobody will mourn – people will spit on your grave until you are forgotten. There isn't a person in the world who truly loves you or cares if you live or die.'

Wyverne's eyes were wild, and his weapon was no longer pointing at anyone in particular, due perhaps to an over-abundance of possible targets. It was clear that nobody had ever defied him in so open a manner before, let alone three people in succession, and he was finding the experience most disagreeable. 'I'll tell the world I had you, bitch!' he spluttered at last. 'I said I would, and I will. I'll say your father begged me to fuck you to get a better price for the necklace, and you must have got a taste for it because now you're letting my whelp—'

This sentence too was destined to go unfinished, because Fred, who hadn't taken any part in the conversation thus far and whose presence Lord Wyverne had entirely disregarded, stepped forward and floored the older man with a punishing right that almost lifted him off his feet.

'I don't, as a general rule,' he said, looking down at Lord Wyverne in a measuring fashion and poking him with one massive foot, 'approve of the knocking down of elderly coves and those as weren't expecting it. But I don't like your dirty mouth, old man, and I don't like what Nate's told me you did to him when he was a green young shaver and you was a swell blade old enough to know better. Proper wicked, that was.' He paused, his voice choked by some strong emotion, and then gathered himself and turned to Rafe, saying in a more level tone, 'If you should feel the need to take up cudgels in your pa's defence, my lord, it'd be a pleasure to stand up against you, even if I'm not the man I was when you saw me go to it with Jem Belcher.'

'And even then he knocked you down and you stayed down, as I recall, despite that famous right of yours,' said Lord Drake equably. 'But that was before poor Belcher lost his eye, of course. No, I'm not likely to be leaping to Wyverne's defence, man. Far from it. I've never come so close to laying hands on him myself, which would still be a shocking thing however much he deserved it. So I owe you my thanks, for sparing me the necessity. And it was very neatly done.'

'Happy to do it,' said Fred gruffly, clearly most gratified. 'And sorry, in a way, not to have a chance for a set-to with you. You're a rare gorger, and no mistake, unlike *him*. If he'd stand up, I might just put him down again. He's not had all that's coming to him, not by any means. What's one blow to the muzzler.'

There didn't seem to be any immediate prospect of Fred getting his wish. Lord Wyverne was still groaning upon the floor, not insensible but nearly so, and there was plainly no question of him taking any further part in the discussion, or making any move to prevent his half-brother leaving with the bag of jewels.

'I don't think he's fit to walk back to the house,' said Rafe. 'He won't be for a while. I'll go and find someone to carry him back – a wheelbarrow would seem appropriate.'

'What will you tell them?' asked Sophie, tucking the priceless jewel back inside her gown and buttoning her pelisse securely over it. 'There'll be a bruise for everyone to see.'

'I should say there will be. I'll inform Kemp that His Lordship must have tripped and fallen while alone – that we came upon him upon the ground in a sad state. I imagine that you will be gone when I return,' he said, addressing Nate and Fred.

'Ashamed to own me, nevvy?' asked his uncle with a sardonic smile.

'Certainly not. Anyone who has spent thirty years as that man's son must be more or less dead to shame by now. You'll have to work much harder at if you desire to be known as the most disreputable member of this family. But I would have thought it might be awkward for you to be seen here by any of the staff, and raise questions in their minds that would be better left unconsidered. I don't suppose anyone would think to suspect *me* of knocking him down, while you and the Fancy, on the other hand... But it's as you wish, of course.'

'You're right in a way,' said Nate. 'Quite a few members of your household would know me well enough, even after all these years, and if they thought I'd laid the old bugger flat I wager they'd sooner cheer me on than hand me over to the constable. But they don't know Fred, and perhaps on reflection it's best they never do make his acquaintance.'

Fred, solid as the tower that loomed behind him, had so very much the aspect of someone who'd just knocked a man down, enjoyed it, and was prepared to do it again that Lord Drake and Sophie could only agree. 'I'll take my leave, then, Uncle,' said Rafe. 'It's been interesting, that's undeniable. I don't know if our paths will ever cross again. Good luck to you.'

They shook hands, and Fred engulfed the Viscount's hand in his great paw. 'It was a pleasure to meet you, Drake,' Nate said. 'I'm quite glad to know – I must be getting sentimental in my old age – that this place will be in safer hands when Wyverne's dead. My father, the old Marquess, wasn't what you'd call a saint, but at least he did well enough by me and my mother, and all his other by-blows. He'd have had something to say if he'd seen how his precious heir has turned out.'

Rafe smiled briefly at this, and then said quietly, 'I'm assuming – hoping – that you'll still be here when I get back, Sophie.'

'I will,' she said. She couldn't leave him in such an abrupt fashion. She probably should, but to do it was quite beyond her in this moment.

He strode swiftly away down the hill on hearing her reassurance, and she turned to face her companions. 'You did it, Sophie,' said Nate, smiling. 'Everything we planned, and more. I'm proud of you. I'll not soon forget Wyverne's face when you told him what you thought of him. I hope it felt good.'

'It did,' she said. 'I'm happy I pulled it off, and happier still that he knows it was me, and that some at least of his atrocious behaviour has come back to bite him. But my family will never know I did it, and it won't bring them back, will it, Nate?'

'No. Nothing will. Listen, my girl,' he told her, taking her by the shoulders, 'you're still young, and you can choose which path you take. You're free to do that now. If you want to come back to us, we'll be very happy to have you, won't we, Fred?' Fred rumbled assent. 'But you don't have to. You've got other options, it seems to me.'

'I can't sit and take tea and mind my sewing and be a respectable lady,' she said, hovering between laughter and tears. 'I'm surprised you of all people would suggest as much to me. It's far too late for that.'

'But do you know he wants you to?' Nate asked reasonably. 'It doesn't seem to me that he's so much as raised an eyebrow at anything you've done. I'd call that rare. There's not many men could cope with a woman like you. I'd have done so easily, of course, if I'd been in the petticoat line, which as you are well aware I'm not.' Fred snorted. 'But then I'm an exceptional man in many ways. Maybe my nephew is too.'

'I don't know,' she said. 'He may be, I suppose. But I won't be responsible for ruining him, even if some part of him wants me to. And it's high time you were gone from here. Take care, won't you?' She stepped forward and hugged them both, a thing she'd never done before, and then watched as they headed off down the hill, Fred carrying the bag full of jewels, in the opposite direction to that which Rafe had taken earlier. I wonder if I'll ever see them again? she mused, as the apparently ill-assorted pair vanished into the trees. It felt like an ending.

## 35

A few minutes later, Rafe reappeared with two of the footmen, and a gardener pushing a large wheelbarrow. Sophie was not astonished to see Lady Wyverne following them, in a state of some dishevelment, as though she had not finished dressing when the shocking news of her husband's collapse had reached her. As she hovered around the footmen, utterly ignoring Rafe and Sophie and berating the young men shrilly for carelessness, Lord Wyverne, groaning, was loaded into the wheelbarrow. It was surely the most undignified form of transport he had ever experienced in his life, but there was no alternative, and at last the strange little procession headed down the hill towards the house. The Marquess showed no signs of fully regaining his senses.

Kemp was waiting at the foot of the steps, and supervised William and James as they carried their master up into the house. 'I will make sure they dispose His Lordship suitably in his bedchamber,' he told Rafe, his face perfectly expressionless. 'The doctor has been sent for, my lord.'

'Thank you, Kemp.' They were like a pair of automata, and Sophie could barely wait for the cortege to make its stately way up the stairs to hiss urgently, 'What if he comes to his senses and tells anyone – tells her? You could still be in danger if he reveals that you had any part in the theft.'

'*We* could be in danger, you mean. I'll face him down, Sophie, and I am not anxious about the outcome, but I think you should temporarily rid yourself of the Stella as soon as possible, hide it somewhere secure. I intend to say, if Wyverne tries to implicate us, that he is delirious and talking nonsense. He's suffered a blow to the head, that much is plain. Who but he would believe I had anything to do with robbing him? It's a crazy idea. And everyone knows he is obsessed beyond all reason with the theft; I'll imply it's turned his brain.'

'I hope you're right, and yes, I'll do that now,' she said. 'Better the doctor does not set eyes on me. I'll go and see your grand-mother afterwards, tell her what's happened.'

'The truth?'

'I don't see why not. The jewels are gone now. I'll ask her if she wants to know, and tell her everything if she says she does. It's her affair too, after all.'

'I'll see you later,' he said, regarding her with a dark, steady gaze. 'Thank you for staying, my dear.'

'It's not the time to talk about it, Rafe, and you know I will have to go soon enough. But I'll be here tonight. I promise I won't leave you without saying goodbye.'

Lord Drake nodded silently and went to wait in the library, and Sophie made her way slowly upstairs to the Dowager's cham-ber. She found the old lady sitting alone, gazing into space, and the expression on Sophie's face must have alerted her to the fact that something extraordinary had occurred, for she said, '*Enfin!* I perceive matters have come to a point, and I need no longer pretend that everything is as usual. Tell me, child, quickly, what has occurred. Is my grandson safe and unharmed?'

'He is,' Sophie told her quickly. 'There is no need to be the least concerned for him. Lord Wyverne is unwell – has fallen – but the doctor has been sent for. I don't believe it can be anything terribly serious, but I do not know for a certainty.'

'Fallen?' repeated Delphine sceptically. 'I insist that you tell me everything.'

'You're quite sure you want to know? If your son should ask you...'

The old lady made a rude noise. 'I've been lying to men for more than eighty years; I should be reasonably proficient at it by now. Everything!'

So Sophie told her – the meeting with Nate, the handover of the jewels, Lord Wyverne's sudden appearance and their confrontation with him, Fred's attack on him. Everything. When she was done, the Dowager murmured, 'My God, Nathaniel Smith – I never thought to hear that name again. You know him well, I collect?'

'He saved me,' Sophie said. 'When I was at my lowest ebb, after my mother and my brother died and I could see only one way to keep myself alive, he rescued me from making that choice, or a worse one. He didn't do it out of compassion, or at any rate compassion was only a small part of it – he thought I could be of use to him. And I have been. But I must still be grateful for what he did. I hate to think where I would be if he hadn't come to see me. Dead, in all likelihood.'

'My dear child, then I can only be very glad he did. Do you think the whole scheme of using you against Wyverne sprang fully formed into his mind when he first met you and realised who you were and what had been taken from you?'

'I have been wondering that. It's possible. But that was eight years ago – it's a long time to wait for a plan to mature.'

'Not if you've already waited more than half a lifetime for

revenge, I suppose. And Wyverne was excessively cruel to him when Nathaniel was a boy. Tormented him, really. I can't say he doesn't deserve what's happened to him.'

'You knew the identities of your husband's natural children?' Sophie asked hesitantly, remembering that Rafe had said there were many of them.

'It was impossible not to know. He flaunted them in my face, in this very house. It was very hurtful at first, when I came here as a bride, before I hardened my heart against him and decided that I could also amuse myself. What is the expression in English about the goose and the gander? It is the same in French: *sauce bonne pour l'oie, est bonne pour le jars*. But all that is ancient history. How distressed I was to know him constantly unfaithful, long ago, and how little it matters now! And Nathaniel was always the cleverest of his brats, and the one he was closest to as a result, which is no doubt why my son loathed him so much. I'm not surprised that he has made a success of his life, albeit in a rather unorthodox manner.' She fixed Sophie with a beady eye, and said, 'Rafael is nothing like that, you know. Nothing like his father, and nothing like his grandfather. If that is a worry for you, you may dismiss it from your mind. You will say I am partial, and no doubt I am, but nonetheless what I say is true. He is very far from being a rake. The woman who marries him will not suffer as I suffered, nor will his children, for that matter.'

Sophie said in a constricted voice, 'His friends must be glad to know it. But it's no concern of mine.'

'My dear child!' said the old lady, laughing. 'I may be old, but I still have eyes!'

'Perhaps I'm a female rake,' Sophie persisted. 'A rakess, a jade. Perhaps I've coupled with half the men in London. Perhaps I was Nate's mistress, and still am. I might have half a dozen of his baseborn children by now. Have you thought of that? You think you know me, but perhaps you don't.'

'Nathaniel must have changed a great deal from the young man who left here nigh on forty years ago, in that case,' said the Dowager with a smile. 'If you wish to shock me, you will have to find a more effective way. And I am not so easily deceived, in any case. I dare say you have had a lover or two, before now – but why should you not, when your life was wrenched so violently from its course and you must have thought there was no going back? I am not the woman to deny a person comfort in their sorrow. I would not be such a hypocrite.'

'There is no going back,' said Sophie. 'You are so far right, madame.'

'No,' said Delphine. 'But there is going forward.'

Sophie had no answer for that.

## 36

There was not to be an occasion for Sophie to have further discussion with Lord Drake that day, whether she wished for it or not. Events of a dramatic and unexpected nature overtook them and kept them apart.

When the doctor arrived and examined his still insensible patient, he took a very serious view of the situation, stating it as his opinion that Lord Wyverne must have suffered a serious paralytic stroke, brought on by the shock of falling and injuring his head. The Marquess was a man of intemperate habits and advanced years, so that such a thing could hardly be a surprise to anyone acquainted with him. He never regained consciousness, lying in a coma for several hours before he apparently underwent another crisis, as a result of which he died later that afternoon. The doctor had had little doubt of the outcome from the start. The Marquess never spoke again, and never had a chance to tell anyone how gravely he believed he had been betrayed. His last words, as was perhaps appropriate given how he had lived, were those angry obscenities he spat out at Sophie before Fred, his brother's lover and faithful companion, knocked him down.

Sophie stayed with the Dowager during this time, and Marchand, who travelled to and fro with the news as long as there was news to be had, remained with them once the death announcement had been issued. During the hours of waiting Sophie had rather tentatively asked if the old lady would like to be carried down to say farewell to her son, though he was insensible and would not know of it, but she had shaken her head. 'We have passed beyond that, I think. It would be ridiculous to think that he cared for me, or would welcome me at his side. And his wife is with him. I should only disturb her. She would upbraid me, or say something cutting – it is her nature to be combative, and that is hardly likely to change now, under such strain – and I might in response to her provocation utter words that I should afterwards regret. It is better not. It must always be unseemly to fall into a heated exchange in such a situation. And who knows what a person can hear in such an extremity, on his deathbed, though he might show no signs of it? No. I shall let him pass in peace.'

'Do you think they loved each other, madame?' Sophie asked now. It was ridiculous to attempt to speak of anything else, to raise some trivial topic of conversation, but it also seemed excessively impertinent to ask the Dowager how she herself was feeling now that she knew her son and last living child was dead.

'I have sometimes asked myself that question,' Delphine said. Her manner was grave, but if she felt deep sadness she was not displaying it as far as Sophie could see; no doubt Marchand knew her better and that was why she was here with her mistress, though she was sitting in the corner occupied with some stitchery and contributed nothing to the conversation. 'Or at least, I have wondered if she loved him, since I am not sure it was in his nature to love but only to possess. It would be so easy to say no, a woman of that kind cannot feel the softer emotions, but thinks always and only of her worldly advantage. I do not know if this is true. They have been married fifteen years, and were lovers before that. I would imagine that must count for something. But I am sure she would not welcome any condolences from me, nor from you for that matter.'

'I wouldn't presume,' said Sophie drily. 'What will happen to her now?'

'I very much hope Wyverne has provided for her with some generosity, and she will be able to leave, to live in some place more congenial to her. It's my belief she's always hated the country and came here only because he demanded it of her. But that is all done with now. There's no dower house on the estate, and she would scarcely care to live alone in one of the follies – the Corinthian Arch, perhaps, or the Gothic Tower! Nor would Rafe wish her to stay here, and he is in charge now, thank heaven. I hope he will not be confronted with the disagreeable necessity of requiring her explicitly to leave when a little time has passed. She will be much happier setting herself up in some watering-place and queening it over people who do not realise that society had never received her and never will, even though she can call herself Marchioness. Perhaps she will marry again quite swiftly. One can only wish her happy, and privately wonder what next will befall her.'

'You will no longer be obliged to endure dinner parties with her, at least.'

'It will be a great weight off my mind, my dear. And the maids will no longer have to be locked away for their own safety when parties are held. Such parties as they were! I'm sure everyone at Wyverne will breathe easier and sleep more soundly tonight. It is a terrible thing, truly...' she said a little fretfully, her thin hands moving in agitation, her manner as much as her words showing some hint of what she was feeling at last. 'My child – my firstborn son, whom I dearly loved once – has died, and yet I know that all anyone can feel or should feel is relief. I feel relief myself, now he can do no more damage in the world. Poor Gervais, what an epitaph: "He can do no more damage now." I think I shall go to bed, Marchand, if you would be so good.'

'Goodnight, madame,' Sophie said, and kissed her soft cheek, the closest thing to condolences she felt able to give.

The old lady took her hand and held it tightly for a second. 'Goodnight, my child. I'm glad that you are here. I know Rafe is too. He should not be alone at such a time.'

Sophie went up to Rafe's empty chamber, though she did not undress. She had an odd reluctance to be anywhere else in the house. It was strange to think that this shabby, comfortable room, furnished with cast-offs and hidden up a back stair, was the refuge of the man who was now master of this whole huge building, and all the lakes and fields, farms and villages for miles around. He'd been a lonely little boy who'd hidden away here, but now suddenly he owned so much, and was responsible for the well-being of so many people. She knew he took this charge with the utmost seriousness, and she could only imagine with what mixed emotions he would be contemplating taking up his heritage. Would he be willing or even able fully to embrace it, or would it always be a burden and a reminder of past unhappiness? She knew he had his own much smaller house a few miles away, which presumably was his real home and had been for years; would he want to go back there for the comfort it would bring, or would he wish to live here, or feel he must even if he did not wish to, and bring his young siblings with him to breathe life to all the chilly grandeur?

One thing was certain: there was no place for her in this palace. Not now. He might wish there could be, she knew he did, and in sober truth so did she, but she could not believe it to be true. The world was as it was. He'd not keep his mistress openly here, flaunting her in the face of the world as even his father had not done, and she could not consent to be hidden away like a guilty secret, nor was he the man to ask it of her. Any other role for her – she refused even to allow the word to enter her mind – would be impossible. Perhaps he'd have realised this for himself by now, and perhaps he'd signify as much by leaving her to sleep here alone for the first time. What an unmistakeable message that would be, so eloquently expressive of the new order of things without so much as a word being spoken: Lord Drake had toyed for a while with the idea of loving her; the new Lord Wyverne now could not.

Or if he came to her tonight, it might only be because he was too good and decent to leave her waiting and wondering, though he must know their time was over. She wanted him to come, she desperately wanted one last night in his arms, though she knew it was weak to want it, and illogical too. She'd said herself that they had no future together. How could she possibly be hurt if he too acknowledged as much?

Having spent hours awaiting his arrival – was that a noise on the stairs? – Sophie finally accepted that he wasn't coming, and, fully clothed, fell at last into an uneasy sleep on top of the cover-let, although it was still early. The day had seemed to last forever, and she was exhausted by the emotion of it.

Downstairs, one Marquess of Wyverne lay cold in his coffin and the other sat in the library with the Reverend Mr Venables. There had been a great deal to arrange, and though Rafe would greatly prefer to be upstairs, holding his love in his arms, he'd only just emerged from a prolonged and very trying interview with his stepmother. Simon had kindly stayed till this was over – he'd presumably been able to hear a fair proportion of it through the closed door – and seemed to feel that he was giving his friend comfort. The new Marquess didn't quite have the energy to send him away. He wanted him to go – he just couldn't in his fatigue find a way of expressing the idea that wouldn't offend the decent old fellow. It was good that his friend was here, and he appreciated the thought – he'd just rather be with Sophie.

Mr Venables was plainly in a state of some unease. His mind was troubled, and his pleasant, open face creased with worry. In his view, it ill-suited a Christian, let alone a gentleman in holy orders, to be pleased that someone, a soul nominally under his care, had died. That would be most unseemly. It was traditional wisdom, of course, to say that the dear departed were going to a better place, and the rector had often employed this notion to console the bereaved. But he hadn't quite been able to bring himself to mention as much to Rafe. Simon cherished a strong private conviction that the late Marquess was going to a much worse place, was probably already there, roasting on a turning spit in the infernal regions, which ought to make his passing a matter for regret. Or ought it? Had he not merely received his just deserts? There was always a place in God's house for a repentant sinner – but it seemed highly unlikely that Lord Wyverne of all people had been the least penitent.

It was all very confusing. How did one, whether as a priest or in the guise of an ordinary human friend, console a man for the death of a parent he'd loathed, and with good reason, and explicitly wished dead? Nothing in his previously uneventful career had prepared Simon for this dilemma.

'Would you like me to go up and speak to your dear grandmother?' he asked rather desperately, as a reaction to Rafe's brooding silence. It had never been entirely clear to Mr Venables if the Dowager was officially a member of the Church of England, and if she wasn't it was probably, at the age of almost a hundred, too late for her to change. He was also slightly frightened of her, but he shouldn't let that deter him from doing his duty to a mother who had lost her son.

'Thank you for the thought, Simon,' said Lord Wyverne with a weary but charming smile. 'But I'm sure she will be asleep, as she tires so easily now. And if she isn't, Marchand or Miss Delavallois will be with her.'

'I'm sure they will give her greater comfort than I could.'

Rafe agreed with him with rather more emphasis and promptness than was strictly necessary. Ignoring this, Simon asked, 'What do you mean to do?' One must make allowances for persons suffering under strong emotions; the man had just learned of the death of his father.

'That's a very broad question. I have a great deal to do, so much that it makes my head ache, but you have reminded me of my duty,' Rafe said, rising to his feet somewhat abruptly. 'I should go and check on my grandmother myself, and see if she is in fact awake. I do not mean to be discourteous, and I am very grateful for your presence, but I haven't had an opportunity to speak to her since...'

'Of course,' said Mr Venables, rising hastily also. 'Shall I see you tomorrow afternoon, then, to finish making the funeral arrangements?'

'Yes,' said Rafe, 'although it must be as simple as possible. It's all very well to talk of his standing in the world, but I think we would make ourselves ridiculous with anything but the briefest of services. I presume the last time my father set foot in a church was at his wedding. One of his weddings. I must go into black for the ceremony, I suppose, but I warn you, Simon, I will not be observing the rituals and conventions of mourning in any other fashion.' He saw unhappiness etched upon his friend's face and said rather impatiently, 'You know what happened here last week

– was it only last week? Do you really think that a man who displays his wife in such a manner deserves...?'

'You may very well be right!' Mr Venables said, blushing, and at last he took his leave.

Rafe sighed, and mounted the stairs.

## 37

The new Marquess found Sophie asleep on his bed, still wearing the demure grey gown she had put on – it felt like months ago – to go to their meeting with Nate Smith. Uncle Nate Smith. No wonder she was exhausted. It was the longest day he'd ever experienced. He'd known many weeks that had passed more quickly.

He hoped she'd dined with his grandmother; she'd know if Delphine had gone to her rest, he supposed. If the Dowager was still up, he would need to go and speak with her this evening, see how she did, even though he had not the least desire to leave Sophie's comforting presence.

It seemed a shame to disturb her, but he must. 'Sophie,' he said gently, and reached out and touched her cheek. She woke quickly, and lay gazing up at his face, her expression undecipherable to him. He thought she was pleased to see him, perhaps a little surprised, but he couldn't be sure.

She sat up, and said, 'I'm so sorry, Rafe.' But she didn't touch him, and he so wished she would. 'I know you weren't at all close to your father, but to lose him so suddenly must still be a shock. How are you feeling?'

'I don't know,' he said, realising the truth of it. 'I've been so occupied, I have not had time to think. And if I had, I'd still be in sad confusion, as was poor Simon Venables, who's been here in his capacity as parish priest, but scarcely knew what to say to me. I'm sure there are words of consolation he would in the normal run of things give to anyone, prince or pauper, who has lost a parent, but none of them seem to apply to my situation. I hated him, Sophie, and I've been wishing him dead since I was fifteen. I can't put on a grieving face now. I won't go into mourning as if he were a normal father.'

She did put out her hand now to take his, and he held it, grateful for her warmth. 'Is there anybody who will expect you to?' she asked. 'Do you have uncles, or relatives of that nature, who might come here and make themselves disagreeable if you do not behave as they think fit?'

'No,' he said. 'No uncles or aunts still living on the Wyverne side. There are cousins only, most of them much older than me, and they won't expect to be invited to the funeral, and probably wouldn't come if I did ask them. My grandmother had another son, and two older daughters, but none of them had anything to do with Wyverne for years – you scarcely need to wonder why – and their children have continued the estrangement with great enthusiasm. It's possible they believe the rumours about me, too – I cannot say, I barely know them. I do have aunts and uncles and cousins from my mother's family, with whom I am in contact, but they would be horrified to be invited, I think, and I can hardly blame them. The Wyverne name,' he finished wearily, 'does not carry a great deal of lustre, you must know.'

'That can begin to change now,' she said. 'Will you call your brother back from Oxford?'

'I've written to him, and to our sister Amelia. If he wishes to come, he may, of course, though she I am sure will not, with her cousin's wedding imminent. But I wouldn't think to insist on Charlie's presence. I shouldn't imagine he has set eyes on Wyverne five times since his mother died. At least my worries for the children's future are at an end now – nobody can question my right to have a care for them. And he can no longer hurt them, with his indifference or in any other, worse manner. We shall not have that concern hanging over Amelia's come-out next year.'

'That's what your grandmother said,' she told him. '"He can do no more harm" – a sad epitaph.'

'You have been with her all afternoon.' She nodded. 'Thank you. I'm glad you were there when I could not be. I had a deal of trouble keeping Rosanna away from her; I didn't think she would have enjoyed that, nor should she be obliged to endure it. How is she?'

'Subdued,' Sophie said. 'Sorry that she is not sorrier, just as you are, and sorry too that her son's life should have come to this. Relieved, and perhaps a little guilty that she is. She's gone to bed, hours ago – she was understandably tired. Marchand will stay with her tonight, I think. She was a little exercised, though, about what would happen to his widow, where she will go. You're quite right, she doesn't want to see her.'

'I didn't want to see her myself,' he said, still holding her hand. 'But obviously I had to.'

'What will she do?'

'I had not known, not being on such terms of confidence with... with my father, what provision he had made for her future. I hadn't seen the will, knew nothing of its contents apart from the fact that most of the property is entailed, thank God, and I did not quite have the heart today to look for his copy of the document. But she experienced no such qualms, and straight away laid her hands on it among his papers so that she could show it to me. He had made reasonable arrangements for her, which knowing his character he might not have done, but he did not give her a life interest in the Brook Street house. This she had apparently expected, claims she was promised, and as a result she is simply furious.'

'Would it have been usual for him to do so? I confess I don't know how such things generally work.'

He shrugged. 'Probably it would have been. The fact that they didn't have children together makes a difference, and – being who she is – she had no father or brother to insist on such matters on her behalf. There were no marriage settlements in the normal sense, and of course she brought no dowry. But he has ensured that she will have enough to live on in some comfort. Whether she is capable of managing within her means is another question entirely. I foresee a future in which I am obliged publicly to repudiate her debts. And of course she has few jewels to pawn now.'

'I can't feel guilty about that.'

'I wouldn't expect you to. I think she knew – she all but admitted as much today in her anger – precisely how the baubles she adorned herself with came into his possession. They were already long married, let us not forget, when Wyverne took the Stella Rosa from your father. I cannot doubt he boasted of it to her. There are probably other similar stories we do not know, and now never shall. She does not deserve our pity, or anyone's. She tried – my God, Sophie, with her husband lying dead in his bed, not yet cold, she tried to seduce me again. As if after all these years and all we witnessed the other night I could possibly want her. Jesus!' He put his head in his hands, realising suddenly how close to collapse he was.

'Let's go to bed,' said Sophie. 'I don't think you need to speak about this any more. You must be exhausted.' He raised his head and looked at her, and something she must have seen in his face made her move to his side and set about undressing him, not with any amorous intention but in a matter-of-fact way, as if he were a child who needed the assistance. In that moment, he found he did. She removed his coat, waistcoat and shirt, and he sat passively and let her do it. When she sank to her knees and began to pull off his boots, it was very much unlike the time she'd done the same thing before, though the image of her naked at his feet would always be seared on his brain. He stood, once she had set them aside, and she began to unbutton his breeches fall. But that, suddenly, was different.

Rafe put his hand on hers. 'Sophie!' he grated out. It seemed he didn't need to say anything else. They were kissing now, clinging to each other in a sort of frenzied desperation that came from both of them, not just from him. Their weariness was forgotten in the sudden mutual need that possessed them. He undid her gown with such urgency that several of the tiny buttons were ripped off, and she urged him on as he stripped her of her undergarments, tearing another chemise in his haste. When at last they were both naked, save for her stockings, they fell onto the bed, embracing, lips locked, her hands tight on his back, his on her buttocks. His hard thigh was between her legs, their bodies pressed together, close as they could be without joining.

He kissed his way down her throat to her breasts, and she fixed her hands deep in his dark hair as he worshipped them with his lips and tongue. 'I want to be inside you,' he groaned against her hot skin, 'as I have never been. Will you take me, if I promise not to spend there? Do you think you might want that too, my love?'

'Yes,' she said with utter certainty. 'Now, Rafe. Do it now!'

He moved over her and she opened herself to him, the sudden rush of pure, fierce sensation as he thrust into her wetness making them both cry out. She locked her heels into his buttocks and they moved together, and the sheer rightness of it made him want to weep, and to forget his promise to her and know the glorious release of spilling inside her as they came together. But he did not. When his orgasm was so close he could scarcely bear it, he pulled out from her and spent himself on her belly in a couple of powerful thrusts. He allowed himself a brief moment of sweet oblivion, his face buried in her neck, murmuring broken endearments, and then he moved down to lose himself in another manner, licking and sucking at her delicious secret places and letting her waves of pleasure engulf him until the last spasm died away and left them both gasping.

He lay with his head on her belly for a while and neither of them spoke – he wasn't sure he still had the ability – and then he dragged himself to his feet and went to get water to wash her, and very tenderly to untie her garters and peel off her stockings. It was dark now, they'd lit no candles, and he could not see what was written on her face in the fitful moonlight that came in through the open window, nor did he know what his own expression would have revealed to her if she could have seen him. They didn't tidy away the scattered clothes, and they fell into bed and let sleep claim them, wordless, spooned together, his hand on her damp skin and her hand covering his. He drank in her scent – not perfume, just Sophie, like a drug to him, an addiction. He could still taste her on his lips, and his last thought before he sank into slumber and left this longest of days behind him was, I cannot lose her. I cannot. Nothing in this world means anything to me if she is not here to share it.

## 38

Sophie woke early the next morning, with Rafe still sleeping deeply beside her, inevitably close as he was a large man and the bed was not roomy. She was glad he was not yet awake, torn as she was between conflicting desires and emotions, foremost among which was her concern for him. Last night he'd needed her, she knew, and this day would not be any easier, nor any of the days that followed until his father was laid to rest. That might at least provide a little relief. It would be a heartless, cruel thing, to leave him to bear all this alone when she could give him the comfort he could not find elsewhere. Nor did she wish, at this time of all times, to be so selfish as to force a conversation about their impossible future. It would be unconscionable to demand he set aside all the hurt, regret and useless anger she knew he was experiencing at this sudden and equivocal loss and insist on talking about herself, as though her feelings were more important than his, or even as important as his, when plainly just now they couldn't be. It was worse than that, though. Even if they did speak of their situation, perhaps at his instigation, was she going to look at him in his current vulnerability and lie to him?

Because she loved him – she had admitted as much to herself in a moment of unwelcome clarity when she'd almost allowed him, begged him, to come inside her, regardless of the potential consequences. She did not want to love anybody, and him least of all. There were a thousand good reasons why she should not. But none of them counted for anything in the face of the undeniable truth. If they had the painful conversation, as eventually they must, and in the course of it he asked her if she loved him, which in his mind would be the only question that mattered, could she really betray him, really lie and say she did not?

She couldn't go, not now at any rate. She couldn't stay. She couldn't speak. She couldn't remain silent, not forever. She was stuck.

Rafe stirred, and instinctively reached for her, and she allowed herself to be drawn into his embrace, where she so much wanted to be, and where she should not be. But it was so seductive... He lay with his head on her shoulder and she smoothed back his sleep-disordered locks with loving fingers. She wasn't leaving him today, nor yet tomorrow. She'd wait until after the funeral, at least. Then she'd pack up her few possessions and go, the next day, after she'd said a painful goodbye. She might as well enjoy – that wasn't the word, but she could think of no other – this short time that was all they'd have together. She wouldn't hold herself back from loving him, nor pepper their conversation with mean little remarks meant to show that none of this was permanent. That would be a low trick – as if she could later say to him, I never made you any promises, remember I did not. No, while she was here, she'd be here fully. Though she would try to prevent herself from telling him she loved him. It was true, but it could do no good. It was not possible, she thought as she held him, to insure oneself, or anyone else, against heartbreak. There didn't seem to be any entirely good choices.

'What must you do today, Rafe?' she asked him.

'A great many aggravating things, when I would rather be here with you,' he said drowsily. 'The lawyer, Mr Barnaby, who drew up Wyverne's last testament will be driving over from Oxford in response to the note I sent by messenger. I've seen the document, of course, thanks to Rosanna, but I'll need to go through it with him. Simon Venables is coming back this afternoon to finish the arrangements for the funeral. I must write a notice for insertion in the newspapers, I suppose – I wrote a prodigious number of letters yesterday, but not those ones. And I must speak to the estate mason about the carving on the stone, so that he can begin on it. I'm not sure how long such things take, or if it can be put in place directly. But I'd like to get it done, and he will know.'

'I had not thought of that. What will you have it say, and where will he be buried?'

'There is a place for him in the graveyard of the church here, beside my mother and his second wife. It will be a plain slab to cover the grave, with his name and dates and nothing more. He had designed no grandiose monument for himself, rather to my relief, and I am not inclined to perpetuate any untruths in stone. No conventional pieties or expressions of affection and regret that nobody feels. Just the bare facts, and let future Wyvernes make what they will of it.'

Future Wyvernes, she thought: his children and his grandchildren. But not mine. 'It sounds a full enough day for you,' she said. 'We should get up.'

'Yes, I fear so. But most important of all, I must see my grandmother. Will you come with me, Sophie?'

'Would she not rather you were alone together? But I will come, of course, if you think I am wrong in that.'

He considered, lying back on the pillow and looking up at her. 'You may be right. Not because she does not care for you or trust you, but just because it cannot be easy for her, this situation we find ourselves in, and she may feel obliged to put a brave face on it for your sake if you are present, when it must be better that she does not, and tells me exactly how she feels. We have no secrets from you, my dear – it's not that.'

'You would be entitled to them if you did,' she told him.

'I disagree. But we cannot speak of this now. And it seems I must leave you alone again today, for which I am sorry. At least I can reassure you that you are free to walk where you please. One of the many things I did yesterday was seek out the men Wyverne had employed to patrol the estate, pay them off and send them on their way. The ones Mr Smith had bribed or otherwise suborned had already taken their leave with extreme promptness. This was one of the many things Rosanna upbraided me for – she is furious that I have no intention to make any further search for the jewels. I expect I haven't heard the last of her grievances, and that she will have thought of more overnight, but I hope you at least can manage to avoid her. Let's go and have breakfast. This is not a day I can face without sustenance, and I can reassure you that it is her habit always to take breakfast in her own chambers. She will not disturb us.'

It would be the first time they'd eaten together in the public parts of the mansion, apart from that appalling dinner party; all the other meals they had shared had been taken in the privacy of this room and he had brought them to her on a tray. She could hardly blame him in his distraction for wanting simply to sit down and eat at table in the house he now owned. It was a less straightforward matter than it might appear, though. It might be more than a little awkward for her, to be waited on in formal fashion by the servants for the first time since she'd been revealed as his mistress. And she didn't want him to think it set any kind of precedent for a future together. But this was the nature of the trap she found herself in, and she would not flinch at it. She agreed.

A short while later, then, Sophie sat in the breakfast room – a light, airy chamber that looked out across the lawns to the lakes – and poured Rafe his coffee. There was a bizarre normality about the domestic scene. They were attended by James and William, and if either of them had any thoughts about her new and most ambiguous situation, they kept them to themselves, and off their faces. They were impassive, and so, as far as she could manage it, was she.

They were just about to rise from the table to go their separate ways when the door opened, and a young gentleman in travelling dress burst in, followed by a plainly scandalised butler who had, it seemed, tried and failed to announce him in a normal manner. At a glance from Rafe, Kemp shooed out the footmen and closed the door firmly behind them and himself, so that the three of them were left alone.

'Good day, Charlie!' he said, rising and embracing the young man. 'I'm glad to see you, though I had not looked for your arrival quite so soon. Miss Delavallois, may I present my brother, Lord Charles? Charles, Miss Delavallois is our grandmother's companion. Grand-mère is well, Charlie, but does not join us for breakfast.'

It was smoothly done, thought Sophie, and gave a spurious air of regularity to what could not be other than an unusual situation. Gentlemen and unmarried ladies did not spend time alone, whether at breakfast or in any other circumstance. But then, it could not be said that Rosanna's presence would have lent a greater respectability to the scene, given her reputation and the rumours that swirled about her and her stepson. Matters in this house had strayed very far from the norm, and her presence as Rafe's mistress would not help to get them back to it.

She greeted Lord Charles, and thought as she did so how little he resembled his half-brother, save in colouring and in the unusual dark blue shade of his eyes, which seemed to be a Wyverne trait. He was a young man of medium height and slight build, and, like so many young gentlemen at the universities and elsewhere, he appeared to be addicted to dandyism: his shirt points were alarmingly high, his coat of an exaggerated cut with peaked shoulders and a nipped-in waist, and his waistcoat was bright enough to make one blink. It was odd to see a countenance that so resembled the late Marquess's – and for that matter also bore a fair likeness to that of Mr Nathaniel Smith – and yet was so youthfully ingenuous, and bore an expression of somewhat vacuous amiability.

'You said in your note that you were writing to the old man's lawyer after your screed to me,' Lord Charles informed his sibling, sinking into a chair and helping himself to a cup of coffee. 'You told me you wrote in haste so that you could send both letters to Oxford by the same messenger. Aha! I thought. So I went round to see him at the crack of dawn and found him just setting off here in his old-fashioned chaise, and got a ride with him. Thought it was damn-dashed cunning of me, but soon wished I hadn't – devilish dull fellow to spend a few hours with. But here I am, all right and tight.'

'Where is Mr Barnaby?' asked Rafe. 'I must go and see him.'

'Kemp put him in the library,' Charles said, his words some-what muffled, as he had loaded up a plate for himself and set to it with a will. 'The old stick didn't think it decent to interrupt the Marquess at his breakfast. Devilish odd to think of you as a Marquess now, I must say, Rafe!'

'It must always have been so eventually,' said his brother drily, 'unless you'd planned to put a period to my existence by some cunning means and take on the title yourself. Which you still could, I suppose. If that is your desire, I beg you not to delay, and then *you* can have the unalloyed joy of dealing with our revered stepmother and all the funeral arrangements, my young cub.'

Lord Charles laughed uproariously. 'As if I would think of such a thing! You are the most complete hand, Rafe!'

'Charlie, I must leave you to what I assume is your second breakfast,' the new Marquess said, rising to his feet once more.

'Third,' said his brother indistinctly. 'Travelling makes me hungry. Had a bite or two when we changed horses. But nothing to touch the food here, naturally.'

Rafe smiled. 'Naturally. Perhaps you will go up and visit Grand-mère once you are done with it; she has seen you so rarely that it must be a surprise and a pleasure to her, and a sign that life at Wyverne is changing for the better. Mademoiselle Delavallois, I hope I shall see you later, and that you pass a pleasant day.'

'Thank you, my lord,' she murmured. 'I hope your duties do not prove too onerous.' She could say no more, with Lord Charles present.

Rafe was almost at the door before he turned back and said expressionlessly, 'Charlie, do try if you can to avoid being alone with Lady Wyverne – with your stepmother. We've spoken of this, you may recall.'

'Anything you say, old fellow,' replied his brother cheerfully, chewing on one of the famous Wyverne sausages with which he had piled his plate.

'He seems to think she's going to leap on me like a wild beast from the menagerie the minute she gets me alone,' the young man said as soon as the door had closed. 'He may be right, of course. Makes a fellow dashed nervous, to tell the truth.'

'I expect he has his reasons,' Sophie replied cautiously.

'You seem to be deep in my brother's confidence, I must say. Have you been here long, ma'am? Thought m'grandmother had another companion last time I sneaked in to see her. Elderly, dusty-looking female. Hard to keep track, though, I admit.'

'I've been at Wyverne just a few weeks,' said Sophie. 'But it's been an eventful time. It feels as though it's been much longer.'

'I'll wager it does. Not...' He coughed, and Sophie thought he was embarrassed, unless it was the sausage. 'Not what you'd call a respectable household, this, is it? Not with m'father and his lady-bird playing off their tricks. Even at Oxford we hear rumours – fellows tease me awfully about the goings-on here. Is she thinking of leaving, do you know? Because I'd imagine Rafe will want to come and settle at Wyverne, and have us with him, m'sister and me. Get us all here together with our grandmother. But he can't do that, not while that woman's under this roof. Amelia makes her come-out next year, you know. I can't claim to be awake upon all suits, like Rafe, but even I know that an innocent chit of seventeen shouldn't be spending any time with a woman like that. Not at all the thing, set all the tabbies gossiping. Come to think of it, not right that you should, either. You're not an ape-leader like the old lady's other companions.'

'I don't know anything about the matter,' said Sophie a little stiffly, acutely uncomfortable and refusing to address the matter of her own status. If only she'd had the strength to leave before Lord Charles arrived, as she should have realised he was bound to. 'If Lady Wyverne has plans, I'm not sure she's shared them with your brother. And he can't put her belongings out in the street, after all. Not that there's a street here to put them in, but you understand my meaning. Your stepmother may be... what-ever she is, but your father only died yesterday. It's not been twenty-four hours, my lord.'

'I'd much rather you called me Charlie,' said the irrepressible young nobleman. '"My lord" is such a mouthful. As is your surname, for that matter. I can just about say it, probably, but I wouldn't care to have to spell it, damme if I would, not if you held a pistol to my head. I'm only a quarter French, y'know.'

She smiled, but said, 'I do take your point, but I can't possibly—'

But she was not to be allowed to finish her sentence, and once again her breakfast was to be interrupted, in a much more unwelcome manner this time. Lady Wyverne surged into the room, leaving the door wide open behind her and advancing towards Sophie at alarming speed. 'You!' she said in the carrying tones that must have served her so well upon the stage. She was dressed from head to foot in black, though her gown was considerably lower cut than was traditional for deep mourning in the daytime. Sophie stood, partly in a show of respect and partly because she thought it unwise to put herself at the disadvantage of being seated and vulnerable if the woman should actually attack her with a coffee pot or piece of flung crockery.

'Lady Wyverne,' she said levelly, though her heart was pounding. 'I must offer you my condolences on your great loss.' Their last encounter had been more than unfortunate, but Sophie had no intention of referring to it, certainly not in front of Rafe's brother.

'I don't want your condolences, you... you trollop!' Lord Charles had also risen at his stepmother's entrance, and was standing regarding her, his mouth half-open and an expression of fascinated terror upon his face. 'How dare you sit here, strumpet, and usurp my position?'

'I'm not,' said Sophie, abandoning civility as a lost cause and resuming her seat. 'I'm just having breakfast, and you must perceive that it's a round table. There's no head or foot.'

'I say, ma'am,' said Lord Charles with some courage, 'making all allowances for your sad situation, and adding my condolences, obviously, but it's not really fair, you know, to address this young lady in that manner. Assure you she's not usurping in the slightest. Just trying to eat her breakfast in peace.' As was I, his expression plainly added. 'Not trying to usurp anything myself, perish the thought, but may I pour you a cup of coffee?'

'Coffee?' bellowed Rosanna with loathing. There was no question; whatever her acting skills may or may not have been – and her theatrical career had not been particularly illustrious in the conventional sense – she'd have been heard with perfect clarity at the back of the cheapest seats and possibly even in the street outside the theatre. 'Coffee? I don't want coffee!'

'Tankard of ale?' suggested Lord Charles hopefully, keen to lower the emotional temperature of the room. 'Sausage? Several sausages?' He brandished one vigorously in illustration, since he hadn't put down his fork when he'd risen reluctantly to his feet.

The suggestion, combined with the gesture, was perhaps unfortunate, given Lady Wyverne's reputation, as was the fact that Sophie choked a little over her coffee, and turned the involuntary sound into a rather unconvincing cough. Rosanna's eyes narrowed. 'Are you mocking me, young man?'

His face was a picture of horror, and he appeared to have been struck speechless. 'I don't think he is, really,' said Sophie, trying very hard to keep her face straight. 'I believe Lord Charles is just wondering if you'd like to join him for breakfast.'

'That's it!' Lord Charles replied fervently, casting a wistful glance down at his abandoned plate.

'I am the Marchioness of Wyverne! I will not sit down to break bread with a woman of easy virtue who has no place here!'

This was undoubtedly intended as her exit line, but it would have had more impact if Sophie had not been laughing. 'Really?' she responded sweetly. 'Would you like me to tell your stepson exactly what took place in the Marble Saloon last week?'

Rosanna was visibly taken aback, but not for long. 'Would you like *me* to tell him what took place in his brother's secret little chamber three days ago?' she shot back. Lord Charles's eyes were jumping from one woman to the other, as at a tennis match. He still held his fork with its forgotten sausage.

Sophie had risen to her feet again now and the two women faced each other, eyes flashing, bosoms heaving, chiefly Lady Wyverne's due to her natural advantages, and Sophie was about to say something most regrettable when fate, in the shape of the new Marquess, intervened. Most unfortunately, he had an elderly gentleman at his heels who must be his legal adviser. This individual looked both shocked and enthralled.

'Lady Wyverne,' Rafe said icily. 'You have an exceedingly carrying voice. It penetrated to the library, where Mr Barnaby and I were in consultation. A respect for common decency has so far prevented me from saying this, madam, but I must say it now: you are no longer welcome here. I would be grateful if you would have your bags packed and make ready to leave as soon as possible. My carriage is at your disposal, and I will ensure you are able to sustain yourself comfortably until all legal matters are settled and your jointure paid to you. But it is time for you to go. And I will not,' he went on, stepping menacingly closer to her and forestalling the vituperative speech that she was quite plainly about to launch into, 'hear another vulgar word from you, least of all if it should be disgraceful, unwarranted and spiteful abuse of my affianced wife!'

## 39

Lady Wyverne was rendered mute by this announcement, and Rafe was not slow to press home his advantage. He said, 'My brother is perfectly well aware of how you comported yourself towards me when I was a boy in this house. Mr Barnaby may not be, but I am quite happy to tell him everything if you utter another syllable. And I am sure that he knows enough of your past history that he will not credit anything you have said in your malice to smear this young lady's good name.'

Mr Barnaby, who plainly knew which side his bread was buttered, murmured, 'Certainly not, my lord!'

'Good name?' began Lady Wyverne.

'If you say another word, madam, I will have the footmen seize you and throw you out by main force, and your baggage after you. It's possible they might enjoy it,' added Rafe thoughtfully. 'And I know I would.'

'You wouldn't dare!' Rosanna seethed.

'Oh, I assure you I would.'

Lady Wyverne took his measure with a glance, and, having

taken it, gathered up the shreds of her dignity, and marched out of the room, slamming the door sharply behind her.

Rafe said, 'I'm sorry, Sophie, that you should have had to endure such a scene. Mademoiselle de Montfaucon,' he told the lawyer with enormous assurance, 'is a young relative of my grand-mother's, who most kindly agreed to come to keep her company quite recently. And she swiftly became much more than that, to my grandmother and most of all to me. It can hardly be a surprise that Lady Wyverne should have taken an instant dislike to her, through no fault of her own, and lost no opportunity to abuse her. But she will do so no longer.'

'Quite, quite,' said Mr Barnaby. 'Most unfortunate, but I am delighted to be able to congratulate you, mademoiselle, my lord. Happier times, we may look forward to happier times, I am quite sure of it.'

Lord Charles set down his congealed sausage and his fork, which he had been clutching all this while, and stepped forward to congratulate his brother, and to kiss Sophie enthusiastically and meatily on the cheek. If he noticed that the name she now went by was not the one she'd been introduced to him under not half an hour since – and it was possible that he did not, since as he'd admitted he was neither awake upon all suits nor proficient in the French language – he showed no sign of it. 'Dashed glad to hear the news!' he said. 'Couldn't be happier for you both! Quite understand why you didn't mention it before, with the old b— with m'father having just given up the ghost.'

Sophie had no option but to accept these congratulations with becoming modesty. She'd lost her temper with Lady Wyverne, and had been lucky, she must admit, that Rafe had stepped in before they had really fallen to pulling caps. She couldn't blame him for what he had said, nor complain that he had been high-handed – it was hard to imagine what else he could have contrived to extricate them from the situation. She *was* a relative of the Dowager's, albeit a very distant one, and it was quite credible that, seeing Rafe's growing attraction to her, Rosanna might have been possessed with jealousy. Mr Barnaby was commendably discreet and respectable in appearance, but must know much more than he showed upon his lined face, given that he'd apparently worked for the late Marquess for some years. If indeed he was currently still labouring under the misapprehension that Rosanna had once been Rafe's mistress, no doubt Rafe would disabuse him firmly of the notion once they were alone again. And as for the spurious engagement, she supposed it could quietly be forgotten, once this crisis had passed. It must be.

And so she smiled, and said all that was proper, and presently found herself being taken up to the Dowager's chamber, at Lord Charles's insistence. 'I'm sure she'd like an opportunity to discuss the good news,' he said confidingly. Sophie admitted with perfect truth that they had not yet found an opportunity to share it with her. 'Well then, all the better! I'll go bail she'll be delighted to hear it – it's not right that she should be the last to know – and to be frank, I'm a little frightened of her, and would welcome the company.'

'Why, Lord Charles?' asked Sophie as they ascended the main staircase together. 'She's always been most kind to me.'

'It's the French,' he confided. 'Don't like to keep reminding her I don't speak it very well. Talks away in it nineteen to the dozen, at the drop of a hat. Know I ought to understand it, but don't. Dashed awkward.'

'She does speak English, doesn't she? I was told she didn't when I first came here, but that isn't true. I'm sure I've heard her speaking to the footmen.'

'She *can*, but she don't care to. Thinks French is better, or some such stuff. It might be, I suppose – not the man to say. But if she does drift off into it, you can always pull her back, or give me a hint if there's something that I should particularly have taken notice of.' Sophie agreed that she could easily do that, and they proceeded on in charity with each other. 'Another thing!' said Lord Charles with an air of having been struck with a delightful and novel thought. 'Now you're marrying Rafe, I don't have to try to get my tongue around your surname. Wouldn't care to attempt it, sounds completely different every time I hear it – just shows you how useless I am at the dashed language. But that's all fine and dandy – I can call you Sophie, and you can call me Charles. Quite the done thing now you're going to be m'sister.'

Sophie agreed rather hollowly that this was so, and by this time they had reached the Dowager's chamber door. They were commanded to enter, and found the old lady sitting *en déshabille*, taking a light breakfast with Marchand waiting solicitously on her. Sophie could hardly doubt that Delphine had already heard tell of much that had passed downstairs; the abigail's skills were close on supernatural in that regard. The old lady greeted her grandson with amused affection, slipping into French almost immediately and causing an expression of panic to appear upon his amiable features. He endured it for a while and then took advantage of the little disruption caused by Marchand's departure to interrupt the Gallic flow and say, 'Sophie – Miss – can't quite recall the name – has some happy news for you, ma'am. I'm sure Rafe would have come and told you himself, but he's tied up with that lawyer fellow and his papers, poor old boy.'

'Indeed?' said the Dowager, patting the satin sofa beside her and inviting Sophie to sit. 'I could perhaps guess what it is, but I shall not. What do you have to tell me, my dear child?' This was spoken in English, and Lord Charles looked quite delighted at the success of his stratagem.

Sophie, to her consternation, found herself blushing. 'Rafe –

Lord Wyverne – has done the honour of asking me, that is he has...'

Lord Charles came to her rescue. 'Dashed unpleasant scene downstairs, ma'am, Lady Wyverne was not herself, said some things... Anyone might be overset by hearing them. Was myself! But Rafe explained it all. Natural, I suppose, that she should not quite like to see herself displaced.' He seemed to realise that this statement might have unfortunate implications in the circumstances, and ploughed on heroically, 'Not that she was, of course. Not a bit of it. No. But yes! The long and the short of it is that Rafe and Miss, Miss Sophie are to be married! Isn't that the most capital tidings you ever heard, ma'am?'

'It certainly is,' said Delphine, smiling patiently. 'Although I must say I am not in the least surprised.'

'Ah, but you're a clever one,' said her grandson in honest admiration. 'Just like Rafe, come to think of it.'

'Perhaps, my dear boy, you might like to leave us two women alone to discuss the good tidings. In French,' the Dowager added, with a wicked twinkle, and Lord Charles was gone from the room as swiftly as was consistent with good manners.

'That foolish boy,' his fond grandmother said, in her native language, as the door closed behind him. 'Thank heaven his sister has his share of brains and more. A pretty young woman, or a plain one for that matter, cannot afford to be half as stupid as a young man of rank can. The world will not make allowances for her. She may pretend to be, of course – that is a quite different matter.'

'I hope you don't think I have manipulated Rafe into offering for me,' said Sophie desperately. 'Because honestly, I haven't. I'd have been gone from here yesterday if his father hadn't died so suddenly. I have not the least wish to marry him. I was astonished when he made that public declaration – but after what Lady

Wyverne had said, I quite see that he had no choice. He was thinking only of my reputation. I was grateful, but the truth is I have none.'

'My dear girl!' the Dowager said. 'Of course I was not referring to you. You have your own resources – and I am very glad that you do, or you would have perished along with the rest of your family. But I beg you, do not lie to me.'

'What do you mean, ma'am?'

'You said you have not the least wish to marry my grandson. But that's not true, is it?'

'No,' said Sophie sadly at last. 'No. Of course it isn't. I'm sorry. I should have said, I have not the least intention of marrying him. That would have been more accurate.'

'That's better. But will you tell me why?'

'It must surely be obvious.'

'Not to me. Indulge an old woman, if you please.'

'Lady Wyverne accused me of being Rafe's mistress.'

'Oh, dear,' said Delphine, preserving her calm. 'Did his brother notice? It can sometimes be hard to tell.'

'I think so, and Mr Barnaby was there too. I expect the servants heard, from the hall. She was very loud. But Rafe spun a convincing tale of her jealousy, said I was your relative, and they seemed to accept it.'

'That was very well done of him,' replied the Dowager in tones of satisfaction.

'But I *am* his mistress! And I had a lover before that,' Sophie said, determined to be understood.

'I have had several,' answered Delphine. 'My husband had many more – well, he was older, and he began it, otherwise I expect I might not have done. Or I might, perhaps. It is far too late to say.'

'It's not the same!'

'No, it is not, my dear, because you love him, don't you? And he loves you. This is exactly what I hoped would happen when I first recognised you.' She sounded excessively pleased with herself.

Sophie hiccupped, something between a laugh and a sob. 'It can't possibly be exactly what you hoped would happen! Lord Wyverne is dead, the jewels gone!'

The Dowager waved one thin hand, in the manner of one who says, Mere details. 'Tell me this,' she said. 'When that dreadful creature so accused you – and I cannot imagine how she had the gall – did Rafe merely say, "No, she is my affianced bride, madam! How dare you so defame her?" It seems most unlike him. He has a temper, you know, though he keeps it well in check. Think how stern he was at first when he disapproved of you.'

'He didn't,' confessed Sophie. 'He told her to pack her bags, and said that if she uttered another word he'd have the footmen throw her down the steps, and her luggage after her. He was most imperious, and she seemed alarmed. She left the room very swiftly, at any rate.'

Delphine clapped in delight. 'That's better than I could have hoped! We shall be comfortable here at last, and I can stop pretending I can't leave this room unless I am forced into it. And it is all thanks to you!'

Sophie shook her head. 'I can't see that. After all the scandal and uproar that Lord and Lady Wyverne provoked, I am quite sure Rafe will want to live a respectable life. He hated being the subject of gossip, I do know that. And I am not respectable. I know you are sorry for what happened, and want to make amends to me, but I assure there is no need to go to such extreme lengths as to marry your grandson to a common criminal.'

'Nonsense!' the old lady said robustly. She appeared to be revitalised by what she had just heard, and her eyes were bright with certainty. 'There is so much wrong in what you say, child, I barely know where to begin. First of all, what Rafe objected to was being unfairly accused of being his stepmother's lover. If it had in fact been true, he'd have faced it down. It's the injustice he minded, quite apart from the fact that he loathes her. What shame, to be known throughout the world as the sort of man who would make love to his father's wife! But he's not by nature averse to a little scandal, not if he has earned it – no Wyverne is. Do you know how the title came about?'

'I've seen a portrait of the first Marquess in the gallery. Rafe showed me.'

'Then you can hardly have failed to notice his strong resemblance to King Charles II,' said the Dowager drily.

'I understand what you are trying to say, and I am grateful for it, but it's not the same,' Sophie insisted. 'These are different times.'

'Let us be plain. My son married his mistress, and she was an actress of low birth and had previously sold herself, to others as well as to him,' Delphine said bluntly. 'That's not what I objected to, in truth. I understand that poor women must live, and all she had was her beauty to trade. I presume she married him for his money and status, and that also I did not mind. Most ladies in society do the same and nobody judges them for it. No. I objected to the fact that, whether through weakness or her own vicious nature, she egged him on to be his worst self. Look at the way they treated Rafe when he was a boy. *That* was truly unforgivable.

'But *you*, Sophie, you bring out the best in Rafe. I understand why he has been so cautious since he grew to manhood, for my sake, for the sake of all the people here and most recently for the sake of Charles and Amelia. So many burdens he has had to carry. But being so careful for so long has damaged him – it is not his proper nature. Left to himself, with no hostages to fortune, he would have damned his father to hell and walked away from here and never come back. And you have given him back that pride in himself. Because of you, he stood up to his father at last, after the jewels had gone, and just now he stood up to Rosanna. This is his best self, not his worst. His true, deep nature. And you have brought this out in him. Do you understand me?'

'It's what I want to believe,' said Sophie distressfully. 'It would be so easy and seductive to credit it. But I can't think that I should, for his sake.'

'My dear child, you know that he loves you. I refuse to believe that he has not made that very plain. It was certainly plain to me, though he has said not a word of it. He is a man grown, he knows his own mind, and he loves you. Though he is a Wyverne, he is constant, he will not change. Can you doubt it?'

'Perhaps he does love me. But he shouldn't.'

'Oh, shouldn't,' said the Dowager with a shrug. 'What he should not do, loving a woman like you, is marry some simpering debutante who wants the title as much as Rosanna did, but is "respectable" so all the world forgives it. And that is what he will come to, make no mistake, if you refuse him. He must marry eventually. You surely cannot think that his fool of a brother is fit to inherit here, or ever will be.'

'Poor Lord Charles,' said Sophie with a twisted smile.

'Poor Rafe, if you do not have him.'

'There will be a great scandal if I do. I don't want that for him.'

'I don't see why. The Marquess of Wyverne marries Clemence de Montfaucon. What could be more suitable?'

'I'm not that girl any more. I can't be her again, it's too late. I'm a thief. I've stabbed people, and not cared if they died of it.' She said desperately, 'There's a picture of me downstairs, half-naked, as Danae with her shower of gold.'

'Oh, how diverting!' said the Dowager rather wistfully. It

wasn't entirely clear to Sophie if she was referring to posing nude, or stabbing people, or perhaps both.

'The artist was my lover!'

'An artist! Was he good to you? I only ask because I have observed that they can often be somewhat self-absorbed.'

'Oh, you are quite incorrigible, ma'am! Yes, he was, for a while. But then as he grew more prosperous he wanted me to be respectable, to forget what I had been. And I can't. I just can't.'

'Very well.' Delphine leaned forward to emphasise her point. 'Talk to Rafe. See if that's what he wants of you. I am almost sure it isn't. He is a nobleman, not a city clerk or an artist with patrons he must please.

'My dear, do not mistake me, we live in the world as it is. I agree that times are changing, and it seems clear that once the poor King and his wastrel sons are dead they will change faster. It may well be that it will be expedient to conceal your past, to deny – if anyone should ever have the temerity to raise the matter – that you are the girl in the shocking pictures. But you can do that. You can do it with aplomb, as the Marchioness of Wyverne. I presume you don't *want* to live in a back slum and pick pockets for a living until you are too old to continue? Is that what you mean to do, if in the end you refuse my grandson and walk away from him? I must tell you in all seriousness that I think that would be perverse.'

'No,' Sophie confessed. 'There's no virtue in poverty for its own sake. It's dirty and dangerous and unpleasant. If I had money and security, I could use my position to help girls who suffer every day as I once did. But you are too persuasive, ma'am, and I should not listen to you. The plain fact is, I care for Rafe too much to want to ruin him, and I would ruin him, I know. And as for my future,' she said with a flash of spirit, 'I must tell you that I am a very good pickpocket!'

'And I am sure you will be an excellent marchioness,' said the Dowager tranquilly. 'I only wish you would get on and do it quickly. I would like to see a great-grandchild or two before I die.'

Sophie had to laugh, despite her distress. 'You are quite shameless, madame la marquise, do you know?'

'Naturally I am aware of it. One does not reach my age without knowing such things. I will stop at nothing to see my grandson happy. I would even lie – but on this occasion there was no need. It is a very simple matter, it seems to me. Talk to him,' she said. 'That's all I ask. Talk, and listen.'

## 40

Though it was notionally a house of mourning, and the funeral of its late master had not yet taken place, there was no denying the fact that the atmosphere at Wyverne Hall became instantly much more cheerful once Lady Wyverne had taken her departure, with her personal maid, looking most unhappy at this fresh turn of events, at her side. The family coach was piled high with bandboxes and trunks, and set off in the early afternoon, trundling down the carriage drive and disappearing in the distance to the regret of precisely nobody.

Sophie had been walking by the lakes, only dimly aware of the beauty around her since she would soon be leaving it behind, as she surely must despite all that the Dowager had said. She climbed the steps slowly to see Rafe standing at the top, tracking the vehicle's lumbering progress until it was out of sight.

'Saying goodbye to your stepmother?' she asked.

'You might describe it rather as escorting her off the premises,' countered the Marquess with a slight smile. 'I thought I wouldn't believe she was really gone until I saw it for myself.' And then he said abruptly, 'We must talk. Not here. Would you be amenable to a short walk, or are you tired?'

'Of course I'm not. I'd sooner not go to the Gothic Tower, though,' she added, aware that the conversation they were about to have could only be painful.

'I'm in complete agreement that we should avoid it for a good while. And also the church – they're digging a grave. May I suggest the Temple of Friendship?'

She assented, and they set off in that direction in silence, both lost in their own thoughts. 'Has it fallen into ruin, or was it built that way?' she asked a little awkwardly as they drew closer. The temple sat on a small rise and had a fine façade with a portico, but the building behind it appeared to be roofless, with trees pushing up where a large room might once have been.

'It was complete once. But many years ago, before I was born, my father held one of his notorious parties here. A fire broke out – I have heard tales, possibly exaggerated, of drunken people, with their garments aflame, running down to plunge into the lake. Though I believe for a wonder no one was seriously injured. He escaped entirely unscathed, naturally.'

'It must have been quite early in the evening, if his guests were still clothed,' she responded drily.

'That's sadly true. Since then it has been left as a folly – just one among many.' They'd reached the pretty, damaged temple now, and by common consent sat down on the broad steps. 'I understand you've been having a tête-à-tête with my grandmother. She upbraided me for not making you a formal offer of marriage, and she is quite right, for I have not.'

'It is impossible that you should. If you were so foolish as to do so, you know I must refuse you. Why should we give ourselves unnecessary distress?' said Sophie with a little constraint.

'The only thing that can distress me now is losing you, and so

I refuse to hear talk of impossibility. I know you do not want me to speak, and I understand why, but Sophie, will you hear me out at last? I think you owe me that much.'

She looked down at her booted feet beneath the drab fabric of her gown. They were surrounded by a beautiful landscape of fine buildings, water and trees, all in perfect harmony of nature, design and execution, but neither of them had eyes for any of it just now. 'Yes,' she answered quietly. 'I will, but I should tell you plainly that I must leave in a few days, as I always planned. I'll stay until after the funeral, but then I must go. Your sister will be back soon enough, and I cannot be here when she returns. Her reputation and her future must not be endangered, and I will not allow them to be placed in jeopardy by any actions of mine. I've done enough damage to your family – I will do no more. I am sure your staff care enough for you to hold their tongues, and if Lady Wyverne talks I doubt anyone will listen to her – no one who matters, at any rate. You will be free to restore your family to its rightful place in the world.'

'And if I said I don't give a fig for any of that, because I need you as my wife, and cannot contemplate life without you?'

'You must contemplate it. There is no other way.'

'I won't believe that. I love you, Sophie. To talk of freedom is nonsense, for what use is freedom without love? With you at my side, I can do anything – without you, nothing. And I know you love me. I know it in my heart and my bones. If you try to tell me you don't, I won't believe you, so don't waste your breath on the attempt. None of this would be so hard for you if you didn't love me just as much as I love you.'

She stood, and turned away from him, gazing blindly out across the peaceful sylvan scene. Why must he make this so damned difficult? 'Very well,' she said, rounding on him. 'It's true. I do love you, even though I don't want to. But it doesn't signify, because love is not enough. It isn't. Your father married a woman with a scandalous past, but she was scandalous in an ordinary sort of way, really. Peers have married actresses before. I'm much worse – I'm a thief as well as a woman of ill repute, and anyone who knows I exist believes me to be Nate Smith's mistress.' She was very distressed, and her voice broke on a wild laugh as she said, 'I'm supposed to be the mistress of your illegitimate uncle, the most notorious thief and master of thieves in England! He trained me to pick pockets, and do worse than that. Can't you see why that might just possibly be a problem?'

'I don't care. As long as you and I both know who we are, we need not heed the opinion of any other person alive. And it is just as well, for all the world believes that I took my stepmother as my mistress, remember, Sophie. What could be more shocking than that?'

'It doesn't matter. You are a man, and so eventually you will be forgiven. I will not. It's not even the world I fear, not really. It's you. You will change your mind, and blame me – it might take twenty years, but you will. I've been here before, remember. Bart would have hated me for giving myself to him, I saw signs of it already creeping upon him after only a year, and one day so will you, who wasn't even my first lover.'

He took her hands in his and said, 'I won't, you know. I understand why you think I will, but you are mistaken. Will you let me explain? You said you would hear me out. I promise if I cannot convince you I will not try to prevent you from leaving, even if it tears me in two.'

She knew she should pull her hands away, but did not quite have the strength to do so. 'Go on,' she said very low. 'Please say your piece, then I can go.' Her heart was breaking at the thought of leaving him, and she felt she could endure only a little more before she must flee.

'Sophie, my dearest love, my heart, I know that you fear I want you to be respectable – Grand-mère told me as much, and I had realised that for myself in any case. But it's not true. If that were all I wanted – to restore the tarnished good name of the Wyvernes, so that not a breath of scandal touches it forevermore, or some such nonsense – I am sure I could go to London, to the Season now in full swing and, despite my undeserved bad reputation, despite my father's deserved one, find any number of good, dull girls willing to marry me forthwith. I could choose one of them in a perfectly cold-blooded way and set about making my life completely miserable. And her life, Sophie. I think that's important too.

'I don't want to be boring and respectable. Perhaps you think I do, because I have not explained myself properly to you yet. It's true that I've lived a staid life compared to that of my ancestors, but that's only partly because I was reacting against my father and trying to keep everyone safe. It's more complicated than that. I'm not like him in many important ways – I have no taste for libertinage, nor for burning down buildings or destroying innocent people's lives. He was a wrecker and I am not. I'd certainly rather not be proverbial throughout the land for wickedness and cruelty. But I don't look forward to leading family prayers and growing big, bushy whiskers either.' She could not help but laugh through her tears at the picture he presented her with, and when she did so he gripped her hand more tightly. 'I want to be wild and wicked, Sophie, but with just one woman – the woman I love. You, my dearest.

'So I'm not asking you to change. I promise I won't ever reproach you for being who you are, or for who you have been, because I love you for it all. It's you I want, not some other woman I don't care two pins for, and not the woman you might have been if your life had turned out differently. I'm not asking you to be

Clemence again, even if that is what your public identity must be if you marry me. You're Sophie. Or you can choose to be some other person, some other name, if you wish, if being Sophie has bad memories for you.'

'It has bad memories, and good ones,' she said. It was true. How badly she wanted to believe him.

He kissed her hand, and held it to his cheek. 'If some of those good memories had me in them, I would be very honoured, and glad. I'm sorry I announced our engagement in front of Rosanna and Charlie, my love. Please believe that I wasn't trying to force your hand. I would never do that. I want you to choose me freely more than anything in the world. It was just that in that moment I couldn't see another way of saving the situation.'

'I know. I don't blame you for it. And that's the point, I think, Rafe. If I marry you, there may be other such moments when you can't rescue matters half so easily. You do know that? I fear you are deluding yourself about the path that lies ahead if I accept you. I want you to be clear exactly how terrible a risk you would be taking.'

'My eyes are open. I'm not expecting miracles. I plan to be very grand and face the world down, if that proves necessary. And if you choose you can be the same, when people whisper behind their hands about *my* supposed past, as they surely will. My grandmother can give you lessons in magnificent unconcern. Or you can just shrug and smile. What a wicked pair they must be, people will say, each as bad as the other. Would you make me the happiest man alive and consent to marry me, Sophie?'

'I had a nightmare the other night. A nightmare about our future together, I suppose, if I married you. I was being presented to Queen Charlotte, and the knife in my garter sheath slipped out, and clattered across the floor to her feet. There was a huge uproar.'

'I can see that there might have been,' he said, smiling. 'I am sorry you have been troubled by bad dreams, but after all there's a simple solution.'

'What might that be?'

'We must design you a more secure sheath for your weapon, one that does not so embarrass you. This is going to involve a great deal of effort and study on my part, but it's a sacrifice I'm prepared to make.' As he spoke, he pulled up her gown and smoothed it back over her legs, shamelessly exposing her stockings, her bare skin and her garter to the spring air. 'Now let me see...' he mused, laying his big hands either side of her thigh and scrutinising it intently.

'Rafe!' she said, conscious of the liquid heat pooling between her legs as her body responded immediately to his touch and the intensity of his dark gaze. 'You presume too much! You make a joke of it, and behave as though the difficulties were small and easily overcome, when they are not. You have most conveniently not mentioned your sister, and the importance of respectability for her.'

He shook his head. 'Look around you – at the house, the land, everything and everyone in it. All the things you can see and all the things and people you can't. The servants and the tenants, my grandmother, my brother and my sister. It is a great responsibility, you are right, and one I take on gladly, because it is in my blood, as my siblings are. I love Amelia and Charlie, and I will always do my best for them. But they are Wyvernes. We all are. That is a legacy that they can never escape, any more than I can. Do not frame my life in such a way, as though if I should be mad enough to give you up, some magic wand can be waved and we will emerge with an unstained name, in a week or a month or a year. I believed that once, even recently, but it was a ridiculous, childish delusion. The past cannot be changed, and we must live with what we have. And I am glad of it now, because none of this means a single thing to me if you cannot be mine.'

She did not speak, her certainty shaking in the face of his desperate eloquence, and he said urgently, 'You must see that I am right. We are not living in a fairy tale, a world of black and white, where my choice is between respectability and love, and I nobly choose love and pay the price. The Wyverne name is already tarnished through no fault of mine or yours, no matter what I do. In a hundred years, in two hundred, when we are all long dead, I dare say a whisper of scandal will still cling to the family. People enjoy being outraged too much to set it aside easily. And knowing that, to choose anything but love would be insanity. Marry me, Sophie, and we will face whatever comes together. Do not make me face it without you. I don't think I can.'

She paused for a moment, but she knew that there was only one answer she could give him. It was hard to believe him after all she'd been through, but her heart told her she must, or she would regret it forever. She'd prided herself on her strength and boldness – now she must take this last and greatest risk. 'I will not ask you if you are sure, for I can see that you are. That being so... Yes! Yes, of course I will!'

'Oh, my love... Thank God! That's... I don't have words to say how much your trust means to me. I promise I will never betray it as long as we live.' He dropped a lingering kiss where the sheath of her knife would be if she were wearing it, then stood and held out his hand to her.

His voice was ragged with emotion, but he was smiling as he said, 'To celebrate our engagement and to seal the unbreakable bond between us, my dearest, I'm going to take you up the steps under the portico and make love to you right here and now. Make love to you properly, as I have not yet, if you do indeed consent to that, my love.'

'You'd like to put a child in me?' she asked bluntly, taking his hand. It seemed to be important to know his intentions completely.

'It's not the main thing on my mind at the moment, but yes, Sophie, I would. It doesn't have to be now, if you don't want that. I have many, many other ideas. What do you think?'

'You *are* quite wild and wicked. I hadn't realised.'

'I'm hoping to be. But would you like a child, Sophie? One day, if not soon?'

'I believe I would,' she said, considering. It was hard to take in the entirely new direction her future had taken. A great sense of excitement was bubbling up inside her like a spring of water that could no longer be suppressed. 'In my life as Clemence I'd always assumed I would have children, and then later, of course, it was vital that I should not, so I determined to put the idea from my mind. I think I'd like one day to have a son and name him in memory of my poor little brother Louis, who barely had a chance at life. But just now I'd like to leave it up to fate. Perhaps I am done with trying to control every aspect of my existence.'

'I promise I won't try to control it either,' he said seriously. 'Apart from anything else, you have a knife.'

She put her arms about his neck. 'You're safe for now. I'll let you know if that changes. So, we go where life takes us, Rafe? No regrets?'

'Yes, as long as we go together. One day I'd like to travel the world with you, if these cursed wars ever come to an end. But just now, my desire is to journey just a few paces up these steps and have you wrap yourself around me.'

'Carry me!' she whispered in his ear. He slid his hands down her back and lifted up her skirts so that she could wrap her legs securely about his waist. She pulled down his head to kiss him, and he fixed his hands firmly on her naked bottom, taking her up the steps without the least apparent effort.

Once there, he set her down on a shallow window ledge that was at just the right height, and while she kissed him with greedy urgency he unfastened his breeches fall and freed himself. 'Are you ready for me, my love?' he asked against her mouth.

'Yes,' she said again. 'Yes, Rafe, I am.'

## 41

Lord Wyverne, his grandmother, his brother and Sophie took dinner together, and the event soon took on the air of a celebration, Mr Barnaby having completed his task and taken his leave once he'd been quite sure that Rosanna was safely out of the way. 'I expect she will be telling anyone who will listen that I turned her out of doors the day after her husband died,' said Rafe, refilling their glasses once the servants had been dismissed.

'Well, you did,' said Lord Charles reasonably. 'Frankly I'm surprised you waited as long as that, old fellow. Horrifying creature, enough to make a man's hair stand on end. Nobody who knows her or anything about her would be the least shocked that you sent her about her business.'

'It is a huge relief to have her gone,' said the Dowager, who had indeed been carried down the stairs by a blushing William but otherwise showed no particular signs of decrepitude. 'I am sure you are right, Rafe, and we will not have heard the last of her, but as Charles says, she is so obviously a woman scorned that her malice can have little effect.'

'I don't suppose that I will ever persuade the world that she has never been my mistress,' replied Rafe ruefully. He seemed so much more relaxed now that his stepmother was gone, Sophie thought. They'd made love with wild abandon in the temple, the first time that intimacy had been entirely unconstrained in either of their lives, they'd realised, and walked back together slowly, hand in hand. He had told her that, while he would always keep the little attic refuge that he'd had for so many years, he would like to move to more commodious quarters now – but not, he'd added firmly, those previously occupied by his father and Rosanna. So they'd spent part of the afternoon choosing adjoining chambers for themselves and arranging for furniture to be moved to their liking; it was not as though their options were limited. Lord Charles and his sister would also need to choose their own rooms now that they could at last make their home here. It would be a fresh start for all of them.

The next few weeks passed in a whirl of activity. Rafe very much wanted his sister Amelia to attend the wedding, and she would not return home for a fortnight or more, so it was decided that they'd have the banns read in the local church, rather than seeking a licence, and use the intervening time to prepare. Sophie had a great need of more suitable clothes, and a trip to London was deemed necessary.

The funeral came first, an extremely quiet affair which Sophie, naturally, did not attend, as women of rank generally did not appear at such solemn events. Rafe and Charles were more or less alone, save for Mr Barnaby and those few of the servants who wished to be present. Some of the local landowners sent empty carriages, as a mark of respect towards the new Marquess rather than the dead man, but none of them saw fit to come in person. And once that day was done with, another weight seemed to lift from Rafe's shoulders.

Sophie, arrayed in her new London finery, found herself a little nervous when it came time for Lady Amelia to return, just a few days before the wedding. She'd established a firm, undemanding friendship with Lord Charles, who was so amiable that it was hard to imagine him being at outs with anybody. But his sister might be a different matter. The Dowager had said she was clever. She might not be quite so ready to accept the insubstantial story Rafe had concocted to explain Sophie's own presence here.

Amelia came to her new home in grand style, one of her outriders cantering on ahead so that Rafe, Charles and Sophie could be on the steps to meet her with due ceremony. But there was nothing grand about the dark-haired, vivacious girl who tumbled out of the carriage to greet her brothers with a flurry of embraces and kisses. Sophie found herself caught up too, and swept inside to take tea.

'I'm excessively glad you are to marry Rafe, Sophie – may I call you Sophie?' Lady Amelia said artlessly, buttering bread. 'It will be much, much better than having stuffy old Aunt Keswick as my chaperon for my come-out next year. She's married Cousin Annabel to a very dull man, though of course poor Annabel is extremely dull herself, but I am *not* dull and I am firmly resolved not to do the same.'

'For once I am in accord with you. I think it may be best if a very dull man doesn't marry into this family,' said Rafe drily. 'He might not like us. God knows, he might not like you, and if he thought he did at first he'd soon learn his mistake. And I'm glad you approve. That's the only reason I'm marrying, naturally, for your greater convenience, Melia. It's my only object in life.'

'Naturally,' she echoed, dark blue eyes sparkling wickedly. 'But you're gammoning me, Rafe. You're in love, I can tell! It's written all over your silly old face. Look at you, blushing and looking conscious! And I am very pleased. It's time you had some fun at last, you poor, sad thing.'

'So am I pleased,' her brother responded, smiling at Sophie as he spoke. 'And I entirely agree. It is long past time I had some fun.'

# EPILOGUE

It was a year, more or less, reflected Sophie, since she'd first met Rafe in his grandmother's chamber at Wyverne House. In that time, her life had changed completely, and so, for that matter, had his. And that was why they found themselves standing in a crowded, stuffy room in Buckingham House, waiting – it wouldn't be a long wait, because after all he was a marquess and she was a marchioness, and rank must be observed in these circumstances – to be presented to Queen Charlotte.

There was already a great deal of whispering among the crowd of finely dressed people, and she could not doubt that much of it was centred upon her. Rules had been broken, conventions set at naught. It was possible to tick them off on one's gloved fingers. The new Lord Wyverne and his family had not gone into deep mourning for their father. It was rumoured that they had not gone into mourning at all, which was shockingly irregular. And then, far from appearing prostrated with filial sorrow, His Lordship had celebrated his marriage, albeit very quietly, some three weeks after his parent's demise. Less than a year had passed since these events had taken place, and here the pair were, bold as brass, in the presence of royalty.

Although the new Marchioness was of illustrious French lineage, nobody could recall setting eyes on her between her emergence into society nine years ago and her most unexpected marriage. It couldn't be supposed that she had as much as a penny to her name. It was known that her parents had died in the missing years, but as to how or where the young lady had lived after her sad bereavement – it was a mystery. The rumour was that she had been a humble governess in some obscure part of the kingdom, though it couldn't be denied that she didn't look in the least like one now. Some people said she'd been an actress, or worse, but fair-minded persons pointed out that this was most unlikely, and might be some form of confusion with her appalling stepmama-in-law, who had recently resorted to treading the boards once more, her circumstances being much reduced. At the mention of *that* woman, ladies still shuddered and rolled their eyes.

And yet... much could be excused, it seemed, even by royalty, if the circumstances were special enough. Lady Wyverne was being presented by her husband's relative, Lady Keswick, whom nobody had ever dared to accuse of immorality, or even of having a sense of humour. The Countess had embarked upon a masterly scheme of rehabilitation, in which she'd told the shocking (and, better still, true) tale of Rosanna's treatment of Rafe to a few dozen of her most intimate friends in strictest confidence. As she had intended, every member of the haut ton knew every salacious detail within three days, and there was no doubt that the revelation altered the case. The question was posed by a few daring free-thinkers – did a parent who encouraged that sort of behaviour and himself perpetrated Even Worse Crimes really deserve the conventional tributes due to a normal, loving parent?

And then, the new Marquess, who'd been so rarely seen in society for many years that most people had forgotten what he looked like, was so very handsome, and much might be excused the handsome. He didn't have the appearance of a man who'd carry on a scandalous affair with his stepmama, being quite austere in appearance until he smiled, and then... and then ladies tended to lose their train of thought, and regret they hadn't met him much sooner.

And his wife, undeniably, was a beauty. Sophie had long since washed out the brown dye that had rendered her hair so unremarkable, though she continued subtly to darken her brows and lashes. Her glorious, shining red-blonde tresses, defiantly unpowdered, were piled up on her head now, and she was wearing a court gown of silver tissue and costly lace. About her regal neck, nestling between her breasts – and perhaps this accounted for some of the whispers – was a magnificent jewel, the spectacular pink diamond known as the Stella Rosa.

The huge diamond sparked fire as Sophie – her true name was Clemence, of course, but it was understood that for some private reason her besotted husband always addressed her as Sophie – sank down into a superbly graceful curtsy before the smiling Queen Charlotte and her many daughters. It seemed as though the room held its collective breath, though this was no doubt an illusion. And then she rose at the Queen's gracious nod, flashing an intimate smile at her husband, and moved forward to converse a little with the royal ladies, who were all friendly condescension. And so it was over.

Having done their duty and taken grateful leave of their sponsor, Lady Keswick, and Lady Amelia, who had accompanied her aunt for her own presentation and would return home in her carriage, Rafe and Sophie managed at last to extricate themselves from the crowded staterooms of the palace and gain the privacy of their own vehicle with the Wyverne dragon crest upon the door.

'Thank God that's over!' exclaimed Sophie as she attempted with little success to arrange herself comfortably upon the seat. 'I've never in my life looked or felt so preposterous!'

Lord Wyverne was seated opposite her. The feathers in Sophie's hair brushed the roof, and the hoop of her court dress was so enormous that it occupied the whole seat and prevented her husband from sitting by her. There had been no question of Amelia sharing the coach with them; there was simply no room for her. 'You look very distinguished and romantic in all your embroidered finery,' the Marchioness said resentfully, 'but I resemble nothing more than a pineapple.'

'A very lovely pineapple,' he responded firmly, lips twitching. 'From the waist upwards, you are entirely delightful, as ever, apart from the feathers, which are undeniably silly. From the waist down... There's a certain perverse charm to it, I admit. I could hide myself away under the hoop, could I not? Set up home there, and never emerge. Bring small pieces of furniture, so that I might be comfortable.'

'Was *that* what you were thinking, as you made your bow and the princesses simpered at you from behind their fans?'

'It was one of the things I was thinking, certainly, my love. But chiefly I was wondering if the new strap arrangement was successful, so that your weapon stayed in place. I must presume it did, since it did not clatter at your feet and frighten the Queen and the whole court.'

'Why don't you go down and check, my lord?' Sophie asked demurely. 'I certainly can't. Look at me! I'm just a helpless pineapple.'

The Marquess said, 'I've always been partial to pineapple,' and pulled down the blinds with a firm, decisive tug.

# ACKNOWLEDGEMENTS

I wrote my first novel in my kitchen in lockdown. I'd never have developed the confidence to do it without the encouragement of all the complete strangers who commented so positively on my Heyer fanfic on AO3. But the real inspiration came from my good friends in the Georgette Heyer Readalong on Twitter. I'm particularly grateful to Bea Dutton, who spent many hours of her precious time setting up and running the readalongs. I can't possibly name everyone – there are too many of us – but thank you all, amazing Dowagers, for your continuing support with this novel and far beyond it. Your friendship is very important to me.

Thank you to all of the reading community on Twitter/X, and now on Instagram.

I've been obsessed with Georgette Heyer's novels since I first read them when I was eleven. They have their faults, but they've provided solace and escape for millions of people in tough times, so thank you, Georgette, even though you would have absolutely hated this book.

Thanks also to my family – Luigi, Jamie and Anna – for putting up with me while I wrote one novel and then another in quick succession. And then another five. Thanks for understanding when I just have to write another 127 words before lunch so I can stop on a nice round number.

My lovely work colleagues Amanda Preston, Louise Lamont and Hannah Schofield, have also been extremely supportive: thanks, Team LBA!

I am very lucky to have a superb agent in Diana Beaumont of DHH. She has believed in my writing from the first time she read it, and will always be my champion. Her editorial suggestions are brilliant, and she's just an all-round star. Thanks too to everyone else on the teams at Marjacq and DHH. I know better than most people how important the whole team at an agency is.

Many thanks to everyone at Boldwood, including Cecily Blench for the fantastic copyediting, to Gary Jukes for the superb proofreading as ever, and to Team Boldwood – Nia, Niamh, Issy, Jessie, Ben – as a whole for your amazing professionalism and unflagging enthusiasm. And of course grateful thanks to my wonderful editor Rachel Faulkner-Willcocks, whose brilliant edits have made this a much better book. One of the many special things about Boldwood is the wonderful spirit of mutual support that the authors share, so I'd like to thank you all, particularly the amazingly talented Jane Dunn and Sarah Bennett, for your generosity and friendship.

Finally, if you're reading this because you've bought the book, or a previous one: THANK YOU!

# ABOUT THE AUTHOR

**Emma Orchard** was born in Salford and studied English Literature at the universities of Edinburgh and York. She was a copy editor at Mills & Boon, where she met her husband in a classic enemies-to-lovers romance. Emma has worked in television and as a Literary Agent, and started writing in 2020.

Sign up to Emma Orchard's mailing list for news, competitions and updates on future books.

Follow Emma on social media here:

X  x.com/EmmaOrchardB

📷  instagram.com/emmaorchardbooks

📌  pinterest.com/EmmaOrchardRegency

## ALSO BY EMMA ORCHARD

A Duke of One's Own

What the Lady Wants

The Viscount and the Thief

You're cordially invited to

The Scandal Sheet

The home of swoon-worthy
historical romance from the
Regency to the Victorian era!

Warning: may contain spice

Sign up to the newsletter
https://bit.ly/thescandalsheet

# Boldwood

Boldwood Books is an award-winning fiction publishing company seeking out the best stories from around the world.

**Find out more at www.boldwoodbooks.com**

Join our reader community for brilliant books, competitions and offers!

Follow us
@BoldwoodBooks
@TheBoldBookClub

Sign up to our weekly deals newsletter

https://bit.ly/BoldwoodBNewsletter

Printed in Great Britain
by Amazon

50774731R00170